ONE S'MORE SUMMER

BOOK ONE OF THE CAMPFIRE SERIES

BETH MERLIN

BOOKS IN THE CAMPFIRE SERIES

One S'more Summer - Book 1

S'more to Lose - Book 2

Love You S'more - Book 3

Tell Me S'more - Book 4

For M & H

CHAPTER ONE

Standing at the stop, waiting for the camp bus, I was amazed by just how little had changed in the almost fifteen years since I was a camper. To my left were the kids who couldn't stop crying. To my right, the ones far too cool to stand anywhere near their parents. Then, the most recognizable group of all—the teenage girls who stood sizing each other up to determine who would be their fiercest competition for male attention over the summer. I took a deep breath and pulled out the clipboard listing the campers who would be on my bus. I put the whistle I'd been given at orientation around my neck and pushed my way through the crowd of duffle bags, trunks, and families. I felt a tap on my shoulder. I turned around and found myself face-to-face with a girl younger than me, but definitely older than the surrounding campers.

"Are you the bus counselor?" she asked.

I nodded and extended my hand, which she didn't shake.

"I'm Tara, your CIT," she said coolly.

"CIT? Oh, right, my Counselor in Training. I'm Gigi, head counselor of the Cedar girls."

"You look young to be head counselor. How old are you?"

I looked down at my outfit of jeans, Converse sneakers, and a Camp Chinooka T-shirt. No wonder she thought I looked young. I couldn't remember the last time I wasn't in stiletto heels.

"I'm twenty-seven," I answered.

"Wow, you're actually *old,*" she said, completely unaware of how rude she was being.

"Excuse me. I'm going to go start rallying the troops now," I said.

I climbed onto one of the trunks and blew my whistle. "My name's Gigi Goldstein. I'm head counselor for the Cedar girls, so hi all," I said, giving a little wave. "We're going to start boarding the buses in just a few minutes, so I need everyone to make sure their bags have been loaded on. If you have any special medications you need for the bus ride, keep those separate, and make sure a parent hands them to me before we leave. I'll be right here checking off names, so start making a line."

The older kids rushed to the front of the line, anxious to board and get their first taste of summer independence. I couldn't believe how much older thirteen looked now than when I was that age. The girls looked like mini versions of my twenty-something friends, decked out in trendy clothes and talking about which boys they were going to hook up with over the summer. When the campers had finished filling the bus, I spotted Tara still on her phone.

"Hey, Tara, we're gonna get going," I said, motioning for her to hang up.

"One sec," she called back to me from the curb. "I'm

saying goodbye to my boyfriend. We get, like, no reception up at camp. I don't know when I'll speak to him again."

Though I knew how important that last phone call was to a seventeen-year-old who thought being apart for the summer meant the same thing as being apart forever, I snickered at the dramatics of it. Forever was knowing the one man you'd ever loved was getting married to your best friend in just two months. Now *that* was worth some dramatics.

When Tara finally climbed on the bus and mouthed the words 'thank you' to me, I knew I'd just made an ally, if only for the three-hour trip we had in front of us. I settled into my seat closed my eyes and thought back to my very first summer at Camp Chinooka.

I was nine years old and had never been away from home before. My mother dropped me off at the bus stop but left soon after to make it to her standing weekly facial appointment. Seeing me alone and upset, a girl wearing a faded Camp Chinooka T-shirt and a pair of cutoff Levi's jean shorts had come over to introduce herself. Alicia Scheinman had shiny blonde hair, piercing green eyes, and a small smattering of freckles across her nose so perfectly placed you'd swear each one was individually applied with a tweezer. Based on the number of arriving campers who'd stopped to say hello to her, I could tell immediately she was one of the popular girls and I was grateful she'd decided to take me under her wing. By the time the bus came, I knew I'd made a good friend. By the time that first summer was over, I knew I'd made a lifelong one.

A few hours later and somewhere in the middle of the twenty-fifth round of '99 Bottles of Beer,' we finally passed the sign for the road to Camp Chinooka. Tara, who'd sulked most of the trip, perked up a bit and offered her assistance picking up the trash off the seats. When the last camper was off, I made my way out of the bus and was able to take a good look around.

Camp Chinooka had opened in the early 1900s and it still retained much of its original rustic quality. There were a few sports fields, a swimming pool that had been added about ten years ago, and several different cabins that housed activities like arts and crafts and woodworking. Down a large hill nestled the camp's namesake, Lake Chinooka. It was my favorite place at camp—maybe the whole world. I used to love sitting on the dock right as the sun was going down and the only sounds were the crickets in the trees and the wind hitting the sails of the docked boats. My whole childhood had been spent in New York City, and until I got to Camp Chinooka, I'd never known that kind of quiet even existed.

On the far side of the camp, past the amphitheater was The Canteen. The Canteen was an old barn that had been converted into a recreational center. On the outside was a window where campers would line up to buy snacks and treats out of their summer allowance. On the inside, was a jukebox, old couches, and a crude bar that had been made by the head woodshop counselor sometime in the 1970s. It was a popular nighttime hangout for the counselors, who made good use of the bar...and the couches.

Some of the bunks had fresh coats of paint on them, and everything seemed just a little bit smaller. Really, though, so little had changed that I could have been stepping off the bus fifteen years ago. As I continued to take in the surroundings, a man with the sexiest English accent I'd ever heard called out my name. I assumed he was part of the Camp America program, an organization that provided international staff to summer camps. The foreign counselors usually spent eight weeks at camp, earning money so they could travel around the US when the summer session ended. When I was a camper all the girls developed huge crushes on the British counselors, who were always far more interesting and exotic than their American counterparts. Looking around at how all the girls were gazing at this guy, I could tell little had changed.

"I'm Georgica Goldstein," I answered, trying to raise my voice above the noise. I pushed my way through the crowd toward a twenty-something guy in khaki shorts wearing his Camp Chinooka T-shirt over a long-sleeved shirt. He had dark, curly hair being held back with a bandana and some of the longest eyelashes I'd ever seen. Across his face was the perfect amount of stubble, making me wonder if he was trying to look cool or just couldn't be bothered to shave.

"I'm Perry Gillman," he said, juggling several things in his hand. "Head counselor for the Birch boys. Figured I should introduce myself."

"Great," I said, staring into his big brown eyes. "I'm Georgica, which I guess you already know. Everyone calls me Gigi."

"Nice to meet you," he replied, looking completely unruffled.

"I'm gonna start organizing the Cedar girls into bunks. I guess I'll see you around?"

"Without a doubt," he replied coolly.

As I walked away, I tripped over a pile of trunks and duffle, wiping out on the gravel in front of everyone.

Perry reached down to help me up. I stood up and brushed the dirt off my knees.

"Might want to pay closer attention to where you're going," he said.

"I'll keep that in mind," I muttered.

I hadn't handled the first introduction to my male equivalent for the summer particularly well. I was caught off guard by his looks and being back at camp, not to mention the number of adolescent girls gathering under the Cedar sign.

"Hi, everyone," I said, making my way toward them. "My name's Gigi. I'll be your head counselor this summer."

A few of the girls rolled their eyes and snickered. I tried not to focus on them, but I couldn't stop my hands from shaking. "I have your bunking assignments on this clipboard. Please listen carefully."

I heard one girl in the back of the group say, "Listen carefully," mimicking the sound of my voice. I wiped the sweat from my palms and swallowed hard. During my interview, the camp director explained that head counselors were required to live in the bunk with the campers. I'd have a co-counselor and a CIT to handle some of the day-to-day stuff, but would be living right there with them, as a way to interact more with the girls.

I read off from the huge list of names organizing the campers, counselors and CIT's into different cabin assignments.

"Okay, last but not least, my bunk, Bunk Fourteen," I said, trying to rev up the remaining girls. "Your counselor is Jordana Singer." I looked back down at the clipboard and realized that Tara was the only CIT not yet assigned.

"Lucky us, Tara Mann's our CIT," I said, smiling at her. "I need the following campers front and center: Emily Barnes, Hannah Davidson, Madison Gertstein,

Alana Griffin, Jessica Jacoby, Lexie Simon, Rachel Stauber, Abby Wexel, and Emily Zegantz."

The girls settled themselves into a line and waited for their next set of instructions.

"Dinner's at six. Go to your bunks, get unpacked, and we'll meet in the Cedar horseshoe for roll call."

The girls took off running to make their claims for the bottom bunks and the best cubbies. I followed behind them with Jordana, who introduced herself as we walked. She was eighteen and going to be a freshman at Brown University in the fall. She'd been a camper at Chinooka and thought it would be fun to work as a counselor before going off to college. She had fair skin and really pretty straight red hair that was held back with a tortoiseshell headband. I could tell immediately we would get along.

"What's your story? Where do you go to school?" she asked as we walked toward the bunk.

"I'm not in college. I'm twenty-seven, actually," I answered.

She repeated the number, understandably a little puzzled by it.

"I know, a little old to be working here," I said.

"Are you a teacher or something, with the summer off?"

"No, I worked as a designer for Diane von Furstenberg up until a couple of weeks ago."

"Wow," she said.

"Don't be too impressed. I was downsized."

It was a lie. I hadn't been downsized. I'd been fired. In fact, the minute Human Resource's number had flashed on my desk phone's caller ID, I knew what was coming. I'd been anticipating the moment for months, and when it finally happened, I had to admit I'd felt relieved.

I remember how I'd trudged down the long hallway to HR, and saw my boss waiting for me in one of the large glass-enclosed offices. I'd offered him a weak smile as I sat down, so he'd know none of this was his fault. The HR rep sat across from us and poured me a glass of water. She slid a box of tissues toward me and placed a manila folder containing what I was sure was my termination paperwork on the table. My boss spoke first, reciting a well-rehearsed speech about how painful the decision to let me go was. Then, the HR rep had launched into her part, rattling off information about COBRA coverage, applying for unemployment, and rolling over my 401K into a personal IRA. I didn't hear any of it. The voice in my head telling me I was a total failure had completely drowned her out.

Two years ago, I'd done something totally out of character and tried out for a new reality show, *Top Designer,* where fourteen contestants competed for a chance to show their collections during New York Fashion Week. Although I had no formal training, I was convinced I could take the fashion world by storm. While there were certainly far more talented people on the show, I believed I had something special—a sense of style that set my work and me apart. The judges had obviously agreed because I made it all the way to the finale. Although I wasn't the ultimate victor, I did win some money to start my own line and more importantly, Diane von Furstenberg had invited me to join their creative team.

I broke the news of my decision to be on *Top Designer* to my parents while we were sitting at Georgica Beach over Memorial Day weekend. Embarrassingly enough, I was actually named for that Hampton's beach. I like to tell people I was conceived during a particularly hot summer following a particularly dull display of Fourth of July fireworks. The unfortunate truth was that my yuppie parents had hoped they'd one day be able to afford a piece of property in the East Hamptons and thought the name would prove inspiring. My grandfather never approved of me being named after a Long Island beach (can you blame him?) and immediately started calling me "Gigi." Fortunately, like any good nickname, it had stuck. Thank God I didn't have siblings, or one might have had the misfortune of being named Martha's Vineyard, another of my parents' favorite summer vacation spots.

As predicted, my parents hadn't taken the news of my reality show stardom well. Although they'd offered to pay the entire cost of a law school education, they'd made it very clear they were not at all interested in contributing to what they saw as a "self-indulgent waste of time." So, I did what any headstrong twenty-something does when faced with what they believe is their own do-or-die moment. I moved out of my parents' apartment and in with my best friend, Alicia. I used every scrap of savings I had to cover my expenses while I was on the show and prayed that all of it would prove worthwhile. The day Diane von Furstenberg offered me a position, it seemed as though I was on my way. And the day they fired me, everything changed.

Thankfully, Jordana knew enough not to ask any follow-up questions relating to my former employer, but her next question was even worse.

"Boyfriend?"

"No," I answered, without even the smallest inflection. "You?"

"I broke up with him a few weeks ago. I didn't want to be tied down this summer. Good thing—there are some really cute counselors this year. Have you met Perry?"

"I just met him a few minutes ago—seems nice," I answered.

"Not my taste, but definitely cute. Some girl will scoop him up."

Before we even walked into the bunk I could already hear the girls arguing over who got what bed and which cubby. Tara's voice was louder than all of them. I looked at Jordana and said, "Here we go." She nodded and pushed her way into the bunk, no easy task with clothes and trunks covering most of the floor. Finally inside, Jordana immediately went to open up some windows, while I took a good look around.

Five bunk beds lined the far wall with stacks of cubbies between each bed. On the opposite side were the two single beds meant for Jordana and me. I threw my bags down on the bed that had my name on it. I turned on the bathroom light and saw two sinks, two stalls, and another row of cubbies for toiletries and sheets. I'd forgotten there were no showers in the bunks. It was nice to see the camp retained some its original rustic qualities, but walking across the lawn, with nothing between the world and my bare behind but a towel... I shuddered at the thought.

Tara had the bottom bunk right across from us and was complaining about not getting a single to anyone who would listen. While the rest of the girls were settling in, making their beds, and hanging posters, I put my own things away.

First, I made up my bed, then turned the top of the cubby into an improvised nightstand. I set up an alarm clock, small lamp, and took out a framed picture of Alicia and me as campers at about the same age as the girls I was now in charge of. I stared at the two of us standing on the porch of the bunk, our hair pulled back with white bandanas, smiles from ear to ear. When one of the campers interrupted my trip down memory lane, I wiped the tears from my eyes.

"I'm Madison—Maddy," she said. She was a slightly overweight girl in shorts and a T-shirt that were both a little too small on her.

"What can I do for you?" I asked.

"I don't have enough room to put away all of my things," she answered.

"Did you see the cubbies in the bathroom?" I said, pointing to the back of the bunk. "There should be two assigned to you."

She crossed her arms and spread her legs apart. "I already filled them."

"Well, how much more do you have to unpack? Maybe you can just refold some of it a little smaller?" I suggested.

She pointed toward her bed, which was covered in piles of clothes.

"Give me a few more minutes to finish getting settled, and then I'll come over to see what I can do."

She had stopped listening and picked up the picture frame off my nightstand. "Who are they?" she asked.

"I'm the one on the left, and the girl next to me is my friend, Alicia," I answered.

"No way that's you," she said.

"I swear, that's me when I was about your age."

"But you were ..." Her voice trailed off.

I knew the word she was too polite to blurt out, so I said it for her. "Fat."

"Yeah, you were fat," she mumbled. Her eyes were wide open, and she was still staring at the picture. "Are you still friends with that other girl? She was so pretty. Is she still really pretty?"

"She is."

I took the picture back from Madison and looked at it. Instantly, I thought of how Alicia'd look with her hair elegantly slicked back into her wedding veil in a few weeks. More tears flooded my eyes as I imagined her standing there, alone, in her white dress, her parents delicately lifting up the veil and kissing their daughter on the cheek before escorting her down the aisle to meet Joshua. I wouldn't be there to see it.

I was *avoiding* being there. What kind of person does that?

"So what about all of my stuff?" Madison whined, snapping me back to reality.

Jordana, seeing the tears rolling down my cheeks, came to my rescue.

"You're Maddy, right?" she asked, climbing over her bed to sit next to me on mine.

"Yeah?" Madison replied.

"Whatever you don't plan on wearing in the next couple of weeks, keep packed in your trunk, okay? Then, in a few weeks, rotate."

"I'll try it," Madison replied reluctantly.

Jordana put her arm around my shoulder. "Homesick already?"

"Maybe," I replied.

"Pull it together. You're our fearless leader," she teased, trying to get me to smile.

I went into the bathroom and washed my face. When I came out, Jordana had all the girls sitting in a circle on the floor of the bunk so they could introduce themselves to one another. After I told them a bit about myself, I went outside to the horseshoe for roll call.

Within seconds of yelling "Roll call," almost fifty girls came streaming out from the five Cedar bunks, all of them raring to go. The counselors lined them up by bunk and then counted off. When each counselor nodded to me that they had the appropriate number of campers, I took my cue to speak. This was my make-it-or-break-it moment. In the next few seconds, they would either see me as their friend, big sister, and mentor, or the person who stood in the way of them having a good time this summer. If it was the latter, their sole mission would be to get me to resign before the summer had even begun. Unfortunately, I knew this from personal experience.

"v"

I was losing them. I sounded like every other patronizing adult I used to hate at their age. I quickly changed my approach. "A little birdie told that the Cedar girls haven't won the Gordy Award in over five years. Well, I don't know about you, but I think that it's our turn."

A few of them perked up. The Gordy Award, aptly named for Gordon Birnbaum, the camp's director for the last thirty-plus years, was given to the group that showed the most involvement and spirit during the summer. The winning group got to choose between a trip to Boston, Washington DC, or New York City and the competition usually got pretty heated. Birch had taken it the last few summers, and from what I'd heard on the bus, were intent on winning again this year. I wasn't about to let that happen.

My years of working in the corporate world had taught me that nothing bonds a group together faster than having a common goal, and even more than that, a common enemy. I'd become close with two colleagues when management hired a manipulative, tyrant-esque VP for our division whom we all hated. Our common disdain for him was the glue that forged our friendship, and getting him fired sealed it.

If I could divert Cedar's attention to Perry and his boys, pitting them as the enemy, I would, if even just by default, become their friend. It was a desperate tactic, but these girls were going to look for every possible way to get me to resign, just as I'd done to all of my head counselors when I was a camper.

At their age, Alicia and I snuck into our head counselor Mindy's bunk while she was sleeping, covering her in shaving cream, toothpaste, and whatever else we could find, just like the scene from the movie *The Parent Trap*. We hoped when she woke up, she'd be too preoccupied with the mess to notice that we'd sneaked over to the boys' side of camp.

We continued our barrage of practical jokes and torments through the first half of the summer until Mindy was so fed up she quit. In hindsight, I realized how awful and immature we'd acted just to have a few moments alone with the boys, but I was not about to let what happened to her happen to me. "I want to remind you ladies that if we win, we get a three-day trip to DC, Boston, or New York, not to mention bragging rights for the rest of the summer," I added. A few of the girls whispered to one another and I could tell I'd stirred up some excitement.

"So, I ask you, are we gonna win the Gordy this year?" I shouted in their direction. I heard a few girls grumble the word yes and I raised my voice. "I can't hear you. I said, 'Are we gonna win the Gordy this year.'"

A few more yelled out the word 'yes.' Jordana made eye contact with me and then nudged some of the quieter girls to speak up.

"Are we gonna kick the Birch boys' asses and take the Gordy?" I screamed out like a maniac.

They yelled the word "yes" at the tops of their lungs.

"Good. So now I want you all to repeat after me: We are Cedar, we couldn't be prouder, and if you can't hear us, we'll shout a little louder. We are Cedar, we couldn't be prouder, and if you can't hear us, we'll shout a little louder."

By the third verse, all the girls joined in, and I started our march toward the dining hall. When the counselors saw my signal, they prompted the girls to follow. We headed to the Great Lawn, screaming the chant, and continued cheering all the way into the dining hall. When we walked in, we had the attention of the entire room. Perry's eyes were fixed on me. He looked upset we'd already gotten the upper hand and made a beeline in my direction.

"Throwing your hat in the ring for the Gordy?"

The girls were still screaming the cheer behind me.

"Maybe?" I said, shrugging my shoulders.

"You know Birch has won it for the last three summers," he said very matter-of-factly.

"Yeah, I think I heard that somewhere," I replied.

"Well, it'll be nice to have a worthy adversary for a change."

"I'm guessing you're the one who led them to victory last year?"

"Last year and the two years before," he answered. "I'm planning on continuing our streak this summer."

"Whatever," I said, feeling a bit argumentative. "There's a new sheriff in town."

"Rubbish," he answered. "Or, as you American girls say, *whatever*."

"We don't say that. I mean, I just said *whatever*, but it's not a fair generalization."

"*Whatever*," he teased.

"Stop saying that. If you think Americans are such *rubbish*, why are you here?"

"I'm working on my doctorate, so I have my summers off. Although I have to put in some time on my thesis."

Attractive or not, he was a little too self-satisfied. Before I could respond, Gordy made his way up to the microphone stand in the center of the room. I didn't know if it was the Chinooka air or water that preserved him, but he hadn't aged one bit. The entire room quieted, and he started to sing the Camp Chinooka alma mater into the microphone. Within seconds the rest of the room joined in. It was amazing how I remembered every word and every inflection, able to sing it effortlessly. When the song was over, Gordy welcomed us all to the centennial summer and invited everyone to enjoy the meal.

The first dinner at Chinooka was always a banquet, but after that, we'd be served cafeteria style for the rest of the summer. The food was just as inedible as I remembered. I picked at some roasted chicken and some lumpy, gray mashed potatoes before pushing the whole plate aside. After all the tables had been served, Gordy made his way back up to the podium to make other announcements. He talked about the new amenities that had been added over the winter, including the new dock and the inline skating rink. He let everyone know that the camp production would be *Fiddler on the Roof*, and because it was the camp's one-hundredth year, we'd be putting on a special performance of it in the newly built outdoor Lakeside Amphitheater. Then, he introduced some key staff and some of the other head counselors from the younger groups, Maple, Pine, Oak, and Elm.

When he got to Perry, I noticed all of the girls in my group whispering to each other. He was by far the best-looking staff member. When Gordy introduced me, I stood up and did a quick wave and the girls in my group cheered. Had I won them over with my spirit and promises of a Gordy victory? Maybe this wouldn't be so hard after all.

Who was I kidding? This whole thing was crazy. Who walked out of their life and went to work at their childhood sleepaway camp at twenty-seven years old? As Gordy finished introducing the last members of the waterfront staff, that answer became painfully clear—only someone with nothing left to lose.

CHAPTER TWO

After leaving Diane von Furstenberg's corporate office, I decided to meet Alicia to celebrate her engagement to Joshua, as planned. I arrived at the bar, and in typical fashion, Alicia wasn't there yet. One of the few women hired into her class of twenty at New York's top investment bank, it was clear she felt the pressure of the distinction. During her first year working, she'd kept crazy hours, and even when I was her roommate, I was lucky to see her once a week. In the last few years, her hours had improved somewhat, but she was still notoriously late for almost everything.

You'd never know by looking at her that she routinely worked eighteen-hour days. Alicia was always polished and perfectly put together. She claimed that because of her long hours, she'd been forced to turn one of her desk drawers into a makeshift bathroom cabinet and therefore had the means to do constant touch-ups. With or without the makeup, she was still just as stunning as when we were young.

Alone at the bar, I ordered myself a much-needed

glass of white wine and turned to the commotion at the door. It was Joshua and some of his Wall Street buddies. He slipped some money into the bouncer's hand, and moments later, a scantily clad girl came out and escorted him and his entourage inside.

"Seems like a popular guy," the bartender said, commenting on all the drinks that Joshua was ordering for the crowd of people trying to sit at his table. I turned back around and tried to blend in, hoping he wouldn't see me. I thought I'd succeeded until I felt a tap on the back of my shoulder.

"Hey, stranger," Joshua said with a sweet smile.

He looked flawless in his made-to-measure Paul Stuart suit and Turnbull & Asser shirt. Twice a year he had them custom tailored to his body, a fact that didn't go unnoticed by the other women in the bar.

"I guess Alicia isn't here yet?" I said, looking past him to the entranceway, hoping she would magically appear.

"I don't know why I bother meeting her at these things when I spend most of them waiting for her," he said, pushing a piece of hair out of my eyes.

My hands started trembling so badly I had to put the wineglass down on the bar so he wouldn't notice. Why did he always have this effect on me?

"I'm sure she'll be here soon. In the meantime, I'm sure you'll be fine hanging with your buddies. Excuse me," I said, trying to push past him and into the mob of people fighting their way inside. I'd told myself I'd give Alicia another few minutes to show up before I went home. Joshua followed closely behind me. He put his hands on my shoulders, and I leaned back into him. He had the slightest hint of cologne on his shirt. I breathed it in, remembering all the mornings I'd watched him dab it on while getting ready for work.

"Are you going to hate me forever?" he whispered into my ear.

I turned around to face him, and he lifted my chin so that I was looking straight into his big beautiful eyes. "As if I could ever hate you," I answered.

"You're right, we've been friends far too long for that."

"Friends?"

"Aren't we? Haven't we always been?"

I searched his eyes for any suggestion of insincerity but couldn't find a trace. I bit my lower lip and looked up again. "Of course. Of course, we are."

He took my hands in his. "Why don't I believe you?"

"Joshua, what do you want from me?"

He stepped toward me but turned when he heard his name being called from a table in the corner.

"It's okay. Go to them. Can you tell Alicia I wasn't feeling well and I'll call her later?"

"Gigi…"

"Congratulations. I really am so happy for you both," I said, gently moving past him and disappearing into the crowd.

When I got home I had two messages on my phone. One was from my mother, asking if we were still meeting in the morning to pick out an engagement gift for Alicia. The second was from Alicia, apologizing for being late to the party and letting me know she was leaving for a business trip to Singapore in the morning but would phone when she returned next week.

I erased both messages and pulled a carton of coffee ice cream from my freezer before collapsing onto the couch. I wrapped an afghan around myself and rummaged through my movie collection, an assortment of tapes and DVDs ranging from *Pretty Woman* to the entire BBC *Pride and Prejudice* miniseries. Consisting of six separate VHS tapes, the miniseries was the main reason I still held onto my ancient VCR. Colin Firth's Mr. Darcy was one of the few men us women could always forgive. I was digging through the drawers of my entertainment unit looking for all six tapes when I spotted my yearbook videos from my summers at Camp Chinooka, all seven years.

There they were. My seven years of summer camp, captured on video. I carefully took the first video out of its box, blew off the accumulated dust from the top, and popped it into my VCR. As the crude graphics scrolled across the screen and some unrecognizable rock song played in the background of the video, I was transported back to Camp Chinooka and Milbank, Pennsylvania. I sat on the edge of my couch, mesmerized, as the camera cut to different footage of the camp. The lake where I'd gotten my Red Cross certification in sailing, the softball field where I hit my first home run, the theater where I'd been in at least four productions of *Fiddler on the Roof,* and the gazebo where I'd received my first ever kiss from Aaron Harris and Alicia had received hers from Joshua.

Just as I thought about him, the camera panned to his face. There he was, nine years old and just as charismatic. He spoke straight into the camera and told anyone watching that he was Joshua Baume, the best soccer player at Camp Chinooka.

A flood of memories came rushing back as the camera focused in on different campers around the grounds. Nine-year-old Aaron playing basketball, and my very first counselor, Deborah, waving. Alicia and I walking hand in hand across the Great Lawn toward the dining hall. I looked like a disaster next to her. Chubby, with a mess of brownish-black uncontrollably curly hair. My polo shirt was untucked with a very visible stain on it.

Even though I looked very different now, it was hard not to think of myself as the girl in the video. Clothes were probably the biggest part of my transformation. At around twelve years old, I'd realized that the cute and trendy clothing Alicia and the other girls my age wore didn't come in my size, so I began to improvise. I created my own versions of the outfits they wore, first by mixing in aspects that flattered my figure. When that no longer satisfied me, I'd learned to sew. The concept of making my own clothing had absolutely horrified my mother, who viewed it as a complete act of rebellion. She referred to it as something only hippies living out of vans did. She constantly pleaded with me to go to a "normal" department store. I knew there was no point. The clothes in the stores were never the right size or cut. My own designs always fit.

Even when I lost the weight, I continued to design and sew most of my own clothing. In college, the other coeds realized my talent, and I ran a small business out of my dorm room. The only person who never asked me to make her anything was Alicia, who really didn't care much for fashion. For someone who cared so little, she was an icon to most of the girls I grew up with. She would wear a plain white T-shirt and jeans to school, and the next day it would be the uniform.

Even in the video, she looked effortlessly cool in a pair of cut-off jean shorts, a light pink polo shirt, and Birkenstock sandals. I was in a similar, albeit much larger, version of the very same outfit.

I spent the rest of the night captivated by the videos. I watched all of them back to back until my eyes were completely glazed over. I was mesmerized, and probably for the worst possible reason. The videos reminded me of what it was like when all I had was a massive crush on Joshua. I hadn't acted on it and hadn't betrayed my very best friend.

At that moment, I would've given just about anything to be transported back to Camp Chinooka and be given a clean slate. I fell asleep with the videos playing in the background and forgot to set my alarm for brunch the next day with my mother.

She was already seated when I walked into the restaurant. Her dark hair, the same shade as mine, was pulled tightly into a neat chignon. Her cherry red lipstick, the Chanel color she'd been wearing for years, was neatly applied. She left lipstick stains on almost everything whenever she wore it. You always knew where my mother had been.

She waved me over to the table.

"So, this is nice, us ladies having brunch," she said, folding the napkin onto her lap as I sat across from her.

"Very," I said, trying to gauge her mood. "Sorry, I must not have set my alarm clock."

"It's amazing to me you function in the real world at all. What if you showed up forty-five minutes late for work, would they be okay with that?"

"Amazingly enough, that hasn't ever happened," I said.

"How's your *job*?"

I hated the way she said the word *job* as if I was doing something truly reprehensible, like prostituting myself or selling drugs. When I was younger, she used to say that the only thing worth being was a noun. "Be a lawyer, be a doctor, be something that stands alone," she would say.

I worked for a design house. I was artistic. I wasn't a noun. Therefore, to her, I was expendable.

I used to wish that Diane von Furstenberg had a take your mother to work day, so she could see what I actually did. It was too late now. Now, I was without a *job*. My stomach was in knots. I ordered a chamomile tea from the waiter.

"My job is great," I lied.

"You know, Gigi," she said, between sips of her Bellini, "entertainment lawyers do all sorts of things with the fashion industry."

"Uh-huh, let's order," I said, picking up my menu so it blocked out most of her face.

She forced the menu back down toward the table. "When will you see that I'm on your side?"

"When you are," I muttered under my breath. I wasn't sure she heard me, but she dropped the conversation anyway.

I was relieved when our entrees came. I hoped eating would distract from the awkward silence, but I only got a minute's reprieve.

"So, how is the dating situation?" she asked.

"Same as usual. I've gone on a few bad dates this month. Maybe one of them will call and ask me out for a second one?" I said somewhat sarcastically. She didn't pick up on it.

"Gigi, did I ever tell you about when you were in second or third grade and Mrs. Madison called me in for a parent-teacher conference?"

"It must have been second grade. I had Mr. Kleinman in third grade."

She ignored me and continued, "Mrs. Madison was

concerned because all your drawings from coloring time were in very dark colors. Blacks, browns, and grays. Not oranges, reds, and yellows like the other kids in your class. So, when you came home, I asked you why you only used dark crayons. You looked me squarely in the eye and said, 'Mommy, I sit at the end of the row. By the time the box of crayons gets to me, all the good colors are gone and only the yucky ones are left.' Gigi, do you see where I'm going with this story?"

"Not really, no," I said, sipping my tea.

"You were the last in line to pick, so you took whatever crayons were left in the box. Instead of getting out of your seat and asking to use the red or yellow crayons, or even demanding them, you accepted what was left. And while I understood it then, I don't think you should still be settling for the dull colors now, do you?"

"Mom, I'm really not following."

"I guess what I'm saying is that you should get out of your seat and demand to use all the colors, whatever colors you want. Don't wait for the crayon box to come to you. Go to the crayon box. The right guy is out there for you, you just need to be more proactive. Look at how happy Alicia is. Why? Because she went to the box and pulled out Joshua."

Her anecdote eerily hit the nail on the head as an allegory for what had been going on in my life. I was fired because my designs had lost their edge, focus, originality, and vitality. They were dull, boring, and dark, not unlike the pictures I'd drawn in the second grade. It was almost as if the last few months following the end of my relationship with Joshua, I was eight years old again, and the last in the row, willingly accepting whatever was left. My designs, once lauded as innovative and fashion-forward, became ordinary and complacent. The work of someone just settling. With every sketch and every one-night stand since Joshua, I hadn't even been looking, let alone demanding, better from myself.

"I hear what you're saying, I really do," I answered.

"Good, because I just want you to be happy," she said, putting her hand over mine.

We left the restaurant and headed to Bloomingdale's to pick an engagement gift for Alicia and Joshua from their registry. I'd only agreed to go when I realized it would look strange for me not to be embracing this milestone in my best friend's life. When we got there, the registry department was packed with brides. Dozens of twenty-something girls walked around with registry guns, scanning china, crystal, flatware, bedding, and kitchen gadgets. I secretly wished one of those guns had real bullets that could put me out of my misery. My stomach actually lurched when I read the sign over the computer that printed out the registry lists: *They've Found Everything They've Dreamed Of. Now It's Your Turn to Choose From the Heart.*

"Isn't that nice?" my mother said, commenting on the sign. She leaned over the computer terminal. "So how does this work?"

"You just put in their names and print out the list," I answered impatiently.

She used one finger to type Alicia and Joshua's names onto the screen. It took forever for her to finish and even longer for their long list of items to print out. I took the papers off the printer, and we headed farther into the store to see what our options were.

"Now, I want to get her one great thing. I hate when

people give a whole mishmash of different items," she said.

I shook my head. "I know, Mom."

"What about you? What are you thinking of getting her?"

"I'm not sure," I said, shrugging my shoulders.

"Well, if I can make a recommendation, you should get them something that stands alone, so that when they take out that platter or teapot, the two of them will know it came from you. If you give them a place setting of china, when they take it out on a holiday or family dinner, they'll never be able to distinguish who gave it to them."

A single place setting of china actually sounded ideal. The last thing I wanted was to give them a gift that gave Joshua any cause to think of me when he took it out at Thanksgiving dinner.

"It's really crowded in here. Why don't we divide and conquer? You take some of the list and I'll take some. We can cover more ground that way."

I wandered into the bedding department, far away from where I knew my mother would shop. She thought that giving bedding as a gift was unseemly and actually abhorred the idea of it being included on a registry. In this instance, I agreed with her, but curiosity got the best of me, and I had to see what Joshua and Alicia had picked out.

I wandered around the bedding department until I spotted the most expensive bedding set Bloomingdale's carried. The sheets were 1500 thread count Egyptian cotton and stark white. Joshua currently owned a very similar set. Staring at the display, my mind drifted back to the first night I'd spent wrapped up in them at his apartment.

Joshua called me at work and offered to make me dinner so that we could talk about the mistake we'd made days earlier. Having no time to freshen up, I did what many women living in New York City did when faced with that situation. On my way to his apartment, I made a detour to a retail chain store selling makeup and other beauty items. Best of all, they encouraged you to sample the products. I dabbed some perfume on in the front of the store and then continued to the back, where I applied new eye shadow, mascara, and lipstick. At work, I'd changed into a fantastic dress that wasn't even in production yet.

We ended up in his stark white bed fifteen minutes after I got to his apartment and didn't leave it until the next morning. We never got around to talking about the huge mistake we'd made the weekend before, or the even bigger one we'd just made. In fact, we hardly talked at all. It was the best, most passionate and exhilarating twelve hours of my life.

I was so absorbed recalling it that I didn't hear my name being called behind me. When I turned around, there was Joshua, standing in the Bloomingdale's bedding department.

"I've been calling your name for the last two minutes," Joshua said. "What has you so preoccupied?"

God, he was beautiful. He looked even better in his casual weekend attire than he did in his three-piece suits. His dirty-blond hair was perfectly tamed, with just a light amount of stubble on his face suggesting he hadn't shaved that morning. He was always more relaxed when Alicia was out of town.

"Nothing. What are you doing here?" I asked.

"Alicia's in Singapore for work," he answered. "She

sent me to do some wedding errands. What are you doing?"

"Looking for an engagement gift, for you actually. My mom's somewhere in fine china. I should go find her," I said, pushing past him.

His eyes softened. "Gigi, why do you keep running away from me? We did nothing wrong. Alicia and I were over when we... Please just—"

"We should keep up appearances in front of Alicia, but it's probably just better if you and I keep to our separate corners." I stared at the ground, trying not to let him see the tears that formed.

"Sweetheart, Gigi, you know—"

Before he could finish his thought, I heard my mother call my name, and we both turned to her.

"Joshua, honey, what a great surprise. Where's Alicia?"

"Working in Singapore this week," he answered quickly.

"Well, this is wonderful. Now you can tell me and Georgica exactly what we should get you. You and Alicia have such exquisite taste that I was having a difficult time choosing." She took him by the arm and directed him toward the china and kitchenware area. "So, tell me about all the wedding plans," she said, totally oblivious to the fact that she was meddling.

"Well, actually, we set a date in August."

"So soon? Why so soon?" she asked.

"The timing works out perfectly with Alicia's promotion. We can get married, take the honeymoon, and when she returns, she can start in her new position. She has a planner working out all the details anyway. It seemed to make the most sense," he continued explaining, looking directly at me.

"Well, when it's right, it's right. No reason to wait," she agreed.

I was stunned. They were getting married in four months. I'd thought I would at least have a year to resign myself to the idea, but no, they'd be husband and wife before the summer was over. I leaned against a display to steady myself and knocked over a glass vase in the process.

"Georgica!" my mother shrieked. I knelt down to pick up the pieces. A salesman rushed to our aid.

"I am so sorry," I said, handing him the pieces of broken glass. The salesman didn't answer me and continued to attend to the mess.

My mother stood off in the corner, embarrassed to be associated with the whole scene. Joshua stepped forward.

"I'll go deal with this. It was my fault," Joshua said, kneeling down next to me.

The salesman looked as though he really didn't care, as long as someone paid for it. Joshua followed him to the register to settle the matter, and my mother and I waited for him.

"Such a gentleman," she gushed. "Somebody raised that young man right. Alicia's a very lucky woman."

"Lucky," I mumbled.

She leaned in close to me. "You know, I never thought I would see this side of you."

"What side?

"You're jealous. It's perfectly understandable. Your best friend's getting married, and not just to some guy, to a great guy. I suppose I'd be jealous, too."

Not wanting to delve into the issue, especially with Joshua so close by, I simply agreed with her. She pushed a piece of hair behind my ear.

"Gigi, remember what I told you at brunch. You could be that happy, too. Don't settle. Go after what you want."

If only it were that simple. What I wanted wasn't up for grabs.

Joshua returned from the register and rejoined us. My mother prattled on about what a gracious gesture he'd made and how we would now, of course, have to get him whatever he and Alicia wanted for an engagement gift.

"Well, I'm not sure what Alicia wants, but I'm hoping someone buys us our comforter," he said.

"If that's what you want," she said uncomfortably.

"Since you both have everything all figured out," I interrupted, "I actually have to be going home."

"Gigi, wait, I'm heading back uptown. I'll go with you," Joshua said.

"I'm not going uptown. I have to stop by my office and pick up some sketches," I lied.

"I'll walk you out to the subway, then," he said.

My mother stood watching the exchange with a puzzled look on her face.

I put on my most genuine smile. "Great."

I leaned over and kissed my mother's cheek and told her I would call her later.

"Bye, Mrs. Goldstein," Joshua added.

"How many times have I told you, it's Kathryn," she said.

"Kathryn," he repeated. He leaned over and gave her a kiss on each cheek. She lit up immediately.

I rushed out of the store, and he could barely keep up with me as I weaved in and out of people and around counters.

"Gigi, slow down," he shouted from behind me. He followed me until we reached the first floor. "I'll make a scene if you don't let me talk to you, you know I will," he said with a mischievous smile.

I thought back to the morning after that first night at his apartment when he'd practically chased me through Central Park trying to convince me that what happened wasn't a mistake and we shouldn't feel guilty exploring the feelings we might have for one another. The more I pushed him away, the more ardent he'd become, until a small crowd gathered to watch the scene play out. I was so mortified, I eventually gave in to him. After that, we'd spent the rest of the day picnicking and making out in the park like teenagers.

Now I pulled him out of the crowd and over to a quieter corner of the jewelry department. "Fine, talk," I said, shifting the weight back and forth from leg to leg.

"Let's walk and talk. Where are you really going?" he asked.

"Home."

We left Bloomingdales and headed up Lexington Avenue in silence, neither of us quite knowing what to say. We'd gone about three blocks when I finally spoke. I dug my hands into my pockets and spun around to face him. "You were so adamant about speaking to me. So speak."

"Give me a second. I thought I knew exactly what I wanted to say to you, but now, I'm not so sure," he said.

By the time we got to my block, I was the one making the scene.

"August, Joshua? You're getting married in *August?* What, you thought if you waited any longer you wouldn't be able to go through with it?"

He paced back and forth running his fingers through his hair. "You begged me not to tell her, Gigi. Maybe if we had, things would have been different."

"I don't believe that," I said, fumbling in my bag for my keys.

"So here we are again, at an impasse."

"No, we're at my apartment, and I'm going inside."

I put down my bag and knelt on the ground to dig for my keys. Before I could stop him, Joshua grabbed me by the arm and pulled me up toward him. I didn't fight him off.

I kissed him back, missing how good it felt to be held and wanted by him. I'd thought about this moment thousands of times since the night we ended our relationship, mentally playing out every possible scenario, almost convincing myself I'd be able to resist him. But now, with his arms wrapped around my waist and his lips working their way up my neck, I surrendered.

I took my keys and let us inside, his lips never leaving mine. We stumbled to my bed and just as I was about to let him right back in, my heart receptive to all of it, his phone rang. It was Alicia calling from Singapore. He hit ignore and placed the phone on my nightstand. He picked his shirt off the floor, slipped it back on and went to the kitchen for a glass of water.

I turned to my side and stared out my open bedroom window. My apartment faced the street, making the rent a little less expensive than it was in the other units. While we were together, Joshua hardly ever stayed at my place because he worried the commotion of Lexington Avenue would keep him up all night. Funny, it'd never bothered me before, yet suddenly all I could hear were taxis honking their horns and sirens rushing by. "The symphony of the city" my father always called it. Now it just sounded like noise.

He sat back down on the bed. I rolled back to face

him. "You know what I was thinking about? Remember how we'd sneak down to the dock at Lake Chinooka—me, you, and Alicia? We'd dangle our feet in the water and talk and laugh until we got called to the dining hall. Remember how quiet it was?"

He slipped a pillow behind me. "What made you think about that?"

Inhaling deeply, I leaned back. "When Alicia got back from London, we decided it was best to hit the reset button and just go back to how it always was. Now we all need to live with our choices."

"But what if I chose wrong?" he asked.

His phone rang again and he reached up to hit ignore.

"You should get that. It's almost five. I'm sure Alicia just wants to say good morning."

He looked down at his watch, "Strange. She's getting up to start her day in and ours is coming to an end."

Although there were a million things I wanted to say to him, the truth was we'd said and done more than any two people in our situation should have. He bent down to kiss my forehead as I handed him his phone. I pulled my knees close to my chest and waited for the thud of the front door as it shut behind him.

I went to the open window and watched as Joshua walked out of my building onto Lexington Avenue, the phone tightly pressed to his ear. Just as he turned the corner up 67th, two fire engines and an ambulance came screaming down the street. I pulled the window closed, but it didn't make one bit of difference. I could still hear it all.

CHAPTER THREE

As head counselor, I had to sit on duty—OD—the first night with one of the other counselors. Every night, the camp required two counselors be staked outside each division to make sure the campers behaved and to be available in case of an emergency. It was a necessary part of the job, but a task none of the counselors ever wanted. To keep it fair, I'd set up a rotation schedule that had each counselor on duty only once a week.

Traditionally, the first night of camp, all the counselors hung out at The Canteen, where a lot of the flirtations that dominated the rest of the summer would be put into motion. Jordana had made a pretty big sacrifice when she offered to sit with me instead of going. I wondered which counselor would stake her claim for Perry until I remembered that as head counselor for the Birch boys, he'd be sitting OD as well.

As the girls were settling in for the night, Jordana and I lit a campfire and made ourselves comfortable on the old rotting picnic table next to it. After a few hours, we walked to each of the cabins and told the girls it was lights out. Although a few of them were asleep, worn out from the long day, most were wide awake, unhappy that we were cutting into their good time by turning off the lights. When I got to Bunk Fourteen, I was surprised to see most of them were in their pajamas settling into bed.

"Well, girls," I said, turning off the light, "hope you had a great first day."

"Night, Gigi," a few of them said in unison.

"Night," I said, closing the door behind me.

Jordana was building up the fire when I got back to our post.

"How were the little terrors?" she asked.

"Surprisingly well behaved."

"Really? I thought they'd be bouncing off the walls or at least hanging from the rafters."

"Me too, but they were quieting down, getting ready to go to bed."

"Great. Maybe tonight won't be so bad. You and I can sit here, gossip, and stuff ourselves with marshmallows," she said, pushing one into her mouth.

We were so wrapped up in our gossip session that I jumped at least two feet in the air when I heard, "OD, Bunk Eleven!" being screamed across the field. I looked at Jordana, who was also startled by the shriek. She started to get up from the bench.

"I got this one," I said.

"You sure?"

"Totally. You were nice enough to sit with me the first night. Don't worry, I got it," I answered.

I turned my flashlight on and aimed it at the rocky, uneven ground that led to Bunk Eleven. I followed the slightly carved-out path, and when I got to the door a small girl with strawberry blonde hair opened it.

"You yelled for OD. What's the matter?" I asked.

"That," she said, pointing up at the rafters.

I shined my flashlight in the direction she was pointing but didn't see a thing.

"There's a bat up there," she said.

"Did you see it?" I asked.

"No, but we heard rustling," a girl chimed in from where the rest of the girls were huddled together.

"So nobody actually saw a bat?" I asked.

"No," they replied together.

"Girls, these cabins are empty ten months out of the year. It's completely likely there's a mouse or squirrel up there." The girls started shrieking before I could even finish my sentence.

I rolled my eyes. "As I was saying, there might be a squirrel or mouse in the rafters, but I really doubt there's a bat. Whatever it is, it's harmless and very high up. So, why don't you all get back to your beds, and I'll make sure maintenance comes here tomorrow and does a thorough sweep of the bunk for creatures of all kinds, okay?"

"Absolutely not," said a very tall and thin girl from behind the rest of the bodies on the bed.

"What's your name?" I asked. She looked a lot like a younger version of the model we'd booked in the last Diane von Furstenberg campaign. I would have told her that, only I had the feeling she didn't need her self-esteem inflated any more than it already was.

"Candice," she answered.

"Candice, I guarantee it isn't a bat. But I promise we'll do a full investigation into this in the morning."

She crossed her arms. "There's absolutely no way I'm going to sleep on the top bunk with rodents only inches from my head."

"The rafters are way higher than any of your beds, so unless whatever's up there is a performer in Cirque du Soleil, there's no way it's getting anywhere close to where your head will be."

"You can't know that for sure," she said. "I'm not going to sleep until you get a maintenance person in here. Do you know how much my parents pay for me to go to this camp? Do you know what they'd say if I told them that I was subjected to sleeping with bats my first night?"

"Now there's more than one bat? Don't you think you're being a little overly dramatic?"

"No, I don't," she answered. "If you don't want to call a maintenance person, that's fine. We'll just keep calling you in here all night to check for it with your flashlight."

I took a deep breath and walked out. These girls were impossible. When I got back to the table, I saw Jordana had finished almost all of the marshmallows. She looked a little bit queasy.

"You don't look so hot," I said.

"I don't feel great," she replied. "If you don't mind, I'm gonna go back to the bunk for a few minutes."

"Sure. I have to go over to the main office and see if any of the maintenance crew are around. There appears to be a bat or a rat or a something in Bunk Eleven, and the girls have declared mutiny until it's removed."

She nodded and then hurried back to our bunk. I hiked through the camp's grounds, and by the time I got to the office, I was absolutely fuming. Worse, as anticipated, nobody was around. The office was empty and dark. I took my time walking back, trying to calm down and regroup. It was only the first night, and already, these girls were getting the best of me. I'd just taken orders from a thirteen-year-old who was using a two-hundred-dollar James Perse outfit as pajamas.

I was twice their age, with twice their life experience. *I* was in charge of *them*, not the other way around. I was going to march back into that bunk and let those girls know I was no pushover and that we were handling the situation my way, end of story. I was so fired up by the time I got back to the table that I almost walked right past Jordana. She was standing waiting for me, her hands on her hips, shaking her head. I rushed over.

"What's the matter?"

"I went back to our cabin to get some Pepto-Bismol, and when I walked in, all but three of the girls were gone."

"What do you mean gone? "I asked.

"Gone, nowhere to be found. Gone," she answered.

"Who stayed behind?"

"Alana, Madison, and Abby," she answered.

"Where are they now?"

She shook her head. "They're in the cabin, but they're not talking."

"Oh, yes, they are," I said.

"I didn't know when you'd be back. I didn't want to leave the rest of the girls unattended to go look for them," she said frantically.

"You did the right thing," I reassured her. "They aren't missing. I'm sure they're sneaking over to the boys' side. I'll go talk to the three of them and confirm."

When I opened the door, the three girls were sitting together on a bottom bunk bed, whispering to one another. All three of their heads turned to look at me when I came in.

"So, Jordana tells me you aren't giving up the location of the rest of your bunkmates," I said as calmly as I could. "I respect that. But you should know a few things. If they tried to sneak over to the boys' side and Gordy catches them before I do, they'll get kicked out of camp. So I hope the three of you really do like each other and stick together, because you may be all each other has this summer when the other girls get sent home."

I was bluffing. Gordy wouldn't kick the girls out for their first offense, but it certainly wouldn't do much for my reputation and job if, on the very first night of camp, girls from my group—let alone my cabin—got caught bunk hopping.

"So, who wants to tell me how long ago they left?" I asked, looking at each of them.

Abby spoke up first. "They left about a fifteen minutes ago when Bunk Eleven called OD."

"Okay, so how'd they do it? Did they sneak out the window in the bathroom?" I asked, remembering how Alicia and I used to sneak out of our bunk.

"No, they went out the front door," Alana answered.

I looked over to the door. "How'd they do that without us seeing them?" I asked.

"They waited for Bunk Eleven to call OD and walked out the front door when Jordana was turned the other way."

"So let me understand, they *waited* for Bunk Eleven to call OD, meaning they knew it was going to happen ahead of time?" I asked.

The girls didn't respond and instead looked at each other for permission to tattle. Madison broke the silence.

"Bunk Eleven was in on it. They were supposed to distract you by saying they saw a bat in their rafters so the girls from our bunk could sneak out. If it worked for us they were planning to try it next week."

I balled my hand into a fist. "Stay here and don't give

Jordana any more trouble tonight. I'll deal with you all when I get back."

"Us? What'd we do?" Alana whined.

Madison shot Alana the same look I'd just given her, and she didn't say another word. I slammed the bunk door behind me.

I didn't bother filling Jordana in on what was going on. The most important thing was finding the girls before anyone else did. I had one huge advantage. I'd been in their shoes. Having been a camper at Chinooka, I was pretty sure how they were going to get to the boys' side. There was only one way they could do it without being seen—the hidden trail in the woods around the lake. Alicia and I had used it half a dozen times to sneak over and meet Joshua. I grabbed my flashlight off the picnic table and set out after them.

The girls had a bit of a head start on me, so there was no point in trying to catch up. I'd be better off waiting for them to emerge from the woods on the boys' side. Unfortunately, in order to do that, I had to walk straight through Perry's division. There was no way around it. I decided to play it cool. I'd walk over like I was dropping by to casually say hello.

When I got there, Perry was playing the guitar while the other counselor was throwing small branches into the dying fire. I stepped on some dry leaves, and they both turned to look at me.

"Announce yourself," Perry said, jokingly squinting past the fire to make out who I was.

"It's Gigi, from Cedar," I said, approaching them slowly.

"You may enter Birch, Miss Gigi," he said in a deep, bellowing voice. The two guys were laughing. "What can I do for you?" Perry asked.

"I'm just on rounds, making sure things are okay over here," I said as confidently as I could.

"We've got things under control. Right, Eric?" he asked, turning to the younger guy on his left.

"Right," Eric answered.

"Okay, good," I said, unsure how to get past them to the clearing where the girls were sure to appear. I needed to kill some more time. "You know, I don't think we got off to a great start this morning. Maybe we should start fresh?"

Perry forcefully zipped up his sweatshirt. "That's not necessary."

"What's that supposed to mean?"

"It means that I don't need any further introduction. I know all I need to about you."

"You don't know anything about me," I said.

He jumped off the bench so he was face-to-face with me.

"Let's see," he said, using his fingers to count. "You're a city girl, born and bred. You took this gig as way to escape real life for a few months. You have a boyfriend at home, but you needed your space and are hoping absence makes the heart grow fonder?"

"I grew up in New York City, so I guess you're right about that."

He raised his eyebrows. "And the rest?"

"None of your business." His arrogance was really beginning to irritate me.

He circled me like a hawk. "So why did you really come over here, especially so late? Miss me?"

I crossed my arms. "Hardly."

He narrowed his eyes and stepped even closer to me. "It's not in our job description to make rounds."

"I wanted to apologize if you thought I was stepping

on your turf this afternoon. I wanted to get the girls excited and thought a friendly competition would get them fired up. But if you're gonna be an *ass* about it..."

He shrugged his shoulders and backed away. "*Whatever* you say," he said, mocking me, as he'd done earlier in the dining hall.

"You know what? I take back my apology. I'm not sorry, and I hope my girls wipe the floor with your boys this summer."

"Which girls?"

"My girls. The Cedar girls," I answered.

He pointed to the clearing, where all of them had come into view. "Oh, I thought you meant those girls?"

I pushed past him and trudged over to where they stood. Dressed from head to toe in black, they looked shocked that they'd been caught.

"Hi, ladies," I said, approaching them. Perry followed up behind me.

"Wandered a little far from home tonight, didn't we, girls?" he said, smiling and waving at them.

"I got this. Thanks for your help," I said.

"Really? 'Cause if you had this, they probably wouldn't be standing here. They'd be back in their own bunk, sleeping."

"Girls, let's get back to the bunk. We'll discuss this back on our side," I yelled.

"Good idea. Why don't you follow Gigi back the way you came, and I'll pretend I never saw you." His accent almost made him sound sincere. I could see all the girls gazing at him.

"And why, pray tell, would you do that?" I asked.

"Cause I'm a hell of a nice guy," he said, flashing a smile and two dimples.

"No, really, what's your angle?"

"It might be fun to have something to hold over your head," he said smugly.

"Come on, girls!" I yelled. "Let's go. NOW!"

I took the lead, and they followed me back the way they'd just come. I could hear them whispering to each other behind me. I turned to face them.

"Enough talking, let's just get back to the bunk."

They nodded, and we walked the rest of the way in silence. When we got back to our side, I could see Jordana pacing nervously by the fire. She ran over to us. I motioned for the girls to get inside the bunk and told them to wait for me there.

"What happened?" Jordana asked.

"I caught them. Well, actually, Perry caught them trying to sneak into his division."

"Did he rat us out?" she asked.

"No," I said through a huge yawn, "but he was definitely happy to have something he could hold over me. I'll read the girls the riot act before they start plotting their next great escape."

It was only midnight, but I was totally exhausted. In my New York City life, I'd be getting ready to go out at this time of night. Now, I was counting down the hours until I could go to sleep. When I got into the bunk, I noticed that the girls were smart enough to have changed out of their camouflage and into pajamas. I sat down on my bed and waited for them to quiet down before I spoke.

"Look, I was a camper here once upon a time. I know your tricks and the secret paths and passages. You should know that the woods you crept through tonight aren't completely safe. Chinooka owns a lot of those grounds, but there's no way to patrol them all or keep local campers or drifters out of the area. Long story short, do not try it again. If you do, I'll walk you straight to Gordy and turn you in myself, got it?"

They nodded back at me. "The rest of you should thank Madison, Alana, and Abby. Even under unrelenting torture and questioning, they didn't give up your whereabouts. I had to figure it out without their help."

I heard Maddy let out the deep breath she'd been holding. "I'm content to pretend this never happened, if I get your unconditional promise it won't happen again."

Emily B spoke up first. "We're really sorry, Gigi, it won't happen again. We just wanted to see if we could make it to the boys' side."

"Congratulations, you made it. Now, if no one else has anything to say for themselves, it's time for bed."

I shut off the lights in the bunk and went to join Jordana outside. She was anxious to hear how it went and told me she thought I'd handled the situation well. I was glad to hear it. After how completely reckless I'd been the last year, suddenly being accountable for not only my own decisions but also for the choices and actions of impressionable teenage girls was a pretty daunting task.

About an hour later, the rest of the counselors from our division came staggering back to their respective cabins, and Jordana and I decided we could abandon our OD post and call it a night. When we returned to the bunk, we were grateful to find all the girls asleep, including Tara, who'd already passed out on her bed in her clothes. Jordana and I washed our faces in the bathroom and changed into pajamas, trying not to stir anyone.

"We did okay tonight, partner," Jordana whispered as we crawled into our beds. I wrestled with the sheets for a few seconds before noticing that Jordana was struggling to get into her bed, too.

"They short-sheeted our beds," I said, on the verge of hysterical laughter.

"What does that mean?" Jordana asked, trying her best to continue to whisper.

"It's a prank. They folded the sheets so that we can't stretch out our legs."

"I don't understand," she said, wrestling with her comforter.

"Pull the sheets and blankets out on all sides and just remake the bed in the morning. Trust me, it will be easier than trying to make sense of it right now."

We both got out of our beds and practically tore them apart in order to be able to get back into them.

"You have to admit, it's a little bit funny," I said, lying back down on top of my bed, not even bothering to climb underneath the blankets.

"A little bit," she said, laughing.

"Could've been worse," I said.

"Really?"

"Trust me. A lot worse," I said, remembering the time that Alicia and I had left a dead mouse in one of our counselor's beds. She quit the very next morning.

CHAPTER FOUR

A few weeks after getting fired from Diane von Furstenberg, I went for drinks with one of the few friends I'd stayed in touch with from *Top Designer*, Jamie Malone. Jamie was now working for The Gap but saw himself as a sellout. He designed mainstream clothing, but in his free time, he created some of the most outrageous and incredible pieces of wearable art I'd ever seen. Jamie had the distinction of being the first one kicked off our season of *Top Designer* following a disastrous challenge where we were asked to make a wedding gown out of toilet paper. It was his very minor claim to fame, but he milked it for all it was worth —usually very little.

We decided to meet for drinks at midnight at one of my favorite bars in his neighborhood, Schiller's. The bar held some sentimental value, as it was one of Joshua and my favorite haunts.

At first, I'd loved how my relationship with Joshua forced us both to step outside of our comfort zone and usual routines. Joshua couldn't bring me to his favorite five-star restaurants or company box seats since he and Alicia frequented all of them. I couldn't take him to any fashion shows or industry parties because I routinely scored Joshua and Alicia places on those guest lists. We realized that in order to stay under the radar, we had to become anonymous.

As a couple, Joshua and I had been strangers to a more underground version of New York City, always on the lookout for some obscure restaurant, show, or gallery opening. I'd lived in New York my whole life without doing half the things he and I did over those few months.

Schiller's was a favorite. It was an old-style liquor bar that seemed transported from a small town in France. The wine was served in emptied-out Coke bottles, and french fries and mussels were available twenty-four hours a day. It wasn't completely hidden, but it was off the beaten path enough that we never worried about getting caught when we ate there.

Walking in the door, I spotted Jamie sitting at a booth near the front. He waved me over and gave me a kiss on each cheek.

"Sit," he said, motioning me into the booth. "I ordered us shots of vodka."

I took off my jean jacket and inched onto the long bench. "So it's gonna be one of *those* nights?"

He took both of my hands in his and leaned in. "So I'm just going to say it. When I didn't hear from you, I called your office. Whoever answered told me you're no longer working at Diane von Furstenberg. Something you want to tell me?"

I pulled my hands back and downed the shot of vodka in front of me. "I got fired."

"Okay, so they downsized. It's no big deal," he replied.

"Not downsized. Fired. I dried up creatively or something," I said, shrugging my shoulders. "I sat at my workstation day after day just staring at my sketchpad and nothing came. It's a block. Or maybe I don't have it and never did. Either way, it wasn't the company's fault. They gave me a dozen opportunities to redeem myself. I couldn't."

"Gigi…" he said.

"It's fine. It was a job, and people get fired from their jobs. Look at you. You got kicked off *Top Designer* first in front of millions of people, and you're doing great," I teased.

"We'll need another shot," he said, calling to the waitress.

"And a plate of fries—actually, two plates," I said, calling out after her.

Suddenly Jamie looked very serious. "Can I ask you a question? Does this have anything to do with the married guy?"

After things started with Joshua, I'd been absolutely bursting at the seams to tell somebody about it. Jamie had sensed a change in me and began to question my newfound happiness. Although I'd wanted to tell him the truth, Joshua and I had decided we weren't going to tell anyone about our relationship until Alicia got back from her program in London and we could tell her in person. So, I made up a story about how I was seeing someone I worked with. It wasn't so far-fetched, and some of the made-up story really did parallel what was going on in my life.

"He went back to his wife. You knew that, right? The

two of them have completely reconciled." All the alcohol rushed to my face. "Are my cheeks red?"

"A little. Gigi, stop," he said.

I threw back Jamie's shot of vodka. "Stop what?"

"I know the guy is Joshua. I saw you here with him," Jamie said.

If my cheeks weren't red before, I was sure they'd just turned a bright shade of crimson. "You saw us?"

"It was a few months ago. You were in that booth back there," he said, pointing to the corner. "Does Alicia know?"

"No," I answered. "They're getting married in August."

The waitress brought out our plates of french fries, and Jamie asked again for the second round of shots she'd forgotten. He put his hands over his mouth. "You're still seeing him?"

I shook my head. "No, no of course not. We ran into each other in the registry department in Bloomingdale's of all places, and he dropped that bomb."

"Gigi, how did this thing with him even start?"

There were so many answers to his question. In some ways, it had started when I was on the bus my first summer at Camp Chinooka. Never having been away from home before, I was terrified. Joshua had sat down beside me and we'd talked the whole way to camp. I first fell in love with him that day.

Maybe things really began during our senior prom, when we were standing outside the Sheinmans' apartment building taking pictures. Joshua was Alicia's date, and I'd gone with a friend. As we made our way toward the limo, Joshua had turned to me and told me that he'd never seen me looking more beautiful. After that, my own date hardly existed to me.

Or three years later at a New Year's Eve party, when Joshua had kissed me in a dark corner of the crowded dance floor while Alicia was getting a drink from the bar. It wasn't a full-on passionate kiss—more like a peck between drunk friends—but I knew I was in trouble when I realized how much it had meant to me.

Then, when I moved in with Alicia, my feelings only seemed to intensify. On the nights Joshua was over waiting for Alicia to come home from work, we would talk for hours. I'd hold my breath every time I heard the elevator door open in the hallway, silently praying it wouldn't be her. Of course, she always returned, and it was as though those stolen moments had never happened.

After that, I'd kept my distance, fearing that my feelings would be obvious to one or both of them. Alicia would invite me to join them for dinner or a movie, and I'd make up excuse after excuse so as not to have to be around Joshua. I was actually relieved when Alicia announced she'd be spending at least a year in London for work. I was certain that Joshua would have no need to visit our apartment, and I'd finally be able to get over him.

Then, the completely unexpected happened. Alicia broke up with Joshua before her trip. After dating him most of her life, she'd decided she needed a clean break and the opportunity to explore other relationships. Within a month, she was seeing someone new. By the two-month mark, she was calling to tell me she was considering moving to London permanently. I'd hung up the phone, my heart pounding, because for the first time since I'd known him, Joshua was free.

I gave Jamie the simplest explanation I could. "It

started last year when Alicia was in London. When she got back, it ended."

He gave me a look that said he didn't quite believe my straightforward answer.

"I've been the third wheel in their relationship since we were kids. When Joshua wanted to know what to buy Alicia for a birthday or how to surprise her for an anniversary, he came to me. When she was mad at him for one reason or another, I made it right again. I don't remember when I first fell in love with him because I can't even recall a time I wasn't."

He rubbed my forearm. "So, what are you going to do?"

"You know as well as I do, it's gonna take some time before any fashion house is willing to look at me. I have some of the money I won on *Top Designer* saved, but I'll have to figure something else out in the next couple of weeks."

"There's always Mama and Papa Goldstein," he suggested.

"I'm almost twenty-seven years old. I'm not asking my parents for help unless I'm completely desperate. Besides, they've been waiting for this since I threw all those law school acceptances away. I can't give them the satisfaction."

"You know you can always crash at my place if you need to. It's not big, but we'd make it work."

I reached across the table and gave his hand a squeeze. "You're a good friend, Jamie."

He gave me a reassuring smile. "Have you seen Alicia since the engagement announcement?"

"She's been in Singapore this last week for work. She doesn't even know I was fired, and I'm not planning on telling her."

"What?" He practically spewed his vodka across the table.

"I just need to get away for the summer. Maybe I'll travel? Backpack through Europe? I need to disappear. If she thinks I'm getting ready for the fall fashion shows, she'll get over the fact I can't go to the wedding. She puts work ahead of almost everything. She'll understand."

"You know, just because you convince yourself she'll understand, that doesn't make it true," he said.

"No, she will," I said firmly.

"Maybe you should fess up? Shouldn't she know what she's getting in a husband?"

"It's not like that. Joshua loves her, not me. He has since we were children. I was just a distraction. A way of getting over her," I answered.

"Did he ever outright tell you that? "Jamie asked.

"No, never," I said.

Jamie raised his eyebrows. "Well?"

"Either way, in a few weeks, I'll be out of the equation, and things will go back to the way they were."

"You don't really believe that, do you? Things like this can never go back," he said.

Over the past few months, I'd fervently held onto the belief that if I could put enough time and distance between Joshua and me and what we'd done, our actions could be forgotten. It was the only thing that had enabled me to be around Alicia without being suffocated by guilt. I clung to that hope. I staked everything on it.

Jamie looked me squarely in the eye. "You should tell her."

"Why hurt her? It's done now."

"If you still have feelings for him, how can it be done?"

"They'll get married like all of us always knew they

would, and I'll take up the role of the single friend they invite over for holidays. It's a foolproof plan." I looked up at Jamie. "Do you think I'm a terrible person?"

He another sip of his drink. "We can't choose who we fall in love with."

"I could have chosen not to act on it, though," I said.

"I know it's hard because you still love him—and her, for that matter—but you didn't *really* do anything wrong here. They were broken up. *Alicia* ended it. He didn't leave her for you, and you didn't cause their relationship to end. You took a chance on a love you've always harbored with a guy who's always been there. What's so wrong with that?" Jaime took a breath and continued. "And you forget there were two of you. You should tell him how you feel, Gigi. Don't let him dictate the ending to this story if you want a different one." He grinned and leaned over to muss my hair. "You'll be okay, kiddo, I promise."

I smoothed my hair back into place. "Kiddo? You're only a few years older than me."

"But decades wiser," he said, winking.

The waitress brought our bill, and we continued to talk until we were interrupted by an obviously drunk couple who'd placed a bet on whether or not Jamie had been a contestant on *Top Designer*.

"What do you have riding on my answer?" Jamie asked them.

"If she wins, I have to buy her a shot. If I win, she has to go home with me tonight," the guy replied.

"Which one of you thinks I was on the show?"

The guy pointed to the girl next to him. "She does," he answered.

"Sorry to disappoint you. I've been told I look like the

contestant from the show, but it wasn't me," Jamie responded.

"Sorry to bother you, dude," the guy said, taking the girl by the hand and walking away.

"That was generous of you," I said.

"Being on *Top Designer* should help someone get laid," he joked. "Even if that person isn't me."

I leaned way over and gave Jamie a kiss on the cheek. "What a sad pair we are. What happened to the two young eager designers ready to take on the world?"

"We did reality television," he said, laughing. "The exact moment we sold out is probably playing in the form of a *Top Designer* rerun marathon right now. But, darling, there's always tomorrow," he said, taking my hand to help me out of the booth.

"And after all, tomorrow is another day," I said, finishing the famous quote from *Gone with the Wind*.

Gone with the Wind was Jamie's favorite movie and a constant source of inspiration for him. Although his design school professors had advised him against it, he'd been adamant that his final show before graduation be inspired by the film. He'd proved all the skeptics wrong, sending the most incredibly outrageous hoop skirts and gowns down the runway. The original dresses had inspired his designs but he'd reconfigured them in such a way that they were completely fresh and new. The publicity he'd received from that show had garnered him both his job with The Gap and his spot on *Top Designer*—both career moves he wished he could take back.

"Promise? "I asked.

"Cross my heart," he said. "Now let's get you into a cab."

Jamie and I staggered out of Schiller's, and after trying to hail a cab for what seemed like hours, one finally stopped and agreed to take me all the way back uptown to my apartment. Jamie gave me a kiss on each cheek and made me promise to text him when I got home so he would know I was safe.

After a few minutes, the steady rocking of the cab began to lull me to sleep. I rolled the window down for some fresh air and fished around in my bag for my keys. As I dug deeper into the bag, my hand brushed against my phone. I yanked it out and, in my alcoholic haze, decided to break the one and only rule I'd established for myself during my virtually rule-free affair: no drunk dialing. Ever.

Drunk dialing, also known as a DUI (dialing under the influence) was the most pathetic of all possible acts someone could commit, but at that moment, I didn't care one bit. I was drunk and Jamie's words about not letting Joshua dictate the ending were reverberating in my head. I wanted to hear Joshua tell me—to reassure me—that even if he couldn't be with me for all the reasons we'd agonized over for the last year, he at least recognized what he'd given up in letting me go, and would always be sorry for it. Before I could second-guess my decision, I dialed his number. He picked up on the second ring.

"Ali?" he said groggily.

I'd woken him out of a sound sleep, and he assumed it was Alicia calling him at this strange hour from Singapore. I stayed silent on the other end of the phone and waited for him to say her name again.

"Ali, is that you? Are you okay?" he repeated.

"It's Gigi," I answered.

He sounded more alert and awake. "Is everything okay? You never call me on this number."

"Yeah, fine, everything's fine," I replied, my voice quivering.

"Gigi, what if Alicia answered my phone?"

"She's in Singsapore—I mean, Singapore," I said, slurring my words.

"Are you drunk?"

"I'm fine," I answered. "Are you alone?"

"Of course I'm alone. As we just established, Alicia's in Singapore. Sweetheart, this isn't like you. What's going on?"

The vodka acted like a truth serum. Finally, I had the courage to tell him the thing I'd hinted at, alluded to, and danced around, but never been able to say. "Choose me," I said through trembling lips. "If you think you chose wrong, then choose me now."

The minute the words came out of my mouth, I knew I'd put myself on a course from which there was no turning back. I swallowed hard and continued.

"Joshua, I've loved you ever since I was that homesick little girl whose hand you held all the way to Camp Chinooka. I know it sounds crazy, but even with all of our secrets, I've loved you more honestly than anyone in my life."

Then, with my next sentence, I crossed our line in the sand. "I can tell Alicia now. I'm completely prepared for the consequences as long as I have you." I inhaled deeply and waited for his response.

"Georgica, sweetheart. It's so much more complicated than that."

Déjà vu. I'd heard those very words from him before. I thought back to the previous summer, when we'd sneaked away for a weekend at my parents' house in the Hamptons, while they were off visiting friends on Martha's Vineyard. Since their house would be empty, we'd jumped on the Jitney and at the chance to escape reality and the hot and stifling city. The Hamptons was never really my scene, but my parents had achieved their dream of owning a beautiful and secluded home off Georgica Pond. It was an ideal locale for a couple looking for a weekend getaway.

Joshua and I took full advantage of our privacy and freedom, lounging by the pool all day, and then cooking gourmet meals and eating them on the patio at night. Our third night, after we finished putting away the dishes from our makeshift clam bake, we'd decided to go for a late-night soak in the hot tub beside the pool. We'd polished off our second bottle of champagne and were making out heavily in the water when I heard my father's voice coming through the pathway that led from the front lawn to the back of the house. A few seconds later, my father had walked in arm in arm with a woman who was most certainly my age, if not younger. There'd been no way to hide from them, and they'd noticed us immediately. I pulled myself out of the hot tub and wrapped a towel around my waist. Joshua stayed in the water, completely silent.

"Mom told me you were going to be in Martha's Vineyard this weekend."

I noticed the girl on my father's arm staring at Joshua, and it had only infuriated me more.

"She went. I didn't go," my father answered.

"I can see that," I snapped back at him. I suspected this wasn't the first time my father had cheated on my mother, only the first time he'd been caught.

"No, Gigi. You don't understand," he said calmly. "This is Samara. She's a paralegal with the firm."

"What's he paying you?" I questioned her. "Don't forget to ask for time and a half. I mean, he did drag you all the way to his empty house in the Hamptons."

He took two steps toward the hot tub. "Gigi, that's enough."

Joshua climbed out and stood beside me to lend support.

My father put on his glasses. "Joshua, right?"

"Yes. Hello, Mr. Goldstein," he answered.

"Aren't you Alicia's friend?"

Checkmate. My father knew perfectly well that Joshua had been Alicia's boyfriend. My father was the top litigator at the most prestigious law firm in New York City. He made his reputation on his uncanny talent for being able to dissect any situation into cold hard facts. He'd just caught me in an equally compromising situation to the one I'd caught him in, and we were, for better or for worse, evenly matched in our wrongdoings.

"I think we should call it a night and head back to the city," Joshua suggested.

My father walked past us and around to the front door of the house. "That would be a very good idea," he muttered.

Samara stood there trying desperately not to make eye contact with me, which only made me feel worse. In reality, she and I weren't all that different. Simultaneously, I was the other woman *and* Alicia all rolled into one. It was a complicated paradox. In that moment, when the realization of the situation mixed together with the two bottles of champagne we'd just finished, I knew I was going to be sick.

I ran inside, and Joshua followed me into the bathroom where I threw up dinner and continued to dry heave until there was absolutely nothing left in me. I broke down and cried on the bathroom floor while he held me in his arms and kissed my head.

"I just don't understand. How could he do that? "I sobbed.

"Shhh, try to calm down," he said, smoothing my hair.

"Do you think he loves her?"

"Georgica, sweetheart, it's far more complicated than that."

"I should go," I said, picking myself up from the bathroom floor. "We should go. There's no reason to stay here, not now."

As I rose, Joshua wrapped his arms over my shoulders and around my neck, pulling me into his chest. I leaned my head back into him, and he rocked me back and forth.

"I'm not sorry," he said turning me around. "For any of it. Are you?"

"I'm sorry for all of it," I said.

"I'm sorry to hear that," he whispered in my ear.

Suddenly, the line from the movie *Love Story*, "Love means never having to say you're sorry," came into my head—a line I'd never fully understood until now. If love meant never having to say you were sorry, and here we both were expressing regret for all we'd done and all we'd been, this couldn't be love. What it was, though, I wasn't sure.

Over the next few months, I'd agonized over that question. From that point on, I'd obsessed over every word he and I exchanged and every glance he threw my way. I clung to his promise that maybe our separation was only temporary. My work suffered, my personal life suffered, and by the time Joshua and Alicia announced their engagement, I was unrecognizable, even to myself.

Now, almost a full year later, I was hanging on at the other end of a phone, having laid all my feelings on the line. I couldn't take back what I'd just said to Joshua, and because it was the last time I'd ever plead for his affection, I didn't regret a single sentence.

"Maybe it was complicated, but now it's simple. Joshua, choose me," I repeated.

"I can't," he answered, his voice losing all power.

"Can't or won't?"

"Gigi, please get home safe, okay?"

"Please Joshua, wait—" I whispered to the dial tone.

I hung up the phone and sobbed so hard that the cab driver pulled over to the side of Second Avenue, where I pushed open the door and preceded to throw up vodka and french fries into a storm drain. The driver helped me back into the cab and then took me to my apartment, where I stumbled inside and passed out on the couch.

In the morning, my apartment felt stuffy and small, the guilt and shame of the night before completely suffocating me. I stood up to open some windows and noticed a packet with the Camp Chinooka logo peeking out from the pile of mail on my coffee table. I slowly pulled it out from underneath the large pile of bills I'd been avoiding and opened the envelope. Inside was a brochure, job application, and letter from Camp Chinooka's director, Gordon Birnbaum.

Dear Camp Chinooka Alumni,

As we enter into our 100th summer, we need you more than ever. We're looking for hard-working, fun-loving, energetic, and enthusiastic former campers to return to Chinooka as counselors or head counselors. If you think you have what it takes, and are looking to recapture a bit of your youth in the beautiful Poconos, enclosed is an application. Come join us for our amazing centennial year! We look forward to welcoming you back to the Chinooka family, your home away from home.

Sincerely,
Gordon "Gordy" Birnbaum

The answer was so simple and now, staring me in the face. I could work as a counselor at Camp Chinooka for the summer and get away from everyone and everything. I needed a job and a hideout—this was both. I needed time to mend my broken heart and figure out what to do with the rest of my life. Most of all, I relished the notion that I could actually revisit a time and place in my life where not every decision was life-altering and the possibilities had seemed wide open. I sat down at the kitchen table and filled out the application, and before I had time to second-guess my decision, slid it into my building's mail chute.

Weeks later, I received a phone call from Gordy's secretary, inviting me to Camp Chinooka's New York offices for an interview. I'd already put my apartment on some sites for subletting and spoken to potential tenants about renting for the summer. The morning of the interview, I stood at my closet for what seemed like hours, trying to decide what to wear. A suit seemed too formal, but slacks didn't seem formal enough. I finally settled on a wrap dress I'd made for myself a few years before. It was perfect.

My interview wasn't with Gordy but with one of the other camp directors, Suzanne Tillman. Suzanne was in her mid-forties and had been the drama counselor back when I was a camper. She didn't remember me. She did, of course, remember Alicia.

"So, let's see," she said, flipping through my application. "You were a camper at Chinooka?"

"That's right," I answered.

"Wonderful. I was working as the drama counselor back in those days," she said.

"I worked backstage in one of your productions of *Fiddler on the Roof*."

She scrunched up her nose. "Really?"

"My friend Alicia played Hodel in that same show," I said.

"Alicia Scheinman?"

"Yes."

"Our best Hodel to date. Are you two still close?"

"The best of friends," I replied.

"Wonderful. So, Georgica," she said, changing the subject, "Why are you applying to be a counselor at Chinooka?"

"You can call me Gigi. Everyone does."

She nodded and leaned in, waiting for my answer.

"As a kid, camp was the one place you could reinvent yourself. Truth is, I've always wanted to go back and work as a counselor. Each summer, something else just seemed to get in the way of me doing it," I said.

She leaned in even closer. "What's different now?"

"I'm at a bit of a crossroads, both personally and professionally," I said.

She was making notes all over the application. "Can you elaborate?"

"Up until a few weeks ago, I was a designer with Diane von Furstenberg. I was let go. Now, I'm not really sure what I want to do with my life," I answered.

"And personally?"

"Alicia Scheinman's getting married in a few months to a really great guy. I'm still very single."

She pushed her hair behind her ears. "Say no more. I completely understand."

I glanced down and noticed she wasn't wearing a wedding ring.

She continued, "We have an opening for a head

counselor for Cedar. Think you'd be up to the challenge?"

The Cedar girls were notoriously one of the worst behaved groups at camp. Thirteen-year-old girls, full of hormones, convinced they were too mature to be told what to do but too immature not to be. They took any chance they could to push boundaries and challenge authority. Only a small number of counselors had ever lasted the whole summer with them, but I was so desperate for the chance to get away, she could have told me I'd be looking after convicts and I probably would've accepted the job.

The interview lasted another half hour. When it was over, Suzanne told me that, pending the background check, the job was mine. I thanked her profusely for the opportunity.

She called out to me as I was leaving. "Gigi?"

I turned around. "Yes?"

"You know it's just a temporary means of escape, right? Your same life will be waiting for you when you get home."

"I just need one more summer," I replied.

She nodded and said, "I'll send all the employment documents when the background check comes through."

Armed with a plan for escaping the summer, I was ready to face the world. I just had one hurdle left—facing Alicia.

CHAPTER FIVE

After my night chasing the girls around the grounds of Chinooka, I was awakened by Gordy blasting music through the camp's speaker system. His routine hadn't changed one bit. He turned the music down and screamed into the microphone, doing his best impression of Robin Williams. "Goooooood morning, Camp Chinooka. It's 0600 hours. What does the 'O' stand for? Oh my God, it's early. It's time to rise and shine. It's a beautiful seventy-two degrees and sunny. Breakfast is in one hour. Last one there, gets *no* eggs."

The entire *Good Morning, Vietnam* reference went right over the kids' heads, but he continued with it anyway.

"Competition for the Gordy is already underway, with Cedar taking a slight lead. What are you gonna do about it, Perry?" Gordy asked before blasting *Eye of the Tiger*.

I looked over to my right, where Jordana was mumbling the lyrics to the song in her sleep. I threw my pillow at her. "Hey, rise and shine."

"I feel like death," she muttered back.

"Between the short-sheeting and my impromptu hike around Chinooka last night, I'm not feeling much better myself. But guess what? We got a shout-out this morning."

"Why?" she asked, crawling out from underneath her comforter.

"He said we're in the early lead for the Gordy."

"Great," she garbled and rolled back over.

"Jordana," I shouted.

"I'm up, I'm up," she said, sitting upright in her bed.

"Okay, now we just have to get *them* up."

"I'll take the left. You take the right," she said grudgingly.

I popped out of bed and stepped onto the cold wood floor. Goose bumps rose up and down my arms and legs. I tiptoed across the room and flipped on the light switch. There was a collective group of moans. Several of the girls covered their heads with their pillows and sank more deeply under their blankets.

"Good morning, girls," I said as cheerily as I could. "Time to get up. We have a lot to do this morning." More groans.

I walked back over to my area and got dressed while Jordana and Tara went around to each of the sleeping girls and basically shook them awake. I took my hair straightening iron into the bathroom and had just started to try smoothing out the mess on my head when the lights in the bunk flickered. I ignored it until they shut off completely.

"What just happened?" I yelled.

"We blew a fuse," Tara answered.

"How is that even possible? All I plugged in was my hair iron."

"Your hair iron, but their alarm clocks, fans, and iPod chargers. It's too much for the old wiring," Jordana said as she flipped the switch in the fuse box.

"Girls, please unplug some of your things so I can use this real quick." They all stared at me blankly. "Now!" I insisted.

I waited a few seconds and plugged the iron back in. The lights flickered and went out a second time. I pulled the cord out of the wall, walked over to the fuse box, and flipped the switch again.

"I don't think you can use your hair iron in the bunk, Gigi," Tara said.

"Thank you for your observation, Tara."

"No problem."

"What's the matter?" Jordan asked.

"Nothing," I said, looking enviously at her stick-straight red hair. I threw my own hair up into a bun and pulled out the work wheel from one of my cubbies.

"For those of you who may not know, this is a work wheel," I said, gesturing Vanna White style. "You'll notice that I included my name, Tara's name, and Jordana's name on the wheel. We live here too, so I thought it was only fair that we help out."

A few of the girls raised their eyebrows, surprised we would volunteer ourselves when we didn't have to. "I'm going to give it a spin, and let's get this party started," I said, giving the wheel a good turn. I doled out all of the chores and clapped my hands to get the girls moving. "All the cleaning supplies are under the sink. Let me know if you need anything."

After I finished cleaning the bathroom (lucky me), I went outside for roll call. A lot of very tired-looking campers and counselors lined up in front of me.

"Hope you girls had a great first night at camp. Bunk

Eleven, I hope you girls slept well. No other bat incidents?" I asked, smiling. Brooke and Michelle, Bunk Eleven's counselors, looked incredibly confused. "I'll be in the gazebo after breakfast to do activity sign-ups. We already have a slight lead on the Gordy, so let's keep it up going into the dining hall. Repeat after me: 'Cedar girls, Cedar girls, we've got the spirit. Cedar girls, Cedar girls, come on, let's hear it."

The girls half-heartedly repeated after me. After a few more rounds, they joined in the chant, which grew in volume with each repetition. Perry was waiting for me outside the dining hall.

"Morning, Princess," he said, leaning back into the wall.

"Morning," I grumbled back.

"You look like you could use a latte."

"You have no idea."

He held the screen door open for me. "Well, there's cold, watery coffee inside—enjoy," he said.

When I got into the dining hall, I noticed the Birch boys were dressed head to toe in Chinooka blue and gold and were sitting silently at their tables. When they spotted me, they started singing. "We love you, Gigi, oh, yes, we do. We don't love anyone as much as you. When you're not near us, we're blue AND GOLD. Oh, Gigi, we love you."

They repeated the song several times, and Perry joined in. After the third verse, I motioned for my girls to stand up and recite the cheer from earlier. The two groups were yelling as loudly as they could until Gordy got up to the microphone and motioned for silence.

"Seems like we have a heated competition this year for the Gordy. Keep it up," he said excitedly. "I want to welcome everyone to their first full day at Camp

Chinooka. We'll be following the normal schedule. Activity sign-up will be in the gazebos right after breakfast. *Fiddler on the Roof* auditions will be at 2:00 this afternoon for the girls and at 4:00 for the boys. Have a great day and enjoy breakfast."

As soon as Gordy stepped away from the microphone, Birch went right back to singing. I spotted Perry in the corner, laughing.

I stood up on my tiptoes. "Okay, enough with the song, guys. I know you love me," I yelled in their direction. The singing just got louder. "Can you stop this?" I shouted at him.

"Ask me nicely, Princess," Perry shouted back.

"Can you pretty please with a cherry on top stop them from singing?" I said, rolling my eyes.

"Sure," he replied.

And just like that, with a single nod of his head, they stopped. It was infuriating. I got my tray and filled a bowl with cereal. I grabbed a banana off the center table and sat down with the rest of the Bunk Fourteen girls, who were busy eating their breakfast.

"He likes you," Tara said to me as I unloaded my tray.

"He does not," I replied.

"Yes, he does," Rachel, a camper, chimed in.

"Well, if I don't like him, it doesn't really matter, does it?"

"Do you have a boyfriend?" Madison asked.

"Girls, enough," Jordana reprimanded. "Let Gigi eat her breakfast in peace."

I sneaked out to the gazebo before breakfast ended to wait for the girls. I called each bunk over to choose their first week of activities and took down the names of the girls planning to audition for *Fiddler on the Roof*. Hannah

Davidson, one of my campers, told me she'd tried out for the role of Hodel the summer before but was too young. This summer, she was finally the right age and desperately wanted the part.

After the last girl was signed up for activities, I dismissed the different bunks back to their cabins to change for instructional swim and went to the office to drop off the activity sheets. Gordy was at his desk doing busy work. I smiled at him and went to my mailbox. Inside was an envelope from my mother, along with a schedule of the Cedar evening activities. I quickly folded the envelope in half and stuffed it in my back pocket. Then, I looked over the calendar. Tonight's activity was the Dating Game with Birch.

"What did you stuff in your pocket, Princess? Letter from your boyfriend?"

"What? Huh?" I said, spinning around to face Perry.

"The thing you just stuffed in your pocket," he said, pointing to the envelope sticking out of my pants.

"It's a letter from my mom, and stop calling me Princess."

He looked down at his clipboard and scanned it. "So I see we have a date tonight?"

"What?"

"Your girls and my boys, the Dating Game at the Lakeside Rec," he said, pointing to the calendar.

I yawned. "Oh, right, yeah, I just saw."

"Tired?"

"A little."

Perry intentionally raised his voice louder. "A late night can do that," he said.

Gordy looked up from his papers and I shot Perry a dirty look. "I'm just adjusting to the schedule."

"Getting up before noon must be tough when you aren't used to it, Princess."

"You don't know a thing about me. And *stop calling me Princess.*" I emphasized the words through gritted teeth.

He snapped the top of his clipboard closed. "Oh I know enough," he said in his posh accent.

"Just because someone is daring to challenge you for The Gordy for the first time in three years doesn't mean you should lash out in frustration."

He laughed. "Is that what you think I'm doing?"

"Isn't it?"

"I'm just having a good time giving you a hard time, Princess—I mean, Gigi. See you tonight."

Gordy chuckled behind me. I turned to face him.

"What?" I asked.

"Nothing," he answered, still laughing.

I stamped my feet close together. "Gordy, what is it?"

"I like listening to the two of you. It's going to be one fierce competition this summer."

"If I don't kill him," I said.

"You won't," he said.

"Don't be so sure."

"None of the other ones have."

Not that I imagined someone as good-looking as Perry hadn't had his share of summer flings, but I was utterly unimpressed that he was using Chinooka as his own personal hunting ground.

"Well, just for the record, he's not my type at all," I answered.

Gordy laughed again. "Dost thou protest too much? Maybe you're just as wrong about who he is, as you seem to think he is about you?"

"Well, he *is* wrong about me. But I highly doubt I am about him," I answered.

"He's a good guy, Gigi. One of the best. He's just working through a few things."

"Like what? How to be civil to another human being?"

"Like I said, it's going to be a good competition this year."

I picked up the rest of my paperwork and added it to my clipboard. "We have this one in the bag. Speaking of which, let me go make sure the girls are at instructional swim like they're supposed to be."

Although there was a pool, most of the activities and even the swim instruction was done at Lake Chinooka. Since it was only late June, the water hadn't fully warmed up yet, and I could see the lifeguards were having a tough time coaxing the girls into the cold water. I was grateful this was one battle I didn't have to fight. To keep an eye on everything, I sat down at the shore on a wooden chaise lounge, which was probably as old as the camp. Leaning back, I felt the envelope I'd forgotten in the midst of my spat with Perry. I pulled it out of my pocket and ripped it open.

And there it was. The thing I'd been dreading. Alicia and Joshua's wedding invitation. I slowly pulled it out of the larger manila envelope and read it line by line.

MR. & MRS. THOMAS SCHEINMAN
REQUEST THE PLEASURE OF YOUR COMPANY
AT THE MARRIAGE OF THEIR DAUGHTER
Alicia Leigh Scheinman
To
Joshua Adam Baume
SATURDAY, THE FIFTEENTH OF AUGUST

EIGHT O'CLOCK IN THE EVENING
THE ST. REGIS HOTEL
NEW YORK, NEW YORK

Seeing their names printed together, embossed on white card stock that would be mailed out to several hundred guests, was a finality I was not ready for. I was in the midst of wishing the chaise lounge would clamp down and swallow me whole when Tara shook the back of it, causing me to jump several feet in the air.

I put my hand over my heart. "Jesus, Tara, you scared me."

"Sorry, you seemed sort of distracted," she said, taking a seat at the end of the lounge. "Whatcha doing?" she asked in a sing-songy voice.

"Reading something. What do you need? Shouldn't you be watching our girls down at the lake?"

"They're covered. Jordana and the lifeguards are all over it."

I tilted my head to the side. "So what is it I can do for you, Tara?"

"I just wanted to know if you'd mind if I went after Perry?"

"What?"

"Perry, the head counselor of Birch."

"I know who he is, Tara. He's probably a good ten years older than you," I said.

"So you like him? Okay, fine, I'll stay away."

"What about your boyfriend? The one from home? Brian, right?"

"We're on a break for the summer," she said.

I thought back to the scene she'd made before getting on the camp bus. "Weren't you just sobbing into a cell phone, telling him how much you'd miss him?"

"Some of the campers told me you like Perry," she said, completely ignoring my question. "If you do, I'll stay away."

"I don't even know him. But either way, you're way too young for him. Why don't you set your sights on someone more age appropriate, like one of the other CITs?" I asked, pointing to where a few of them were standing on the dock.

"Perry likes younger girls. Michelle told me."

"Michelle, the counselor from Bunk Eleven, Michelle?"

"Yeah, she told me that last summer she heard he was seeing Brooke, who was only eighteen at the time." Tara leaned in closer. "He also supposedly had a pretty hot and heavy relationship with a counselor a few summers ago. They took some crazy cross-country road trip together after the summer was over."

I'd had a feeling he was a player, but getting his kicks going out with girls almost ten years his junior put him in a totally different category. "Tara, I'm not your mother, but I have a feeling it's prohibited for a counselor to date a CIT."

"But you're sure you aren't interested, right?"

"No, Tara, I'm not interested," I replied.

"So you have to help me, then."

I shook my head. "Help you? I'm definitely not going to help you."

"Gigi," she whined.

I sat up in the lounge chair. "Seriously, how could I possibly help you?"

She walked behind me to try to get a glimpse of the clipboard on my lap. "What's tonight's activity?"

"The Dating Game," I answered.

"Perfect. Okay, you have to put me in it," she said.

"Play a couple of rounds with the campers, and then do a counselor round. Have Perry be the bachelor, and I'll be one of the contestants."

"I'm not doing that," I said.

"Gigi, please," she begged.

"Tara, there's no point."

"Please," she said again, getting on her hands and knees.

"I'll think about it, but he really is too old for you."

"Don't be so serious, Gigi. I'm not marrying the guy. I'm just looking for a summer fling. You are familiar with the concept of a fling, right?"

"Vaguely familiar, yes," I answered.

"So, will you set it up for later?"

"I told you I'll think about it, okay?"

Tara went running back toward the lake, probably to tell Michelle and Brooke about her small victory. I wasn't surprised that Perry liked younger girls, given how immature he seemed. Maybe he kept returning to camp so that he could date people who'd be deemed wholly inappropriate back home? Either way, it really wasn't my concern. If he wanted to spend his time with girls like Tara, that was totally and completely his prerogative, and I was staying out of it. Well, not completely out of it since I'd just agreed to consider rigging the Dating Game so she could have a shot with him.

After instructional swim, the girls went off to their morning activities. I walked around, making sure they were exactly where they'd signed up to be so we didn't get any Gordy points deducted. Cedar had a reputation for cutting activities and smoking behind abandoned bunks and The Canteen. The whole practice was ridiculous since they invariably got caught. But, as a rite of passage, a whole new set of girls tried to be the first to get away with it each year. I started my rounds at arts and crafts and was relieved to see all ten of the Cedar girls happily tie-dying T-shirts behind the cabin.

From there, I walked over to the archery fields, where another five of my campers were slated to be. Instead, I found Dominick, the archery instructor, a really muscular Irishman, fuming.

"I'm missing five of your girls," he shouted at me as I crossed the field toward him.

I started jogging. "I have a good idea of where they might be. Don't deduct any points yet. Get started with the rest of the kids, and I'll get them."

I rushed down from the fields and over to the abandoned bunks, which were a good distance from the rest of the camp. The girls weren't there, so I hurried to some other spots I thought they might be. Finally, I made my way to the total opposite side of the camp and saw smoke wafting out from behind The Canteen. When I heard girls giggling in the distance, I knew I'd found them. I crept up and saw Candice, the tall, willowy girl who'd given me a hard time about the bat in the bunk, and four other girls from Bunk Eleven passing around a cigarette. When they spotted me, Candice threw the cigarette on the ground into a pile of dried leaves. The pile immediately started smoking, and the girls started shrieking. I ran over and stomped out the emerging fire.

"This is why there's no smoking allowed on camp grounds," I shouted at them. I realized from the smell of the smoke, they weren't passing around a cigarette, but a joint. "Are you girls smoking pot?"

They started laughing again.

"Where'd you get this?"

Candice stepped forward. "I brought it from home. I took it from my father's stash. Geez, you look like a mess, Gigi," she said, commenting on my disheveled clothes and the sweat that was now pouring off my forehead.

"I just spent the last forty minutes running around this camp like a lunatic and you've been right here smoking your father's pot?"

She flipped her hair back. "He never notices. It's *so* not a big deal."

"It's a huge deal. It's definitely against camp rules, and all rules, actually. It's illegal," I said, lifting up my T-shirt to wipe the sweat off my face.

"God, Gigi, you're so old school," she said.

"So, Candice, you tell me, how should I handle this?"

She crossed her arms. "Call it strike one?"

"This is strike two, actually. Strike one was when you conspired with the girls in my bunk so that they could sneak out last night."

Candice looked around at the other girls for support. "Okay, so strike two, big deal."

"I would definitely say it's a big deal. The five of you are going to be sitting out of evening activity tonight and the rest of the week. You should also plan on missing the first half of the camp social so we can talk about the hazards of drug use."

They looked miserable. I'd just taken away two very crucial social events. "If we hit strike number three, well... I don't have to explain what happens at strike three. Just know that I won't hesitate for one second to tell Gordy about all this. Don't test me. Got it?"

"Got it," they mumbled.

"Got it?" I repeated.

"Yeah, we got it," Candice answered for them.

"You're expected in archery. Now!"

The five of them went running back to the archery

fields, and I collapsed into a pile of leaves. I felt disgusting. Sweat was dripping from everywhere. The last time I was this hot was over a year ago when Joshua invited me to meet him at a Bikram Yoga class downtown. Yoga wasn't my thing, but it was the first real date he'd ever asked me on and I wasn't about to say no.

The morning of the class, I'd woken up extra early to get ready to meet him. Although my body was far from perfect, my spandex outfit had done an excellent job of sucking everything in. I flat ironed my hair until it was stick-straight and applied my makeup so I looked natural, but with a glow.

I met Joshua in front of the yoga studio. He looked adorable in Adidas tear-away pants, a white T-shirt, and a gray zip-up hoodie. His hair was slightly tousled from sleep, but I always liked it better like that than when he tried to tame it. He handed me my own bottled water. I thought it was a sweet variation on the flower-giving date ritual and told him so.

"I didn't know if you would know to bring it, and you'll definitely need it for hot yoga," he said.

"So what's so hot about it anyway?" I asked in my most seductive voice.

He zipped up his hoodie. "What do you mean?"

"You said it was a hot yoga class? What makes it so popular?"

"It's not that popular. It's Bikram Yoga. I tried to get Alicia to go a couple of times, but she likes efficiency in her workout—on and off the treadmill in forty minutes, nothing extraneous."

"Oh, right, Bikram Yoga. I've been dying to try it," I said.

I didn't have a clue what Bikram Yoga was. We went

inside and waited for the class to begin. The instructor gave us each mats and started with some basic stretches. It wasn't so hard at first, but then it began to get really warm in the studio. At first, I thought it was just me, but everyone else was sweating profusely, too. I looked at Joshua. His shirt was soaked through with sweat, but he looked like he couldn't be happier. When we were in Downward Dog, I turned to him. "Joshua," I said in a whisper, "I'm roasting in here."

"It's great, right? All your muscles feel loose and your whole body feels centered?"

My whole body felt sweaty, and I was feeling a little light-headed.

"Maybe we should come back and do this when the air conditioner is working?" I said.

"Gigi, this is Bikram Yoga. It's supposed to be this hot."

"Oh, right."

I spent the next forty-five minutes the most uncomfortable that I'd ever been, with sweat coming out of places I didn't even know I had. I later found out that during Bikram Yoga, the room temperature was pushed up to 105 degrees, so that you could supposedly cleanse your body of all toxins. When the class was over, I made a beeline to the ladies' room to wash my hands and face and whatever else I could stick under the faucet in cold water. I had makeup smeared everywhere, and mascara was running down both my cheeks. My once pin-straight hair was a curly, matted mess, and my cute spandex outfit was almost transparent from sweat. I was horrified. There was no way I was going back out to face Joshua looking the way I did.

I scanned the bathroom for a window I could climb out of but realized, sooner or later, I'd have to leave the ladies' room. I washed the makeup off my face the best I could and smoothed my hair into a bun. When my cheeks were no longer an embarrassing shade of crimson, I bit the bullet and emerged.

"You look—" he started to say before I interjected.

"Disgusting, I know. I lied to you. I had no idea what Bikram Yoga was. I wasn't prepared for what just happened in there," I admitted.

"I was going to say that you look beautiful," he finished.

"Really? 'Cause I feel anything but."

He handed me his gray hooded sweatshirt, which I gratefully zipped up over my exposed self. "You look perfect. So what'd you think of it?" he asked.

"The class? I think I didn't know what I was missing."

"Are you lying to me again, Ms. Goldstein?" he teased.

"No, I'm completely serious. I didn't know what I was missing, and now that I do, I can keep on missing it," I teased.

He laughed, flashing his white smile.

"Wanna grab breakfast?" he asked, putting his arm around me.

"I need to shower first," I answered.

"Okay, so let's go to my place. We'll take a shower and then go."

We never made it to breakfast. We didn't leave his apartment all day.

The following day, I met Jamie for brunch. As soon as I sat down, he said, "You absolutely had great sex last night. Or a facial. You're glowing."

I told him I'd tried Bikram Yoga, which seemed to pacify him. Little did he know I'd followed it up with great sex. The truth was, I wasn't just glowing. Something had shifted. After that morning, Joshua and I couldn't write off what we were doing as a one-time mistake. For the first time ever, I was making the conscious choice to put my own needs and feelings ahead of my friendship with Alicia. The realization had shaken me to the core then and still did now.

I picked up the joint from the ground, pressed on the ends a few times so it relit, and took a few drags. The sound of Gordy's voice over the loudspeaker announcing that the auditions for the show were starting at the Lakeside Amphitheater in a few minutes snapped me right back into reality. I threw the joint back on the ground and stamped it out.

The amphitheater had been built especially for the Camp Chinooka Centennial Celebration. It was a beautiful theater in the round, set against the backdrop of the lake with trees surrounding it on all sides. Any production put on there was going to be an event. I scanned the crowd of girls waiting patiently to audition, and I spotted Hannah pacing nervously in line. I went up to wish her luck.

"I'm gonna be sick, Gigi," she said, leaning against the backstage railing.

"You'll be fine, sweetie. Just take a few deep breaths," I said, rubbing her back. "They're calling for you. Break a leg, or whatever people say." I pushed her toward the stage.

Hannah looked up, took a deep breath, and then stepped onto the stage, where she sang a flawless rendition of 'Far From the Home I Love.' When the song was over, the show's director gave her a standing ovation, and we both knew she'd gotten the part.

"I think it went well," she shrieked as she ran

toward me.

"You were fantastic," I answered.

"That means I have a shot, right?"

"You have more than a shot. It's in the bag," I said, hugging her.

"I really hope so." Hannah squealed and went running to her friends.

I walked down to where the director and assistant director for the show were sitting and taking notes about the auditions and introduced myself.

"I'm Gigi, head counselor of Cedar," I said extending my hand.

"Hi, I'm Jackie, and this is Davis," a woman close to my mother's age, with a British accent, answered and introduced her counterpart, a twenty-something guy.

"I'm really in awe of this location," I said, looking around. "I don't know if you've given any thought to the costumes, but I had a few ideas. Do you know the Marc Chagall painting that people say inspired the show? Maybe you could start there. The colors are amazing. So vivid and beautiful. They're really different than the dull grays and browns people expect."

"To be honest, Gigi, we hadn't really given the costumes much thought. Usually, the campers just provide their own. We make do. Thanks for the suggestion, though," Jackie responded, barely looking up from her clipboard before walking away.

"Do you have any experience with costume design?" Davis asked.

"A little. I was on this reality show where one of the challenges was to design a costume for the Broadway revival of *Cats*. They ended up using mine for the show."

Davis's whole face lit up. "That's why you look so familiar. You were on *Top Designer?*"

"I was, yeah."

"What was that guy's name? The one who got kicked off first with that toilet paper wedding dress challenge? I always felt really bad for him."

"Oh, my friend, Jamie. He's a good guy and a great designer, actually."

"Look, I'll talk to Jackie. Maybe we can find some budget for costumes, especially if I tell her we have a celebrity in our ranks."

I opened my mouth to protest, but it was too late. He was already rushing off to speak with her.

After dinner, the girls made a beeline for the shower house. The cabin was chaotic as they got dressed, borrowing each other's clothes and drying their hair with the one hairdryer that didn't blow our fuses. The room was buzzing with excitement as the girls chatted away about which guys were "hot," which were "not," and everyone in between. Tara confessed her not-so-secret crush on Perry, and Emily Z announced to anyone who would listen that she was making a play for one of the more popular guys in Birch, Alex Shane.

"That's enough, girls," Jordana chimed in after Tara started detailing her make-out session with one of the other CITs the night before. Tara shot Jordana a dirty look and lowered her voice to finish telling the story.

"Seriously, Tara. Not appropriate," Jordana said, crossing her arms over her chest.

I chimed in. "Let's keep the talk G-rated, okay, ladies?" I picked up my clipboard and headed out of the bunk for roll call.

The girls came rushing out of their cabins, freshly

showered and wearing their cutest outfits. I saw more designer labels than I was used to seeing at some of the trendiest bars in Manhattan. After spending the better part of the last hour organizing the line for the showers in order to avoid fights, I'd had no time to shower myself. I felt pretty gross from the day and even grimier seeing them in their chic ensembles.

"Hi, girls, you all look very nice," I said, peering over my clipboard. "Tonight's our first activity with Birch, the Dating Game. I need some volunteers to be the bachelorettes."

Very few hands went up in the air. The game show was a little before their time, and they didn't want to sign up for something they didn't understand. After I laid out the rules of the game, a few more hands shot up.

"There's also going to be a counselors' round, so I need a few volunteers for that," I added.

Tara's was the only hand that went up. "Okay, I'll just pick the campers for now and worry about the counselors later."

I randomly chose a few of the girls to participate in the game and led the rest of Cedar to Lakeside Rec to meet up with Birch. As we filed into the room, I was disappointed that Perry's boys were already seated and waiting for us. He was such a show-off, trying to get under my skin by highlighting just how well behaved his group was. Unfortunately, after the day I'd just had, he succeeded. I marched up to him. "You win. Your boys are angels."

"I don't know what you're talking about," Perry said, shrugging his shoulders.

He'd apparently had time to shower and freshen up after dinner and looked great in dark jeans and a fitted T-shirt. He smelled even better. I, on the other hand, was in the same exact army fatigue shorts and black tank top he'd seen me in this morning.

"Oh, come off of it," I spat back at him.

"Is that an American expression like *whatever*?" he teased.

"No, but this is," I said, sticking my middle finger up at him. I hadn't flipped anyone off since I was twelve, but it felt good.

"I just cannot believe you just flipped me off. Are you seven years old?"

"Can we just get tonight over with?" I asked.

"*Whatever,*" he said, jumping onto the stage.

I made my way back over to where Cedar was seated and called out the names of the girls competing in Round One. "I need Emily Zegantz, Colleen Starston, and Laila Brownstein."

Perry sidled up next to me and announced the bachelor for Round One. "I need Ben Lewin front and center."

A tall, good-looking boy with a backward Yankees cap stood up. He was blindfolded, so Perry led him to a seat in front of the curtain on stage while I guided the three girls to their seats behind the curtain. Perry untied the blindfold and handed Ben a stack of index cards with questions on them.

"The basic rules of the game are as follows," Perry said to the audience. "Our bachelor will ask a series of questions, and each of the bachelorettes will be given the opportunity to answer. Based on those answers, our lucky bachelor, Ben, will select one of the girls as his date."

A few of the guys sitting in the front row snickered.

"Ready? Okay, let's begin," Perry said, transforming into a corny game show host. He put a clip-on bow tie over his T-shirt and even had the American accent down. "Ben, why don't you tell our studio audience a little bit about yourself?"

Ben looked embarrassed. "My name's Ben Lewin, I'm thirteen years old, from White Plains, New York. I like the Yankees, and I'm not sure what else to say..." He looked to Perry for help.

"What's your favorite activity at camp, Ben?" Perry asked.

"I like the Jet Skis," he answered.

"Great. Now let's meet the ladies," Perry said, turning his attention to the other side of the curtain. "Bachelorette Number One, why don't you tell us your favorite activity at camp?"

Silence.

"Bachelorette Number One?" Perry repeated.

"Emily, that's you," I said, tapping the back of her chair.

"Oh, hi. I'm Bachelorette Number One," she answered in a way too mature-sounding voice. "My favorite activity at camp is gymnastics."

"Thank you, Bachelorette Number One. Bachelorette Number Two?"

"I like arts and crafts," Colleen answered.

"And Bachelorette Number Three?" Perry asked.

Laila leaned forward. "I really like water skiing."

"Fantastic. And now I'm going to turn over the microphone to our lucky bachelor, Ben," Perry said, handing Ben the cardboard paper towel roll he was using as a microphone.

"This question is for Bachelorette Number Two," Ben said softly.

"Can you speak up?" I shouted from behind the girls' side of the curtain. "It's not a real microphone."

"This is a question for Bachelorette Number Two," Perry shouted back.

"Bachelorette Number Two, if you were an animal, what animal would you be and why?" Ben asked.

I rolled my eyes. Could the question have been cornier? Perry was responsible for writing the questions for the guys' round, and I was responsible for the questions for the counselor round. It was clear how little time he'd spent on his.

"I would be a butterfly," Colleen answered.

"Bachelorette Number Three?"

"A dolphin," Laila replied.

"Bachelorette Number One," Ben continued, "same question."

"I would be a cougar. No explanation needed," Emily replied quickly.

The boys applauded.

"Next question," Perry interjected.

Ben cleared his throat. "Bachelorette Number One, compare yourself to a movie star. Who do you most resemble?"

"Angelina Jolie," Emily shot back. "We both have seductive lips."

The boys cheered at her response.

"Let's tone it down a bit," I said.

"Number Two?" Ben asked, his voice cracking.

"Umm, maybe Emma Stone," Colleen answered.

"And Number Three, same question?" Ben asked.

Laila was quiet for a few seconds and then said, "Taylor Swift."

The boys all cheered again.

"This will be the final question before our bachelor, Ben, chooses a date," Perry announced, still using the corny game show host voice.

Ben read off the final index card. "Bachelorette Number Three, can you describe your perfect date?"

"Dinner and a movie," Laila answered

"Bachelorette Number Two?"

"Taking a late afternoon hike and then watching the sunset together," Colleen said.

"Number One, same question."

Terrified of what was going to come out of Emily's mouth, I jumped in before she could answer. "You know what," I chimed in, "I think Ben has heard enough to make his decision. Why don't we let him make his choice?"

"Okay, Ben, choose one of these lovely ladies as your date. You have a few seconds to think it over." Perry hummed the music played during the final round of Jeopardy, and the rest of the room joined in. "Ben, we need an answer," he said after some time had passed.

"Okay, I choose Bachelorette Number Three," Ben answered awkwardly.

Perry applauded. "Ben, it's time for you to meet the ladies you didn't select. Please come around the curtain, Bachelorette Number One."

Emily sauntered around the curtain, and Ben looked disappointed he hadn't chosen her.

"Bachelorette Number Two," Perry continued, "meet Ben Lewin."

Colleen walked around, gave Ben a quick wave, and took her seat in the audience.

Perry handed me the cardboard paper towel roll. "Gigi, can you introduce us to Bachelorette Number Three?"

"Sure, Perry," I said, mimicking his announcer voice. "Bachelorette Number Three hails from Wayne, New Jersey. She's the captain of her school's swim team, and this is her fourth summer at Camp Chinooka. Let's have a big round of applause for Laila Brownstein."

Laila awkwardly made her way around the curtain and gave Ben a hug. They both looked equally uncomfortable as they walked off the stage together.

"We're going to take a short break, and then it's time for the counselor round," Perry informed everyone.

I walked off the stage to where the Cedar counselors had gathered.

"Okay. I need a counselor. Will anyone volunteer to be the bachelorette?" I asked.

Tara's hand shot up again.

I scanned the rest of the counselors. "Really? Nobody else?"

It seemed Tara had begged, pleaded, or otherwise persuaded the other girls not to volunteer. "Jordana?"

"Just let Tara do it, Gigi. She's being impossible," Jordana replied.

"All right, Tara, you can be the bachelorette," I said.

Tara looked ecstatic as I led her to the single chair on the far side of the curtain. I handed her the index cards with my questions and waited to see which male counselors she would be choosing from. Eric, the counselor who'd been sitting OD with Perry, took the first seat, a British counselor named Jon took the second seat, and unexpectedly, Perry took the third seat.

Ugh. What an opportunistic jerk. Did he have to chase every available girl on the campground? Since it was my turn to play the announcer, Perry handed me the clip-on bow tie, which I put over my tank top.

"Who's ready for the all-exciting counselor round?" I asked in my best game show voice.

"You'll have to speak up. That isn't a real microphone, remember?" Perry shouted.

I raised my voice. "You know the rules. Our bachelorette will ask a series of questions to the three bachelors and then, based on their answers, pick her date. Let's begin. Bachelorette, fire away."

"Bachelor Number Two, what do you think is the most important technological advancement in world history?" Tara read off the first card.

"Gigi," Tara whispered, "what kind of a question is that?"

"A great one," I whispered back.

"Bachelor Number Two, your answer, please?" I asked.

"The iPhone. Mine's awesome," Jon answered.

"I'm sure," I replied, rolling my eyes.

"Bachelor Number One, same question," Tara instructed.

"Definitely has to be the airplane. I love to travel," Eric answered.

"And Bachelor Number Three?" she asked.

"The printing press," Perry answered. "Without a technology in place for the cheap mass production of books, the dissemination of ideas would have been virtually impossible, and our world would be a completely different place."

"Bor-ing," Tara whispered to me.

I was actually kind of impressed. It was a really well thought out answer.

"Okay, moving on," Tara said impatiently, flipping to the next card. "Bachelor Number Three, who's your hero?"

Tara rolled her eyes and gave me a look of disappointment. Obviously, she didn't think the questions I'd come up with were scintillating enough.

"Mahatma Gandhi," Perry replied.

"Great," Tara replied, completely disinterested.

"Bachelor One, same question?"

"My mom," Eric answered.

There was a collective "Awww" from the front row of girls.

"Bachelor Number Two?" Tara asked.

"David Beckham," Jon answered.

"Awesome. Now on to the final question," I said, trying to move the game along.

Tara read the card and looked up at me. "Gigi, this is supposed to be fun. We aren't picking a president. I'm picking a date."

Apparently, she didn't like my final question asking the bachelors what they thought the biggest problem facing the United States was. She substituted her own instead.

"Okay, boys," she said in her most innocent voice, "what would we do on our first date? Bachelor Number One, your answer?"

I was relieved that she didn't take it somewhere raunchy.

"Take a day trip somewhere. Maybe apple picking or horseback riding," Eric said.

Tara looked disappointed in his answer. "Number Two?"

Jon sat up in his seat. "Going to a football match or pub to watch a game."

Tara smiled. "Number Three?"

"First, I'd take her for a morning picnic in Regents Park, one of the prettiest parks in London. Then we'd walk along the park's canals to the London Zoo. After that, we'd make our way to Little Venice, passing Browning's Island, an island in the center of the canal named for the poet Robert Browning. We'd end our walk in Camden Lock Market, where we'd sip on hot chocolate. Then, later that night, I'd take her to the Whispering Gallery in St. Paul's Cathedral. It's a really special place. Anything whispered against its circular walls can be heard throughout the whole dome. I'd whisper to her, and everyone there could hear me say what an incredible day I'd had," Perry answered.

I was fairly certain every girl in the room wanted to go to the Whispering Gallery with him. They were all gazing adoringly at Perry, who was oblivious to it.

"Tara, which lucky bachelor is it going to be?" I asked.

All the girls in the room shouted out their choices, the loudest vote going to Perry.

"I choose Bachelor Two," she said confidently.

I was completely shocked she didn't pick Perry, especially after all of the scheming she'd done. "Let's meet the men Tara didn't select. Bachelor Number One hails from New Haven, Connecticut, and is going into his sophomore year at the University of Connecticut. Eric Briggs, come meet Tara Mann," I said.

All the guys stood up and cheered as Eric rounded the curtain to meet Tara. She looked slightly disappointed she hadn't chosen him. He had a great athletic body, and considering we were barely into the summer, already had a fantastic tan.

I continued. "Bachelor Number Three comes all the way from London, England. He's your favorite head counselor, Perry Gillman."

Tara sighed deeply. Perhaps unable to distinguish one British accent from another, it seemed she'd mistaken Jon for Perry. Perry gave Tara a kiss on each cheek before walking off the stage. Tara looked shell-shocked and kept her hands on her cheeks as if she was terrified the kisses would somehow melt off.

"Relieved?" Perry asked as he passed me.

"Absolutely," I answered, "you're way too old for her."

"Now let's meet our winner," I continued. "Straight from Manchester, England, this eighteen-year-old soccer prodigy likes fish 'n' chips, long walks by the lake, and action movies. Tara, please meet your date, Jon Roth," I said excitedly.

Jon, a good-looking guy with a shaved head and several tattoos, crossed the stage and gave Tara a big bear hug, which she seemed to enjoy. He took hold of her hand, and they walked off the stage together. Tara was already gazing adoringly at him, the kisses from Perry a distant memory.

After the Dating Game finished, we led the two groups to the Great Lawn so they could hang out and get to know each other. When everything was well under control, I sat down under a large tree in the corner of the field and rested my head against the trunk, exhausted from my first full day on the job. I dozed off for a few minutes before being awakened by Perry, who slid down the trunk beside me.

"Sleeping on the job, are we?" he asked as he sliced pieces of an apple with the Swiss Army knife.

"Just resting." I yawned.

He wedged out some slices. "Want some?"

"No thanks. What's that?" I asked, noticing the small notebook on top of his clipboard.

"Some music compositions," he said, tucking the book underneath the papers. "So, Princess, what did your mum send that had you all frazzled this morning?"

I'd almost forgotten about Alicia and Joshua's

wedding invitation, now concealed underneath my mattress.

"It was nothing, an invitation," I said nonchalantly.

"And?" he said, leaning into me.

"And nothing. I'd rather not talk about it."

"You know what? You're intriguing," he said, narrowing his eyes at me.

"Intriguing?"

"There is something quite mysterious about you," he said.

"Not really."

"Then what were you hiding?"

"Just leave it alone—it's nothing. It's a stupid wedding invitation."

"Methinks I hit a sore subject. Who's getting married? Let me guess, your mother for the fourth time? Your younger sister, and it's killing you she's getting married first? Someone you shagged? Your boss? An old lover? A young lover? An unrequited crush?" he teased.

I physically winced after his last guess. Afraid that he noticed, I channeled my humiliation into anger. "You guessed it," I spat at him. "I have a big, scary skeleton in my closet and the invitation to prove it."

He stared at me a few seconds, not quite sure whether he should believe my outburst. I continued my tirade. "Congratulations. You figured me out. I am every awful thing you've suggested. Pampered, privileged, and promiscuous. I've heard an earful about you too, though. You like them young, right? What, like eighteen or nineteen years old?"

He sat speechless.

"I guess we all have our crosses to bear, huh?" I stood up and started walking over to where Jordana and some other counselors had gathered.

"Gigi. Hey, wait a minute," he shouted in my direction.

"Just leave me alone."

"What was that about?" Jordana asked, having observed our tiff from afar.

"He just gets under my skin."

"Hey, take a look at that," she said, motioning to a shadowy part of the field, where two campers were locked in a kiss.

"Is that Madison and Alex Shane?" I asked.

"It most certainly is," Jordana replied like a proud older sister.

"That won't end well," I said.

"Why do you say that?"

"Isn't that the guy Emily Z set her sights on? The one she was talking about in the bunk earlier? He's like *the* guy, right? The guy all the girls are crushing on?"

"I think so," Jordana said.

I raised my eyebrows.

"It's just a kiss, Gigi. Maybe he likes her?"

"Maybe," I said skeptically. "I hope she doesn't get hurt."

"Sometimes it's worth it," Jordana said.

"What is?"

"Getting to kiss the Alex Shanes of the world, even if they ultimately break your heart."

"I'm not so sure," I said.

"So who's sitting OD tonight?" she asked, trying to change the subject.

"Michelle and Brooke, but I was thinking I might just sit," I answered.

"You have to go out. You came to camp to have some fun, right?"

I shrugged my shoulders. "I just don't think I'm up

for The Canteen tonight." Imagining Perry making out with one of the younger counselors on the old moth-eaten couch kind of made my stomach turn.

"Well, that's perfect because some of the counselors are going into town to Rosie's. Come on, Gigi," she pleaded. "It'll be fun."

Rosie's was the one and only bar in Milbank. I'd never actually been, but from the time I started going to Camp Chinooka, I'd heard wild stories about what went on there. Back when I was a camper, Rosie's had seemed like the most exciting place to be—even more so than The Canteen, because it was off grounds. Now of legal drinking age and actually allowed to leave the camp premises, curiosity of this once forbidden place got the best of me.

"Fine, but first, I need to shower. I've been in these clothes all day," I said.

"Yeah, you are a little funky," Jordana said, pretending to sniff my shirt.

Fifteen minutes later, I announced the end of evening activity and called the girls back to their bunks for the night. They reluctantly said their goodbyes and huddled together in small cliques to discuss the night's events as they walked back to the cabins. I rushed ahead of them to the shower house so I'd have time to get ready before we left for town.

The Cedar shower house was one of the oldest structures at Chinooka, left untouched since I was a camper. It was nothing more than a cabin that housed about ten shower stalls. Unfortunately, it didn't have working lights, which wasn't a big deal when the girls were showering at five but was more of an issue now that it was dark. Using a small flashlight, I fumbled my way into one of the stalls, where I turned on the faucet. Nothing but freezing water came out. I stood, shivering, waiting for the water to turn warmer, but it never did. Realizing it was a cold shower or nothing, I stepped in and took the quickest shower of my adult life. In complete darkness, I managed to shampoo and condition my hair, shave my legs, and loofah my entire body in under five minutes. As soon as I finished, I wrapped myself in a towel and sprinted across the field and back to the bunk. When I walked in, most of the girls were gathered around Madison's bed, listening to her recount her kiss with Alex Shane.

"And then Gigi yelled that evening activity was over, so he kissed me one more time and told me he would look for me at breakfast," Madison said, finishing up her story with an ear-to-ear smile.

I unwrapped my hair from underneath a towel turban and shook my head, knowing exactly how Madison felt. Having just kissed her fantasy guy, she was completely on top of the world. It would be a long way to fall when she finally came off her high.

Turning my attention away from Madison, I scanned my overstuffed cubbies, trying to decide what to wear to Rosie's. After spending the last twelve hours in the same shorts and tank top, I decided I'd feel better if I stepped it up a notch. I pulled out a simple but sexy charcoal tank dress from the bottom of one of the piles and smoothed it out the best I could. I put it on and modeled it in front of the full-length mirror in the bathroom, looking at myself from every angle.

"That dress is killer," Tara said, coming up behind me. "Where are you going tonight?" she asked, perching against the sink next to me.

"Rosie's," I answered.

"Lucky. I wish CITs were allowed off camp grounds," she said.

"It's just a bar. Not a big deal," I said.

"A bar that all the best-looking counselors hang out at. Is Perry gonna be there?"

"I don't know," I said, applying mascara to my top and then lower lashes. "What do you care anyway? I saw you kissing Jon goodnight."

"He's all right. He's no Perry, though," she said.

"I'm getting over someone. Maybe I'm just not able to be totally objective," I said.

"Really? What happened?" she asked, inching closer to me.

"Tara, there isn't that much light in here to begin with."

She closed the toilet seat behind me and sat down. "So what happened?"

The way Tara was perched reminded me of when I was a little girl. I'd sit on the toilet seat beside my mother, watching her as she got ready for an event.

"Things just didn't work out," I answered.

"Another woman?"

"I guess you could say that," I answered.

"Men are assholes," she said bluntly.

"Men?" I said, shooting her a look.

"Men, boys, guys, whatever. They're all jerks," she said, rolling her eyes. "You should go out and have a good time tonight. You look hot, Gigi. Go make him sorry he ever looked at that other chick. Can I borrow this for the dance?" she asked, picking up the tube of light pink Christian Dior lipgloss from the sink. I nodded and took one last look at myself in the mirror before hurrying out of the cabin to meet Jordana by the front gate.

CHAPTER SIX

Two nights after Alicia came home from Singapore, we met at a trendy midtown sushi restaurant not far from her office. She called to let me know that, as usual, she was running about an hour late. I had a drink at the bar while I waited, hoping to calm my nerves. I was only slightly more relaxed by the time she came tearing into the restaurant rattling off her usual apologies.

"I could not get off this conference call," she said, giving me a kiss hello on the cheek.

She looked stunning. For a woman who'd supposedly been stuck in meetings for the last several weeks, you would have thought she just returned from a vacation in the Caribbean.

"You look great," I said, admiring how sophisticated and elegant she always looked, no matter how frazzled.

"You, my friend, are the one who looks great," she said, taking off her coat. "What have you been doing these last few weeks?"

Deciding to go work at Chinooka had begun to lift

the dark cloud looming over my life, and I was finally starting to come back to myself. Of course, my best friend would notice this not-so-subtle change.

"I've actually been doing quite a bit these last couple of weeks," I started to explain before the hostess came over to tell us our table was ready. We sat down and I continued. "Actually, I'm no longer working for Diane von Furstenberg. I was let go—fired, actually, if I'm going to be accurate."

She put her hand over her mouth in disbelief.

"Ali, I'm fine. It's really for the best, and things hadn't been clicking there for me for a while now," I said.

"But you loved that job."

"It was just a job. I'm a designer. I can still do that, just not under their label."

"I just can't believe they let you go. You're so talented," Alicia said.

I grimaced, thinking how lucky I was to have always had someone in my life who believed in me so completely. A knot of violent guilt tightened in my gut.

"I'm fine. I'll figure something out."

"Of course you will, and of course you can stay with me as long as you need to while you figure it out," she said, putting her hand over mine.

"You're getting married in less than four months. While I appreciate the offer, I can't stay with you. Besides, I have a plan."

"Great, let's hear it," she said, leaning over the table.

"Well, here's the part I don't know how to tell you," I said, trying to recall the speech I'd practiced so many times in my head.

She pushed her hair behind her ears. "Just tell me."

"I ran into Joshua at Bloomingdales and he told me you moved your wedding up to August."

"It just made sense with the timing of my promotion. After dating him for almost my whole life, we figured what's the point in waiting?"

"It makes sense, complete sense," I said, swallowing. "I just don't know if I'll be here for it."

"Not be here for the wedding?" She sank down into her seat and was quiet for a few seconds. She took a sip of her ice water. "Where will you be?"

"I'm not sure. Traveling, maybe?"

I was telling her yet another lie, but in the grand scheme of betrayals, I figured this small fib was part of my greater effort to do the right thing. "I just need to get out of here and get some distance and some new ideas. I need to feel inspired again. I think I need this summer to reinvent myself a bit."

"Then you should go," she replied firmly.

"Do you hate me?"

"Of course not, Gigi. You're like a sister to me. I love you enough to see you need this right now. The wedding's a formality. Joshua and I have been as good as married for years. Who would know that better than you?"

"Right, who would know that better than me," I repeated the words back to her.

"Where will you go?"

"I don't know. Wherever the wind takes me?" I said jokingly.

"Just make sure it blows you back, eventually. I'll miss my best friend too much."

"Thank you for understanding, Ali."

"You don't have to thank me. I see in your eyes that you need this," she said.

"More than anything."

"I don't know if I should tell you this now, but I was

going to ask you to be my maid of honor tonight," she said.

"Alicia ..."

"I understand," she said, taking my hand in hers. For a split-second, I wondered if she really did know more than she was letting on.

We finished dinner and made small talk about Singapore and the wedding. As usual, Alicia was all business, going over every detail like it was some sort of merger. If I were the one marrying Joshua, I wouldn't be worrying about florists or bands, place cards or photographers. I wouldn't need a wedding planner to advise me on how to design the wedding of my dreams. All I would need was Joshua, wholly and completely wanting to commit to me. But, Alicia had that. She had the love of her life wholly and completely wanting to commit to her. Why shouldn't she have the perfect venue as well?

We finished eating, and the waiter came to ask if we wanted to see the dessert menu. I was completely stuffed, but before I could answer, Alicia told him to please bring it over.

"I couldn't eat another thing, but you should definitely order something if you're in the mood for something sweet," I told her.

"I asked Joshua to meet us here, so I should probably order something so they don't kick us out of the table while we wait for him," she said.

I shifted uncomfortably in my seat. I hadn't seen Joshua since the day at my apartment a few weeks earlier and hadn't spoken to him since our phone confrontation. I wasn't at all prepared to sit across a table from him, especially with Alicia there.

"You know, Ali, I should probably get going. I'm not feeling a hundred percent," I said.

"What's wrong?"

Before I could answer, she stood up and motioned Joshua—who'd already walked into the restaurant—toward our table. He leaned over and gave me a kiss on the cheek as a hello. Then he gave Alicia a kiss on the lips before sitting down next to her in the booth. The waiter came over to take his order.

"I'll just have a Grey Goose with a splash of tonic. Ladies, do either of you want a refill of anything?"

Alicia ordered another Chardonnay.

"I'm fine, thanks," I said.

Alicia clinked her fork against her glass. "Gigi has an announcement."

"It's really not that big of a deal," I said.

"Of course it is," Alicia responded before motioning for me to speak.

"I lost my job, so I'm going to take some time for myself this summer and figure some things out. I won't be at the wedding," I said as fast as I could get the words out.

"Where are you going?" Joshua asked, never taking his gaze off my face.

"I haven't completely decided yet. I just need to get away from here and get a different perspective on things," I answered.

"I gave her our blessing," Alicia chimed in. "The wedding's a silly formality. You agree Gigi should get away, right?"

I held my breath, waiting for any small indication that he wouldn't want me to leave.

"Of course she should go," he said.

"See?" Alicia continued. "I knew Joshua would

understand." She put her hand over his. "It's been so long since the three of us have been out together. I'm so lucky to have not one but two best friends," she said, putting her other hand on mine.

Joshua smiled and put his arm around her. She leaned against his chest, and he kissed her forehead the same way he'd always kissed mine.

"Gigi," she said, sitting back up, "I don't know what made me think about this, but do you remember when we were eleven, or maybe twelve, and Joshua and I got married at the Camp Chinooka carnival?"

I did remember. I remembered how I stood watching their pretend ceremony, certain even then that someday I would stand witness to their real one.

"I was your maid of honor and the best man. Of course, I remember."

"And you set up our honeymoon by the lake," Alicia added.

I'd decorated one of the old cabanas at the lakefront with pink and white crepe paper as a surprise for them. Alicia and Joshua had spent about thirty seconds together post-nuptials before our counselor interrupted them.

"I'm sure this honeymoon will be a step up from that one," I joked.

Joshua sat silent.

"Did I tell you where we're going?" Alicia asked.

"No, I don't think you did." I knew she hadn't. It wasn't information I would soon forget.

"Anguilla," Joshua said, chiming in before she could tell me. "Cap Juluca. Have you been there?"

All the blood in my body rushed to my face, and Joshua's gaze seared into my skin. "No. No, I haven't been there," I answered quickly.

I had been there. Last Memorial Day, Joshua had shown up at my office and surprised me with two first-class tickets to Anguilla. He'd arranged for us to stay in a private beachfront villa at Cap Juluca, an exclusive five-star resort. We'd spent the days snorkeling, sunbathing, and taking long naps together in the hammocks on the beach. At night, we got couples massages under the stars and ate dinner on our patio that overlooked the ocean. It was like we were on our own private island, in our own private world.

For the first time in our relationship, we'd been completely at ease with each other, and by the end of the three days, I'd naively begun to believe that, somehow, things would work out. Once Alicia saw how happy and in love we were, she'd approve, or better yet, be so consumed with her new relationship that she wouldn't even care. But on the last day of our trip, just as I was getting out of the shower, I'd heard him on the phone with her. I'd only needed to hear a few words before I understood the purpose of the call.

She wanted him back. She was sorry and she wanted him back.

Moments after he hung up, my own cell phone had starting ringing. I'd hesitated to answer.

"It's Alicia," I said, looking down at the caller ID.

"She'll be home in a few weeks. Mid-July," Joshua said, picking the phone up off the nightstand and handing it to me. It kept ringing, but I didn't answer. I knew the information waiting for me on the other end, I didn't need it confirmed. The look on his face said enough.

"We knew this wasn't forever," I said, my voice, betraying my emotions.

He unwrapped me from my towel and guided me

back to the bed, where we lay in each other's arms, trying to ignore the bombshell that had just dropped on us both.

But I couldn't ignore it. Even if I'd been momentarily comforted by the weight of his arms around me as we stood in the waves of the blue ocean, or blinded to reality by the alluring glow of the Caribbean sun, because of Alicia's call I had no choice but to accept that we existed on borrowed time.

Pulling myself from my memories, I said, "I've heard Anguilla's really beautiful."

"I can't wait. Joshua rented us the most amazing beachfront villa," she gushed.

"It'll be fantastic," I answered, my cheeks heating up again.

Alicia reached over the table and touched my face. "Maybe you are coming down with something. You're very flushed."

"Yeah, I should get going," I said, standing up from my chair.

Alicia rushed over and hugged me. It was so unlike her that it caught me completely off guard.

"Whoa," I said, grabbing the table for support, "what was that for?"

"I'm proud of you," she answered.

"For what?"

"Taking charge of your life like this. Going after what you want."

"Then why does it feel a little bit like I'm running away?" I said it softly enough that Joshua, who was still seated, couldn't hear.

"I know it's a cliché, but sometimes you have to lose yourself to find yourself again," Alicia said.

I hugged her back. Joshua stood up and moved

toward me to give me a friendly goodbye kiss on the cheek.

"It's fine. Stay where you are," I said, motioning him to sit back down. "I'll call you later, Ali. Enjoy the rest of your evening."

I walked out of the restaurant wondering why it didn't feel like a huge weight had been lifted. It was unseasonably humid, the air almost suffocating as I walked toward home. I made it half a block before I heard my name being called from down the street. I turned around. It was Joshua, waving my jean jacket in the air and speeding up to catch me.

"You left this on your seat," he said, slightly out of breath.

"Thanks," I said, putting it on, even though I was uncomfortably warm.

We stood in silence. I held my breath and waited for him to say something—anything—that let me know my leaving town rattled him in some way or another. He remained silent.

"Was I just a distraction?" I said, using up my very last ounce of self-respect.

"What?"

"Was I just a convenient way of getting over Alicia? You didn't have to look hard to find me. I was right there waiting in the wings like always."

"Is that what you think Gigi?"

I looked down at the ground. He lifted my chin up and kissed me hard. Harder and more passionately than he ever had before. I closed my eyes and let the moment wash over me.

Then every emotion that'd been bubbling up for years charged through me like a lightning bolt. I pushed Joshua away and slapped him hard across the face.

He raised his hand to his cheek and looked like a puppy who'd been scolded for bad behavior. I'd never seen him look so hurt.

He rubbed at his stinging cheek and sighed. "Have a good summer, Georgica." The words caught in his throat.

I inhaled deeply, still relishing in the tingle of his lips against mine, which matched the stinging in my palm. I reached out to console him as I'd done so many times before, but it was too late. He was already gone.

CHAPTER SEVEN

Since neither of us had a car at camp, Jordana and I arranged for a local taxi service to take us and a few other counselors to the bar. Rosie's looked exactly the way I'd pictured it. There were booths on either side of the dark wood-paneled walls, and in the middle was a long bar with about ten stools lined up around it. In the entranceway to the bathroom, was a cigarette dispenser straight out of the seventies and an old-fashioned jukebox. In the far left back corner was a pool table, and dartboards lined the back wall. In New York City, a place like Rosie's would be considered one step above a dive bar. To the Chinooka counselors, it was the hottest spot in town.

A few of the other counselors were already sitting in booths drinking pitchers of beer. Jordana sat down with them, and I went up to the bartender. "Can I get a vodka martini straight up?" I asked, digging a twenty-dollar bill out of my purse.

"No mixed drinks, sweetheart," the bartender answered.

"Okay, do you have shots then?"

"Depends what you want," he responded.

"Tequila?"

He poured me a shot and handed me a slice of lime. I downed it and slammed my glass down on the bar.

"Easy does it, honey," he warned.

"Gigi," I said, extending my hand.

"Rosie." He shook my hand.

"*You're* Rosie?"

"In the flesh." He refilled my shot glass.

"Wow." I swallowed the second shot and sucked on the piece of lime.

"My reputation precedes me?"

I spit the lime into a napkin. "Sort of. I'm a counselor at Camp Chinooka. I didn't realize Rosie was an actual person, let alone a man."

"Charlie Roseman, aka Rosie," he said.

"Nice to meet you, Charlie," I said, offering my hand.

"Welcome home, young man," Rosie shouted behind me and across the bar to Perry, who'd just walked in the front door. I turned back around on my stool.

"He's a great guy. Have you met Perry yet?" Rosie asked.

Perry came over to the bar and sat down on the stool next to me. He looked great in a crisp white button-down shirt and dark jeans. His dark wavy hair was perfectly tousled. "What's the lady drinking?" he asked Rosie.

"I'm doing tequila shots," I answered.

"Brilliant," Perry replied.

Rosie poured us each a shot, and I drank mine quickly. Perry didn't touch his.

"A toast," Perry said, lifting his shot glass in the air. "To second chances."

"Not sure I believe in second chances," I said.

"What do you believe in?"

"Tequila," I said, lifting my empty shot glass in the air.

"To tequila," he said, clinking his shot glass with mine. He put the glass down without drinking any.

I eyed his full shot. "Are you trying to get me drunk, Perry?"

"You think *I'm* trying to get you drunk?"

"Aren't you?"

"You seemed to be off to a pretty good start before I got here," he said.

"You think you're so fantastic, don't you?" I said, the tequila taking away all reticence. "What's your real agenda, Perry? Do you have a thing for Jordana? Tara?"

"I don't have an agenda," he said.

I hadn't eaten much all day and the warmth of the alcohol surged through my arms and legs.

"Of course you do," I said. I stood up from my stool and reached back to it for support. "All guys like you do."

He pushed down on the stool to steady it. "Let me help you," he said, extending his hand out to mine.

"I don't need your help," I snapped.

I pushed past him and headed over to the group of guys at the pool table. I introduced myself and joined in their game. They ordered a round of beers, and we drank and shot pool. I'd only ever played once before at a small pool hall in Chinatown with Joshua last summer. Although I wasn't very good, I was starting to loosen up and heed Tara's advice about having a good time. It was easy with these guys. There was no pretense, and as far as I could tell, the only game being played was eight ball.

When it was my turn to shoot, Danny, one of the guys I'd been flirting with, leaned over to show me how to hold the pool cue. Within seconds we were kissing. It was completely impulsive, but I didn't care one bit. I was never going to see him again, so in my estimation, he was the perfect distraction.

When we finished the game, Danny pulled me away from the table and into a dark corner of the bar, where we continued to make out. Out of the corner of my eye, I could see Perry watching us from his bar stool. I closed my eyes and shut him and everything else out, trying to remember what it was like to just kiss someone without it meaning anything more than that.

Danny and I spent the rest of the night going back and forth between the bar and the dark corner by the bathroom. After a few hours, I crossed the line from drunk to absolutely plastered. I looked around the bar for Jordana. She was nowhere to be found, but Perry was still sitting on his stool watching me. I staggered over to him and asked him if he thought I was putting on a good show.

"You should go home," he said firmly.

"You should mind your own business," I snapped back at him.

"Rosie said that guy you've been hanging out with is kind of a jerk."

"I'm sure he doesn't know him very well," I said.

"Neither do you. Gigi, what are you doing?" he asked.

"*Whatever* I want," I said, emphasizing the word whatever. "Stay out of it."

I turned and walked back to Danny, who was waiting for me in our corner. We went back to kissing, and then the Def Leppard song 'Pour Some Sugar on Me' came on the jukebox. The last thing I remembered before blacking out was pulling Danny on top of the bar to dance with me.

Then nothing.

Several hours later, I awoke from my drunken haze in a strange bed surrounded by unfamiliar things. I sat up, rubbed my eyes, and started to take in my surroundings before I was hit with a wave of nausea, followed by a pounding headache.

"Here. Take these and drink this." A familiar voice with a British accent sounded through the darkness, and someone handed me two Advil and a bottle of water. When he stepped into the light, I saw that the familiar voice belonged to Perry.

"Thanks." I took the Advil and chugged almost half of the water. "How did I get here?"

"Well, first you tried to do a striptease on top of the bar, and then you basically blacked out. I didn't think you'd want Gordy to find out about it, so I brought you here instead of your cabin," he said.

"What time is it?" I asked before finishing off my water.

"Almost four a.m.," he answered.

"I have to go. Where can I toss this?" I asked, holding up the empty water bottle. I tried to get up from the bed but got dizzy and had to sit back down.

"I'll throw it into the rubbish bin," he said, gently taking the bottle from my hand and brushing past my arm. "Stay. Let me make you something to eat."

Although I wasn't hungry, greasy food was really the only way to sober up. "Fine, but then I have to go."

"Deal," he said.

He turned on a light, and as my eyes adjusted to the brightness, I looked around the cabin. It had been renovated into a charming summer cottage complete with a modern kitchen, large-screen TV, and air-conditioning.

"So is this what winning the Gordy three years in a row gets you? Deluxe accommodations? How come you don't have to bunk with the campers?" I asked.

"Gordy renovated some of the older cabins a few years ago so he could rent them out during the off-season. When I almost didn't come back this summer, he sweetened the deal and let me stay here instead of one of the Birch bunks so I could work on my thesis. Beans and toast?" he asked, holding up a can of baked beans.

"Beans?"

"Too English for you, I guess? How about two eggs and toast?"

"Extra greasy."

"Extra greasy. You got it." He turned his attention to the stove.

The Advil was beginning to kick in, so I stood up to look around some more. The cabin was practically overflowing with lined sheets of music and vinyl records. They covered almost every inch of spare space. There was even an old-school record player resting in the corner. Leave it to the English guy to tote along his own record player.

"Did you bring all of this stuff on the plane?" I asked, amazed by the sheer amount of sheet music stacked everywhere.

"I shipped them here. To complete my doctorate, I need to write an original composition, but I've resigned myself to the fact that it's my fate to be head counselor for Birch forever. Your eggs are ready," he said, turning off the burner.

I moved to the small kitchen table, which was covered with more lined paper. I made a small space for a plate, and Perry served me two eggs sunny-side up, toast, and some coffee. "Thank you. This is perfect." I took my first bite. "I can't believe how much I drank."

"What was that all about?" he asked.

"What do you mean?"

"You were doing shots at the bar by yourself before I even got there. What are you trying to drink away?" Perry asked.

"Nothing. Can't a girl just have a good time at a bar on her night off?"

"You passed out. I carried you here."

"And?"

"So that's a typical night for you in the big city, Princess?"

I shrugged my shoulders. "No, not typical, but it happens."

"Seemed like you were out to prove something. Nobody drinks that much just for fun."

He was right. So many of the moments I most regretted had been fueled by too much alcohol and a need to be out of control. But the biggest mistake I'd ever made—getting together with Joshua—hadn't occurred in a drunken stupor. Worse. It had happened when I was stone-cold sober. I'd been fully in control of my faculties when I succumbed to my desire for him. Years of pining sated in one reckless moment. I'd spent the last year replaying our relationship over and over in my head, wondering.

If I had it all to do again, would I?

CHAPTER EIGHT

About a month after Alicia went to London for her training program, I was enjoying a night alone with a glass of wine and some bad television when Joshua let himself into my apartment. I was startled by the sound of the door opening but was actually more nervous that it was Joshua entering and not a stranger. He must've come straight from work. He was still wearing his suit and tie from the day and irritatingly looked as pristine as when he'd put them on at least twelve hours earlier. I looked down at my outfit —ripped pajama pants and a Columbia Law T-shirt that'd belonged to my father—and sank a little deeper into the couch.

"Hey. I hope I didn't come at a bad time. Alicia left me her keys, and I was nearby. Must be weird to be here alone, huh?"

"The time will go fast," I said, lifting the remote to turn off the TV.

"Unless she decides to stay in London with the guy she's seeing."

So, that's why he came by. Joshua was looking to unload on his usual sounding board, and I was here waiting for him.

He took off his suit jacket and hung it on the rack by the front door. "At first she said she just wanted a break, but now she isn't returning any of my calls or texts. Why do I feel like I just saw you?" he said, trying to change the subject.

I shook my head. "I don't know. We haven't seen each other in months."

"I remember now," he said, smiling. "I got sucked into a *Top Designer* marathon a few weekends ago."

I rolled my eyes. "I can't wait for the next season to air so they'll stop showing mine."

"Why? You were great. I was rooting for you to win the whole time."

"That's nice of you to say."

"Why wouldn't I say that? We're friends, aren't we, Gigi?"

"Of course we're friends."

He sat down next to me on the couch. "It's funny. I've known you longer than Alicia, but when was the last time you and I went for a drink or a meal?"

"You haven't known me longer than Alicia. We all met at camp."

"I can't believe you don't remember," he said.

"Remember what?"

"Alicia hopping from seat to seat on the bus, talking to anyone who would listen while you were homesick or something."

I shook my head. "That's right. You came and sat with me."

Of course, I remembered. That moment had set into

motion a lifetime of pining for someone who would never be mine. I remembered how I couldn't believe that Joshua Baume had wanted to sit with me. He was the most beautiful boy I'd ever seen and he'd chosen me over Alicia and all the other girls on the bus clamoring to be near him.

"I get it. We go way back. Look, whenever you want to have dinner, we can have dinner," I said.

"Fine, how's now?" he asked, calling my bluff. He loosened his tie and slipped it off.

"Now? Now's great. Just let me go change."

"Sounds good. I'll be waiting," he said, picking up the remote off the couch cushion.

I didn't have a single clue what to put on. Nothing I owned seemed right. I finally settled on a fitted white tee, low-rise jeans, a blue-gray velvet blazer that matched my eyes, and a pair of slingbacks I'd wrestled away from another girl at a sample sale. When I finally walked back into the living room, Joshua was setting our small kitchen table.

"What's all this?" I said, trying to hide the disappointment in my voice.

"I called for some takeout. It should be here in a few minutes," he said, laying out the flatware.

I took some of the dishes out of his hand. "So what'd you order?"

"Well, there's this incredible Mediterranean place right around the corner."

"La Mer?" I guessed.

"Yeah, you have eaten there?"

"It's one of my father's favorites, actually."

"Alicia wouldn't ever go with me," he said.

"Yeah, I know. She doesn't like spicy food."

It was strange talking about Alicia without her being there. It was like we had to bring her name up every few minutes just to keep the conversation from coming to a screeching halt.

"I didn't know what you liked, so I got a few things to try," he said.

"Thanks," I said, looking for a bottle of wine in the very back of the refrigerator. "I knew we still had one. Is white okay?"

"Yeah, white's great," he answered.

While I was uncorking the bottle, the door buzzer rang and Joshua ran to answer it.

"I have cash in my wallet," I said, yelling from the kitchen. "Just take whatever."

"I got this," he replied, signing the receipt in the doorway while the delivery guy waited.

I emptied the food containers into bowls and set them on the table. Everything smelled wonderful. I sat down next to him, and he raised his glass for a toast.

"To us and our first dinner together as friends," he said.

"Cheers," I said, clinking my glass with his. I took a long sip before setting it down. "This all looks really great," I added.

"You look really great, Gigi. I should have told you that when you walked back in here," he said.

I shifted uncomfortably in my seat.

"No, really. You look different. What's different about you?" he asked.

"Nothing's different," I answered.

He turned his chair toward me and pushed some hair out of my face.

"What are you doing?" I asked.

"Nothing. I couldn't see your face," he said, turning

his attention back to the food. "How incredible is this hummus? You seeing anyone?" He leaned farther back in his chair.

"What? No, just sort of dating. Nobody special," I said, admitting the embarrassing truth before I could come up with a believable lie.

"What happened to Mike?" he asked.

"Who?" I said, taking a forkful of falafel.

"The guy you brought to your parents' last Fourth of July party?"

"Oh, Matt? Yeah, we went on a few dates, then it fizzled."

"Not your type?"

"I guess not."

"So what is your type?" he asked, leaning closer to me.

"I don't know if I have a type," I answered.

"Have you ever been in love?" he asked very directly. It caught me off guard.

I put my wine down. "No. Have you?"

"Yes."

"Of course. Alicia, obviously," I said, feeling stupid for even putting the question to him.

"Shira Levy," he said.

"Who?"

"You don't remember Shira? I'm shocked." Joshua threw back the rest of his wine.

I racked my brain for a few minutes before it came to me. "Shira Levy from Camp Chinooka. That wasn't love. That was puberty. She developed boobs at eleven."

"Maybe so," he said, laughing to himself.

"So Shira, huh? What would Alicia have to say about that?" I teased.

"I think she'd understand."

"You're right. I think every camper was a little in love with Shira Levy. If you're finished, I'll clean up so you can get going."

"Is it okay if I stay a little longer? I don't feel like being alone tonight."

A flutter started in my stomach and moved its way into my chest. "Umm…sure, stay as long as you need to."

I reached over him to clear his plate, and he lifted his hand from the table and placed it over mine.

"What are you doing, Joshua?" I whispered.

He took the dishes from my hands and placed them back on the table. Standing up, he pulled me toward him and turned me around. He ran his fingers through my hair and then kissed me.

I thought to push him away, but his arms felt so right wrapped firmly around me. I gave in and kissed him back. It wasn't romantic or even passionate. It was primitive and urgent. When he finally let go, I backed away and almost hit the wall behind me. He kissed me again, and I let him take over, happy to finally relinquish control to the one person who ever made me feel out of it.

My college philosophy professor had once explained that in any relationship involving three people, by default, it became one person's role to mediate between the two opposing or contradictory sides. Ultimately, one of the three would take on the responsibility of interceding between, reconciling, and connecting the two.

I'd held that position for as long as I'd known Joshua and Alicia and with that one kiss, forever abandoned it. Over the course of the next few months, I tried to push that truth as far into the recesses of my mind as my heart and guilt would allow, but it always resurfaced.

Now, in Perry's cabin, being questioned about my most recent behavior and the motives that had incited it, my shame came back to light. I was a million miles away from that night, yet I could still feel the weight of Joshua's body against mine and the way his fingers dug into my shoulder blades when he kissed me. His touch was imprinted on my mind, body, and soul, and I cringed at my own inability to let it go and—worse than that—the mistakes I was continuing to make in trying to do so.

"So you think I'm out to prove something?" I said, in response to Perry's accusation.

"Aren't you?" he asked, still leaning over me, clearing the dishes. He was so close his breath grazed my ear. Even though I'd been repulsed by him only hours earlier, now I wanted him. I wanted nothing more than to pull him close and prove to myself I was over Joshua.

"Maybe," I said softly.

I stood up to face him and leaned in, hoping he'd scoop me up, carry me back to his bed, and help me move on from the night when Joshua and I had crossed over the brink. Instead, Perry backed away from me.

"What's the matter?"

"What are you doing?" he asked.

"Don't you want to?"

"I'm not looking to be part of this game you're playing with your boyfriend back at home, Gigi."

"Is that what you think this is?"

"Isn't it? The guy at the bar? Me? It's all part of some big game for you, right?"

"What do you care anyway? Isn't this the kind of thing that you come every summer for?" I said.

"Hardly," he answered.

All I had to do was look around the cabin to see he was using camp as a means of escape from something, too. "I have to go. I have to get back before my girls notice I didn't sleep in the bunk."

"Let me walk you back," he offered.

"I'm fine."

"It's still dark outside. Let me walk you back."

"I said I'm fine. I was a camper here for seven summers. I don't need your help." I crawled across the floor, trying to find my shoes.

"At least take my flashlight," he said, handing it to me.

I took it from him, slipped my heels back on, and walked out onto the cabin deck.

"Do you need some other shoes?"

"I walked from SoHo to my apartment on the Upper East Side in these shoes during a massive power outage in Manhattan. I can make it back to my cabin, thank you very much."

He laughed, which only irritated me more.

I stood up to face him. "Look, whatever this act of chivalry was tonight, I appreciate it, but next time, just let me be. I'm a big girl, and I would have gotten home from the bar just fine."

Perry was silent for a moment, and then, almost as if he was hearing me for the first time, he said, "You've made that quite clear to me a few times today, so, no problem. From this point on, I'll leave you alone."

"Great."

"Well, Princess, all too happy to oblige." He walked back into the cabin and slammed the door before I had a chance to reply.

When I got back to the bunk, all the girls were soundly sleeping. I took off my shoes and tiptoed across the floor to my bed. I was hoping to maybe get an hour of sleep in before the wake-up call. I changed out of my dress and into a T-shirt and sweatpants so the girls would think I'd slept in the bunk all night and climbed into bed. After a few seconds fiercely battling my covers, I realized I was once again the victim of a short-sheeting prank. I groaned loudly. Jordana heard me and woke up.

"They did it to my bed again too. Here," she said, tossing me a sleeping bag from under her own bed. I unzipped it and turned it into a blanket before wrapping it around me.

"I've been worried about you. I tried to get you to leave with me and the other counselors, but you weren't having it. Perry told me he'd make sure you got home, so I finally left. Where have you been?" she whispered.

"Perry's cabin," I answered.

"What?" She sat up, her eyebrows almost leaping into her hairline.

"Shhh, you'll wake them. It's not what you think."

"What happened?" she asked.

"I had too much to drink and I blacked out or something. Perry took me back to his cabin so Gordy wouldn't find out."

"I guess that was after you made out with the townie?"

"Townie?"

"The guy you were all over? You know, he doesn't work at camp, right? He lives in Milbank year-round."

She made it sound like I'd made out with a convict or something. "Well, at least I won't have to run into him at breakfast later," I said.

"True. So then, what happened after you finished making out with the townie?"

"Apparently, I tried to do a striptease on the bar? That's the last thing I remember before I woke up in Perry's bed."

"Classy." She smirked. "Then what?"

"Then nothing. He made me some eggs, we talked a little, and I left. The last thing I needed were any of the girls seeing me do the walk of shame this morning."

"Coming home from Perry's cabin would be more like a stride of pride."

I tossed one of my pillows at her head.

"Really, Gigi? Nothing happened?"

She sounded surprised by my answer, which only further confirmed my suspicions about Perry's true nature.

"Less than nothing," I said, the moment of rejection still fresh in my memory.

"You have amazing restraint," she said, settling back down into the bed.

"He was the one who didn't want anything."

She was silent. I could tell she was just as surprised as I'd been. Then she said, "His loss," like a supportive best friend. Just like Alicia would have.

"It's sweet of you to try to make me feel better, but honestly, I was probably still drunk when the thought crossed my mind. I'm sorry I woke you. I'm gonna try to get a little rest before the wake-up call."

I closed my eyes, and after what seemed like only a few minutes, I was awakened by Gordy's voice blaring over the loudspeaker system. "Gooooooood morning, Camp Chinooka. It's raining cats and dogs out there, so don't forget to put on your galoshes this morning. Now, a musical tribute to Mother Nature to get you up and going. A chart topper from 1982, the classic, 'It's Raining Men,'" he blasted the song.

"He has got to be kidding," Jordana said, putting her pillow over her head.

"I feel like death," I replied, pulling my own pillow over my face. "Is he playing 'It's Raining Men,' or am I having a Bat Mitzvah flashback?"

"It's no flashback. He's definitely blasting eighties music before eight a.m.," she answered.

"There is something very wrong with that man. Okay, girls, everybody up," I said, tearing myself out of bed.

There was a chorus of moans as the girls stirred. "I don't like it any better than you do," I said as I walked from bed to bed, making sure they were actually getting up.

"You look like shit, Gigi," Tara said, as I pulled the blanket off of her.

I put on my most comfortable sweatpants and staff T-shirt and washed up the best I could. I spun the work wheel, divided up the tasks, and when I was finished, put on a big pair of sunglasses and waited for the girls outside in the horseshoe. The combination of the weather and the hangover was completely draining. I dragged myself to breakfast, the girls trailing behind me. When we got inside, of course, Perry's boys were already seated and in mid-cheer. I rolled my eyes behind my sunglasses and sat down at the table.

Within seconds Perry's group was chanting, "We've got spirit, yes, we do; we've got spirit, how 'bout you?" while looking in our direction. My girls answered them back with the same cheer, even louder. The two groups went back and forth chanting, each time getting a little bit louder. My head throbbed, and I knew Perry had intentionally initiated the contest as a way to punish me for my behavior. I went over to the cereal canisters at the far side of the room, away from the shouting, and poured myself a bowl of Frosted Flakes.

"It's raining outside, and it's dark in here," Perry said, pouring cereal into his own bowl.

"How very astute of you. Hard to believe you still haven't earned that doctorate yet," I said.

"I just meant you look a little out of place with sunglasses on."

"My head feels like it's in a vise, and my brain could squeeze out of my eyeballs at any moment. The sunglasses are just a means of shielding the rest of you in case that actually happens."

"Fair enough," he replied, backing away from me.

"I'm so glad you approve. Excuse me," I said, pushing past him and right into Gordy, who had been hovering nearby, hoping to jump into our conversation.

"I want to grab a word with both of you, if that's okay?" He ushered us toward a quiet corner (if there was such a thing) in the dining hall. He did not look happy. I was pretty sure we were busted, and I was about to be fired from my second job this year.

"I heard things got pretty out of hand at Rosie's last night. A lot of drinking and dancing on tables," he said, rubbing the gray stubble on his face.

I swallowed so hard I could swear that Perry heard it and turned to look at me.

Gordy continued, "Maybe this isn't right of me to ask, but the two of you are a little bit older than the other counselors, so I need you to be my eyes and ears when you're off the camp grounds. Make sure everyone's doing the right thing."

"No problem," Perry quickly replied.

"Is there anyone in particular I need to speak to this morning about their behavior?"

I could have been paranoid, but it felt like he was glaring in my direction. I pushed my sunglasses off my eyes and on top of my head.

"No, sir, nobody I can think of. Gigi?" Perry said, turning to me.

"Me neither," I answered.

"Thanks, kids. My door's always open if anything comes up."

Perry leaned in close to me. "That's it. That was your one freebie. Don't expect me to protect you again."

When I sat down at the table, all the girls were distracted, staring at the entryway of the dining hall, where Madison was talking to Alex Shane.

"What'd I miss?" I asked, setting out my second breakfast of the day on the table.

"Well, Alex sent his friend Todd over here to ask Emily to ask Madison to meet him by the doorway," Jordana recounted seamlessly and without looking up from her bowl of oatmeal.

I shook my head and sighed.

"What?" she said, looking up.

"Do you think Alex will send Todd to break the bad news to Madison when he decides he likes Emily better in a few days, or be a man and do it himself?"

"You're so cynical," Jordana said.

"I just call 'em like I see 'em."

"Then you aren't seeing this," she said, turning my attention back to the doorway, where Alex and Madison were mid-kiss. "Enough to soften even your hardened heart?"

I wanted to tell her my heart wasn't hardened—it

was actually in shambles—but instead, I nodded in agreement.

"Fine, I can't deny that it's very sweet," I conceded. "But I'm electing you to clean up the mess when it all implodes."

"I accept," Jordana said, mocking my serious tone.

Gordy went up to the microphone to make morning announcements, and the room quieted down. As he spoke, I noticed Michelle, one of the Cedar counselors, leaning over Perry and talking to him by his table. He was totally focused on her, ignoring Gordy completely. I was so caught up in watching them flirt that I didn't hear Hannah calling my name from across the table. She threw a banana at me to get my attention.

"Geez, Hannah, you could take my eye out," I teased.

"Gigi," she whined, "Gordy said the cast list will be posted after breakfast on his office door. I'm gonna throw up." She rested her head in her hands.

Oh to be thirteen and have *this* be your biggest problem. "Don't throw up. Go wait where the list will be posted. I'll meet you out there."

When I got to the office, I fought my way through the crowd of campers anxiously gathered in front of Gordy's door and over to Hannah, who was pacing back and forth in her spot. A few minutes later Gordy forced his way through and tacked the list onto the door. The kids swarmed it and then backed away just as quickly, most of them disappointed with the outcome.

Hannah bit her nails and waited until most of the campers had cleared out. I stood back and waited to see her expression. A huge smile crept across her face, and I knew she'd won the role. She ran over and gave me a hug.

She was grinning from ear to ear. "I did it. I got it!"

"I knew you would. Congratulations."

"Your name is on the list, too," she said.

I didn't understand how my name could have found its way onto a cast list for a show I hadn't tried out for. I went over to the bulletin board and ran my finger down the list. I saw Hannah's name next to Hodel and a few other girls from my group listed as part of the chorus. As I got farther down the list, I saw Alex Shane's name next to the part of Perchick, the "bad boy" character of *Fiddler on the Roof*. He was the idealistic, revolutionary student, and Hodel's love interest. In every production, the boy who played Perchick was the object of affection for most of the female cast. Joshua had played that part at least twice when we were campers.

I scanned farther down the cast list and was surprised to see Perry's name next to the part of the fiddler, and then, even farther down the list, my name was next to the words Costume Design. When I'd made the costume suggestions to Jackie and Davis, I was trying to be helpful. I hadn't been offering up my services. There'd obviously been a huge miscommunication.

"I wouldn't have guessed you were someone who could sew a button, let alone a whole rack of costumes," Perry said from behind me.

"Wonders never cease," I replied.

"You realize costume design actually means designing and sewing the costumes, right? It's not just an excuse to go shopping."

"How 'bout you? Trying to score more Gordy points by volunteering yourself for the show?"

"I'm a concert level violinist," he answered.

"Really?"

"Why do you seem surprised?"

"I guess I shouldn't be. It kind of goes with your whole shtick."

"Shtick?"

"Your whole I'm British and artsy and can get any girl I want shtick," I said, mocking his accent.

"This is getting exhausting. Let's agree not to speak again until you have to measure me for my costume, all right? How does that suit you?" Perry said.

"Suits me just fine. I don't think I'll be the one measuring you anyway. I have to find Jackie and decline the position."

He grunted.

"What? You don't approve, I take it?"

"No, I'm just not entirely surprised, that's all."

"I could do it. I do have the technical skills to do it."

He snorted.

"I was named Most Talented Upcoming Designer by *New York Magazine*," I said.

"So then get off your high horse and make the bloody costumes," he shouted at me before walking away.

It was much easier said than done. It had been almost a year since I stumbled into my creative block. During the last several months of working at Diane von Furstenberg, I'd sat staring at blank sketchbooks, hoping the ideas would begin to flow, but nothing came. I missed deadline after deadline, and when I couldn't come up with one more excuse as to why I should be given another chance, I was fired. The irony was that just prior to the block, I had the most imaginative and inspired period of my whole career. I had an unlimited supply of ideas, some of which I was able to incorporate into my designs at work, and some of which went completely against their aesthetic. I had this burning desire to create. So the designs that weren't right for the label, I made at home.

I'd set up a studio in my living room, lined the walls with bolts of unusual and colorful fabrics, and sewed some of the more avant-garde pieces whenever I had spare time. Within a few months, I had about half of my very own collection completed, while I was simultaneously helping to design the fall line. It was as if my relationship with Joshua had breathed new life into my work. I wasn't sure if it was because my feelings for him had spilled into every other aspect of my life, or if maybe (even though I hated to admit it) the exhilaration of behaving in a way that was so outside of myself had changed me.

I was a different person when I was with him, and so my work became different too. I was freer, more passionate, and more spontaneous than I'd ever been before, and it reflected in my designs. It wasn't long before my bosses began to take notice and reward me for my achievements. I was promoted to Senior Designer. Instead of being lumped in under the main label, I actually got individual name recognition for my creations. A few of my pieces were featured in *Vogue* with an article written about me entitled *Avant Un-Guarded*. There was even insider talk about me starting my own line.

Then, Alicia had returned from London and everything ended with Joshua. After that, I'd slipped into a kind of depression. The guilt of lying to Alicia combined with the pain of no longer having Joshua had been almost more than I could bear. The shame had all but consumed me, crushing whatever creative vision I had. It was all I could think about, all I could focus on, and those feelings had eventually taken over.

I was terrified that picking up a sketchpad again would unearth all of the inadequacy and guilt I'd worked so hard to bury. I knew if I was ever going to revive my career, I had to start somewhere—I'd have to face it.

I just wasn't sure if I was ready.

CHAPTER NINE

The rainy weather made the rest of the day difficult. Instead of instructional swim, the lifeguards taught CPR at the Lakeside Rec, and instead of athletics, the counselors organized games in the dining hall. Of course, my girls wanted no part in any of it. I spent most of the day running around in the rain, unearthing them from their hiding spots. They would've done just about anything to be able to stay in the cabins reading their *Us Weeklys* and listening to music.

If I wasn't in charge, that was exactly what I'd be doing. But I *was* in charge, and battling against my hangover instead of snuggling up in bed was a pulsating reminder of that fact.

It was raining so hard later in the day that Gordy did an uncharacteristic thing. He canceled all afternoon activities and arranged for movies to be shown around camp. He dismissed the other groups and announced that Cedar and Birch would be watching *Titanic* in the Lakeside Rec. Though lately, I wasn't a fan of any movie that dealt with star-crossed lovers, clocking in at over three hours, *Titanic* was just long enough that I could probably sneak in a much-needed nap. The campers loaded into the rec hall and carefully chose their seats. The opportunity to sit next to someone of the opposite sex for three hours in the dark was a rare occurrence at Chinooka.

When the kids quieted down, Perry walked around and offered them a choice of chips or candy from The Canteen, and then took a seat next to Michelle. Tara almost fell out of her chair trying to get a better view of them. Almost immediately after the opening credits of the movie, my eyelids got heavy, and I had to fight to keep them open. Within minutes, I fell into a deep sleep and didn't wake up until I heard the ill-fated words, "Iceberg right ahead!"

Lifting my head off of my chest, I noticed a small drool stain on the collar of my shirt. My neck was stiff, and I struggled to even lift it. I moved from side to side to stretch and saw that most of the campers were watching the movie, although a few had also nodded off. Then, I spotted Alex Shane and Madison in a full-fledged make-out session in a dark corner. I jumped out of my seat and headed over to them. I pried them apart before pulling them outside. Perry heard the commotion and followed right behind us.

"What the hell were the two of you doing?" I asked.

"Need me to draw you a diagram?" Alex answered, and Madison laughed.

"No, I don't need you to draw me a diagram. I need for you not to behave like a prepubescent maniac," I responded.

"What's going on?" Perry asked, addressing the three of us.

"While you were cozying up to Michelle, these two were circling second base."

Perry jerked his head back. "What?"

Clearly, he was unfamiliar with the baseball to sex analogy that I was using to describe how far they'd gone during the movie. "I mean, I can't be sure it was second base, but there was something going on," I replied.

"That's not what I meant, Gigi. I'm just wondering how you can stand there all self-righteous, telling me I wasn't doing my job when you just woke up from a two-hour nap."

"I did not," I contested.

His gaze scanned down my T-shirt and stopped right at the drool stain.

"Fine, maybe I dozed for a couple of minutes," I conceded.

"You were snoring. Loudly."

"I was not. I don't snore."

"You were and you do. You snored last night, too. I had to turn on my telly to drown you out," he said, trying to prove his point. Except he'd also just inadvertently let Madison and Alex know I spent the night with him.

"Gigi slept in your cabin last night?" Alex said, catching Perry's misspeak. "Good one." He raised his hand to offer Perry a high five.

"Not so fast, killer. It's not what you think," Perry chided.

"No, it's probably better," Alex answered.

"*Nice,*" I said, giving Alex a sideways glance. "Perry helped me home after we went out last night."

"Alex, drop it," Perry warned.

"I'll drop it if you both drop it," Alex said.

"You two, keep your hands to yourselves and finish

watching the movie. Don't make me repeat this conversation. Now, go inside," Perry said in a tone so firm it took all three of us by surprise. "Now, *you,*" he said, turning his full attention to me, "where do you think you are? Club Med? This is a job, and you're responsible twenty-four seven. Whether you care or not, those girls look up to you. You're the counselor, not the camper. So, whether your head's turned for a second and ten of them go sneaking off into the woods in the middle of the night, or you decide to take a nap while Madison and Alex circle home base, what happens to them is on you. Whatever your reasons for coming here, that's your business. But now that you are here, *be here.*" He slammed the screen door behind him as he went back inside.

Perry's harsh words still ringing in my ears, I thought about my counselors when I was a camper at Chinooka. There was Deborah from Australia who'd introduced us to everything from Vegemite to how to stuff our training bras. Evie from Manchester, who spoke with the coolest cockney accent, had taught us how to apply eyeliner and shave our legs. Meredith, who dated at least ten different counselors over the summer, had shown us how to write the perfect breakup notes and encouraged my first foray into design by wearing a "Gigi Original" to the camp social.

Each and every one of them had a huge influence on my adolescence—the big sisters I'd never had but always wanted. It was funny. I'd come to Chinooka looking for an escape from everything in my life, giving no thought whatsoever to the fact that I'd be in the position to influence anyone else's. But, Perry was right. I had to do better. I owed it to those fifty girls to do better. So, as old

Rose foolishly tossed the diamond necklace into the ocean, I promised myself I would.

Later that night, I took the girls who'd been cast in *Fiddler on the Roof* to the Lakeside Amphitheater for their first rehearsal. Although it had stopped raining earlier in the afternoon, the wood benches encircling the theater were still damp. I laid my poncho out on the bench before I sat down, and the other girls followed suit. Jackie, the play's director, stepped to the middle of the elevated platform of the stage and formally introduced herself. Then she introduced each member of the cast, giving a little bit of background on the parts they'd be playing. When she got to Perry, she asked him to join her on stage.

"For those of you who don't know, this is Perry Gillman, head counselor of Birch. Perry's an accomplished violinist, and we've been fortunate to have him agree to play our fiddler. Tonight, he has graciously offered to showcase a sampling of the score to give everyone a taste of the show's music. Perry, if you would," she said, turning to him.

He stepped forward, violin in hand, and pulled the bow across its neck. His talent hadn't been exaggerated one bit. I closed my eyes to listen, almost forgetting where I was and who was playing. When he was done, the entire amphitheater was on its feet clapping. True to form, he walked off the stage as if what he'd done was no big deal rather than the feat of artistry we'd all just witnessed. Jackie thanked Perry and then continued explaining her vision for the show. At the end of the meeting, Davis handed out the rehearsal schedule for the next several weeks. As the kids filed out, I went to talk to Davis and Jackie about resigning from my post. Jackie was looking down at a set of notes on her clipboard as I approached. I tapped her on the shoulder.

"I wanted to thank you both for the opportunity, but I wasn't so much offering my help with the costumes as I was offering up some ideas."

Davis quickly chimed in. "We talked it over last night, and think you could really be an asset."

"That's nice, but you said there wasn't really a budget for costumes."

"I spoke to Gordy, and I was able to work something out," Davis said. "Plus, I hoped you might know people in the industry and be able to get us some fabric at cost."

"I do know some people, but ..." I started, but Perry sidled up to me with a smug look on his face. Suddenly I just couldn't let him have the satisfaction of being right about me. "But I'm not really sure if we'll need to do that. I can make it work. I'll get the budget from Gordy and figure something out. I'll have some sketches for you by next week."

Jackie and Davis seemed confused by my one-eighty. So was Perry.

"That's great. We'll make sure you get some time with Big Bertha," Davis said.

"Who's Big Bertha?" Perry asked.

"I cannot believe she's still around," I said, shaking my head.

"Yeah, she still has a few good years in her," Davis answered.

"Who are you talking about?" Perry asked again.

Big Bertha was the camp nickname for an old Singer sewing machine housed in arts and crafts. It had once belonged to Gordy's grandmother and even had its original foot peddle. When she died, Gordy couldn't bear to part with it and found it a home at Chinooka long before I was even a camper. I learned to sew on Big Bertha, spending countless hours behind her, crudely stitching together my latest designs for the play fashion shows we staged at night in the bunks.

"As much as I love Big Bertha, I'm not sure if the old girl has enough juice in her for what I need. I'll see if I can get a friend to drive up my electric sewing machine from the city, along with some extra fabric from my apartment," I said.

"So Big Bertha is a sewing machine?" Perry asked a final time.

"Yes, Big Bertha's a sewing machine. What, were you worried that there was a woman on these grounds you didn't know?"

"Hardly," he replied before storming off.

"What's that about?" Davis asked.

"We didn't really get off on the right foot," I answered.

"Too bad. He's a really good guy."

"That's what people keep telling me. So sketches by next Tuesday?"

"That should work," he said.

"I hope I don't disappoint you guys."

"Gigi, it's a camp play, not the Bryant Park tents at fashion week," he replied, making what he thought was a joke. Little did he know, only one year ago, I *had* shown at those very tents.

I offered to sit OD every night for the next week so I'd have time to do the sketches. Under the moonlight, at a rotting picnic table, I finally found the inspiration that had been eluding me for months. When the week was over, I gave my sketchbook to Jackie and Davis to review.

I was almost as nervous as I'd been when Anna Wintour came to see an early preview of the very first collection I worked on for Diane von Furstenberg. A few days later, Davis gave me the green light to go ahead, and I was off and running.

CHAPTER TEN

Having survived the first few weeks as head counselor, the next hurdle was chaperoning the all-camp social. The girls had been looking forward to it since they arrived at Chinooka, debating their outfits and which guys they were planning to make a move on. The night of the social, Bunk Fourteen was a flurry of activity as the girls first tried on their entire wardrobes and then each others'. Even Jordana got into it, asking if she could borrow the dress I'd worn to Rosie's, which I, of course, lent her.

"What are you going to wear?" she asked while digging underneath her bed to find a match for the sandal she already had on her foot.

"I might just stay in this," I said, pointing to my cargo pants and white tank top.

She shook her head. "Gigi, you *cannot* stay in that."

"I have to stay back with Candice and her clique during the first half of the social anyway."

"You've sat OD every night this week instead of

going out. You walk around this place like you're serving some sort of sentence," she said.

I smiled. "Aren't I?"

"There are guys here who have expressed interest," Jordana said.

"Interest in me? I guess they don't know I'm a hundred and five."

"Do all your friends find this self-deprecating thing as annoying as I do? Look at you. Ah, finally found it," she said, pulling her missing sandal out. She spun around in a circle. "So how do I look?"

"Really pretty. Now go snag your Aussie." Jordana had confessed to me about her crush on Jake, the Australian head of the waterfront staff.

"His accent just does it for me. I close my eyes and imagine I'm making out with one of the Hemsworth brothers," she said, spritzing perfume in the air to make a cloud and walking through.

"I know what you mean. Even when Perry's being insulting, he sounds charming. It's not fair," I said.

"Maybe you just misread things that morning in his cabin? I mean, you both had been drinking. Maybe his rejection was something else?" she suggested. "Maybe he didn't want to take advantage of you or the situation?"

"No, he was pretty clear about not wanting me." At least, I thought he'd been pretty clear. Maybe as a means of self-preservation I was forcing myself to find red flags that just weren't there? "Why is everyone so invested in this anyway? All we've done is argue since the day we met."

"'Cause passion is passion, good or bad, and you have to admit there's something there."

"Fine, I admit there maybe could have been

something there, but I'm not looking for anything complicated and he's complicated."

"One of these days, are you going to extinguish it?" she asked.

"Extinguish what?"

"This torch you're carrying for someone who obviously hurt you badly."

"Maybe you're the one who's a hundred and five. How'd you get so wise?"

"I'm the oldest of three sisters. Comes with the job," she answered.

"I have to go out for roll call. Can you make sure none of them walk out of here with anything exposed that shouldn't be exposed? Oh, and can you give Tara this?" I said, tossing my Dior lipgloss at her.

"Are you going to change out of that outfit?"

"I'll put something else on that's not khaki, I promise."

"Or Army green. It's really not your color," she shouted at me as I walked out the bunk door.

I went into the horseshoe and called for roll call, but nobody came. After I shouted a couple more times, a few girls trickled out. After the fifth time, the rest of them finally showed up dressed to the nines. "You all look great. I don't need to remind you that we're currently beating Birch for The Gordy, so keep that in mind tonight, but have fun. I need to see Candice, Erica, Dana, and Jen from Bunk Eleven. Also, Brooke and Michelle, can you hang behind?"

There was a collective groan from the four of them as the other girls left to go to the social. I turned to Michelle and Brooke. "I only need one of you to hang behind for this. Brooke, why don't you head over to the social? Michelle, can you hang back with me and the campers?"

Michelle rolled her eyes and muttered the word "unbelievable" under her breath.

"Problem?" I asked.

"No. Well, actually, yes. I just think it's really petty for you to make me stay behind to keep me from hanging out with Perry," she said.

"Is that what you think I'm doing?"

"Isn't it?"

"Four girls from your cabin were caught smoking pot behind The Canteen. I need one of you here to help me keep an eye on them until we let them join the social. You were standing closest to me, so, congratulations, you won," I said, heading toward the bunk.

"Right," she muttered from behind me.

I spun around on my heels. "If you have something to say, Michelle, just say it."

"It's just a little desperate, that's all."

"Desperate?"

"To throw yourself at Perry the way you do."

"Perry's all yours. He's all yours, *after* you do your job and watch these girls."

After that, Michelle didn't say a word to me. For exactly an hour and a half, we sat in Bunk Eleven in silence. At one point Candice rose to fix her makeup at the mirror, and Michelle shot her a look that made her sit right back down. When the time was up, I released them to go to the social. I started to walk back to the bunk to change but decided there was no point. I wasn't here to impress anyone, so what difference did it make what I was wearing?

When I got to the tennis courts, a slow song was playing, and most of the campers were dancing. I immediately spotted Perry talking to Michelle under a huge floodlight. Jordana was getting herself some punch at the refreshments table. I joined her.

"Why are you still wearing that?" she asked.

"I added a jean jacket," I said defensively.

"Didn't you tell me you were a fashion designer?"

"Give me a break. You don't know the attitude I just got from Michelle for making her stay behind with me. She thought I was intentionally trying to keep her from hanging out with Perry."

Perry came up to the table to get a drink.

"Two, please," he said to Jordana.

"It's self-serve," she replied.

He turned to me. "Gigi, how nice of you to dress up for the occasion."

I scanned the tennis courts. A bunch of the Cedar girls huddled together in one corner, talking and pointing to different couplings. All along the perimeter of the court were the counselors, who were half keeping an eye on the kids and half eyeing each other. The DJ, probably a local kid from Milbank, had his headphones pressed to his ear and was bouncing along to some hip-hop song nobody on the court seemed to know. You had to give him credit—even though most of the campers were acting like they were way too cool to even be there, the DJ didn't seem to notice or care.

"Who's having a good time?" Gordy shouted into the DJ's microphone. "I said, who's having a good time tonight?" A few campers yelled back. "Right now, Cedar is just slightly ahead of Birch for The Gordy. Let's bring Perry and Gigi out to the middle of the tennis courts for a dance-off worth ten points."

I looked at Jordana. "He can't be serious."

"Apparently, he's not only serious but armed with the

spotlight, which he is shining at you right now," she said.

"Oh, God, really?" Looking up, I was almost blinded by the white light.

She pushed me forward. "You better get out there. Nobody keeps Baby in the corner," she said, laughing.

Then, I heard it—the opening of the same song that Gordy had played at every social back when I was a camper at Chinooka. The classic, 'Summer Nights' from *Grease*. "Oh, I have this one in the bag," I said to her over my shoulder.

I knew every word to that song by heart. Apparently, so did Perry because before I could even get to the dance floor, he was already belting the first line of the song into the mic.

I jumped in, took the mic from his hand, and sang the Sandy verse. Not to be one-upped, Perry slid across the floor on his knees giving the audience his very best Danny Zuko. After a few more exchanges, a group of Cedar girls ran over to join me in the center of the tennis courts. Perry motioned some of the Birch boys to join him, and after some pleading, a few of them did.

The DJ turned up the volume and instantly the Cedar girls and Birch boys were transformed into Pink Ladies and T-Birds battling it out in the center of the court. When the song ended, Gordy stepped up to the microphone and announced that Cedar had won the dance off and the ten points. As the girls congratulated each other, I spotted Madison in the corner of the tennis courts, surrounded by a few of the other girls from Bunk Fourteen.

"Hey, Tara, what's that all about?" I asked, pointing to them.

"Alex Shane's been ignoring her. I think he's into Candice now," she replied nonchalantly.

It definitely looked like Alex was into Candice. The two of them were in the opposite corner of the tennis court, slow dancing way too closely. I was about to go over and pry them apart when I saw Perry was already on his way to take care of it.

Afterward, I went to comfort Madison. "Hey, girls, give us a second, okay?" I said, shooing away the small clique from Bunk Fourteen that had her surrounded. "Maddy, are you all right?"

Unable to speak from crying so hard, she simply shook her head no.

"Look, he's a thirteen-year-old guy, and thirteen-year-old guys aren't mature enough to know what they want. Truth be told, experience has shown me that neither do almost thirty-year-old men."

She took a few deep breaths to calm herself down.

"It's not like that," she said through controlled sobs. "Tonight, before the dance, he asked me to be his girlfriend. I told him I wasn't ready for that and that I didn't want to be exclusive. He got really mad and told me it was all or nothing. Now he's dancing with Candice, who looks like a freakin' model," she said, pointing in their direction. "I'm an idiot, right? Every single girl wants to be with him. Why didn't I just say yes?"

"Why didn't you just say yes?" I asked.

"At home, someone like Alex would never be interested in me. You wouldn't understand."

I smoothed her hair. "What do you want to do?"

"Pull Candice off of him and tell him I made a mistake," she said.

"Well, then get out there. You can take her."

She started laughing.

"What are you waiting for? Go bust in on them. He looks like he needs saving," I said.

"She does look a little bit like she wants to swallow him whole," she commented. "Thanks, Gigi," she said, pulling me into an embrace.

"Anytime. It's what I'm here for."

From across the tennis court, I watched Madison spill her heart out to Alex. I knew that no matter the outcome, she would be better for having done it.

After the dance, I left Brooke and Michelle to sit OD and went to The Canteen. My cell phone barely got any reception at Chinooka, and I wanted to use the one payphone on the grounds to call Jamie and beg him to send me my sewing machine. When I got to The Canteen, I was relieved to see there wasn't a line and stepped into the booth to call Jamie collect. He answered on the third ring.

"Really, Gigi, you're calling me collect? I didn't even know that was still possible," he grumbled.

"Nice to talk to you too. My cell gets almost no service up here, and I didn't want to bring a thousand quarters with me to use the payphone."

"It's okay. I'm glad to hear from you. Your cell phone's been going straight to voicemail. How are you? Ready to pack up and come home from the wilderness yet?"

Even though he'd been born and raised in Griffin, Georgia, the epitome of small-town USA, Jamie was now of the mindset that anyplace outside Manhattan might as well not even exist. Except for the Hamptons, South Beach, and LA—he made exceptions for those locales.

"Not quite yet. It's been an adjustment, I'll admit, but

all in all, it's been good for me to be here. I have a lot of time to think and reflect."

"Gigi, you went to work at a sleepaway camp. You didn't run away to a Buddhist monastery," he said.

"I just mean it's been good to be away from everything and everyone."

"Everyone, or one particular person? Out of sight out of mind, I hope?"

"I wish it was that easy, but it's getting easier." I swallowed and asked him the one question I did and did not want to know the answer to. "Have you heard from Alicia at all?"

He hesitated for a moment and then said, "She called me last week and asked me to meet her to look at wedding dresses. I think she just wanted my professional opinion or something."

A lump formed in my throat. "Did she pick one?"

"A *gorgeous* satin, trumpet-style Carolina Herrera gown. She had to get the sample because of the time frame, but fortunately, with her figure, she fit into almost everything."

"It sounds really pretty," I said, trying to keep my voice from shaking.

"Very. Simple, elegant, sophisticated, and timeless."

"Sounds like how people describe Ali." I squeezed my eyes shut and rubbed my chest. The ache of missing my best friend was almost unbearable. "I'm really glad you were there to help her." Tears rolled down my cheeks.

"Camp's how long? Eight weeks? Think you'll be able to pull yourself together by then?" he asked sympathetically.

"I'm working on it," I said, wiping my eyes with my

sleeve. "I guess this is a good segue into the favor I need to ask you."

I was about to ask Jamie about the sewing machine when someone pounded on the door of the phone booth.

"One second, I'm still using the phone," I shouted behind me. Jamie asked what all the background noise was.

"Just some jerk wanting to use the phone." The person pounded again, even harder.

"Look, buddy, I need a couple more minutes," I shouted again.

More pounding. "This isn't prison, asshole. There isn't a five-minute rule. I can use the phone as long as I damn well please," I screamed.

I spun around in the booth, opened the door, and found myself eye to eye with Perry Gillman. "Good evening, guv'nor," I said, mocking his British accent. "How can I help you?"

"Me and all these other people," he said, pointing to the long line that had formed behind him, "would like to use the telly. That is, of course, if you don't mind?"

"Well, I do mind, so you and everyone else will just have to wait." I slammed the accordion door closed. "Sorry about that," I said, getting back to Jamie. "There's this counselor who seems to think he's more entitled to use the phone than I am. He'll just have to wait."

"Gigi, while I admire the newfound I-am-woman-hear-me-roar thing you have going, this call is costing me like ten dollars a second. What's the favor you want to ask me?"

"Sorry, right—well, I agreed to make all of the costumes for the camp play. I really need my sewing machine from home. Can you send it to me with some of the bolts of fabric from my apartment?"

"You want me to mail all of that to you?" he asked.

"I really need it sooner than later, so if you could do it in the next couple of days, that would be amazing," I pleaded.

"Do you have any idea how heavy that machine is and how expensive it's going to be to ship, let alone overnight it to you?"

"Orrrr you can borrow Thom's car and drive it up here? Please, Jamie, I'll really owe you."

Thom was Jamie's on-again, off-again boyfriend. They seemed to be more "on-again" whenever Jamie needed a car to use.

"Okay, fine. I should be able to drive it up next weekend," he said, sounding completely defeated. "Hey, Gigi, what's his name?"

"Whose name?"

"The guy giving you a hard time?"

"Perry. Why?"

"Introduce me when I'm up there. Night, sweetie. See you next Saturday," he said before hanging up the phone.

I put down the receiver and reopened the door to see the long line of counselors and CITs that had formed to use the phone. Almost all of them shot me dirty looks as I emerged from the booth. Perry didn't even make eye contact when he brushed past me to use the phone. He slammed the door closed before I could even form the words to apologize. Tara was waiting near the middle of the line.

"Is it always like this?" I asked her.

"God, Gigi, there is a seven-minute phone rule that *everyone* follows," she said, emphasizing the word everyone.

"Seven minutes?"

"Yes, more than five less than ten. Just enough time to say hello and ask for what you want sent from home before hanging up."

"It's not like there's a sign with the rule," I argued.

She pointed to the sign posted above the phone booth that I had completely missed on my way in.

"This is the first time I've used the phone since I've been at camp, so I must have banked some minutes, right?"

She crossed her arms. "It doesn't work like that."

"Of course it doesn't. I'm gonna get myself a Chipwich. Do you want anything?"

She looked at me like I'd just offered her heroin. "Do you know how many grams of fat a Chipwich has in it?"

I walked away before she could enlighten me. I went outside to The Canteen's ordering window and knocked. I was shocked when Rita Henley came to answer. Rita and Herb Henley had The Canteen when I was a camper. Back then, they were semi-retired, running a small ski shop in Killington, Vermont during the winter and working at Chinooka in the summer. I ordered the Chipwich from her and took a twenty-dollar bill out of my pocket to pay for it.

"Sorry, sweetie, we don't take cash," Rita informed me.

"You don't accept cash?" I questioned.

"I'll go ahead and debit your canteen account," she responded.

"I don't have a canteen account. Unless you're automatically set up for one when you fill out all the payroll forms like direct deposit, in which case, maybe I do have one? Can you check my name, Georgica Goldstein?"

"It doesn't work like that. You have to ask to set up a canteen account with Herb."

"I'm sorry. I didn't realize," I said. "I'll set one up first thing in the morning. Tonight, can you maybe just make this one-time exception and take the money? Or just front me the Chipwich now and tomorrow I'll ensure the three dollars are taken right off of the account?"

She shook her head and told me that her hands were tied. Rules were rules.

"Hey, Rita, put the lady's ice cream on my tab," an all-too-familiar voice said from behind me. "Actually, make it two."

"What, are you following me or something?" I asked, turning to Perry. "Rita, it's okay, don't worry about my ice cream. Just get him whatever he wants."

"Rita, I'll take the two," Perry said, ignoring me. She passed the Chipwiches to him through the window.

"I don't have anything smaller than a twenty. Do you have any change?" I asked, offering the money to him.

"Don't worry about it. I feel bad about harassing you while you were on the phone. Sit here and eat your ice cream with me."

"I was going to take it back over to Cedar."

"Forget to assign someone to sit OD?"

"Michelle's sitting OD. I'm surprised you didn't notice she wasn't around."

"Are you going to sit with me or not?" he asked.

We sat down at one of the wood picnic benches outside The Canteen. "Fine, my ice cream's melting anyway," I said, licking it around the sides.

"So what is this that we're eating?" he asked.

"It's a Chipwich, kind of like a cookie had a baby with an ice cream sandwich. It's no beans on toast, but I like it."

"Did you have a good time at the social?" he asked abruptly. "I saw you talking to Madison for a while. What was that about?"

"You know, typical thirteen-year-old girl drama," I said.

"And I'm sure one of my boys is to blame. Alex Shane, right?"

"No, actually, it was one-hundred percent her. Alex didn't do a thing. Well, he did ask her to be his girlfriend."

"And?" He leaned in toward me like I had some big twist to reveal.

"And nothing. She was unsure about her feelings. She really likes Alex. She just couldn't wrap her head around the fact he was just as into her."

"So she pushed him away? That doesn't make much sense."

"Maybe she thinks she doesn't deserve him."

He raised his eyebrows. "Speaking from experience?"

"Right, like I would spill my innermost thoughts to someone I loathe," I said.

"You loathe me? That's pretty harsh," he said.

"I don't loathe you. I don't even really know you," I said honestly.

"What do you want to know?" he asked pointedly.

"This is your fourth summer working here, right?" I asked.

"Yes," he answered quickly.

"Why?"

"Why what?"

"Why come back here year after year?"

"I told you, I'm working on my thesis," he answered.

"How much time could you really have to work on

it? We're busy all day and night. Why not just hole up in some music room at Oxford for the summer?"

"My thinking is clearer up here. Maybe it's the air or something."

I had to agree. My thinking had been clearer since the minute I set foot at Chinooka. "But still, that's a long time to work as a camp counselor. Or to be working on your thesis, for that matter."

"You think I have some ulterior motives or something?"

"No, I didn't say that," I answered.

"But that's what you were thinking, right? Why would an almost thirty-year-old guy come up here summer after summer?"

"I wasn't judging you. It was just a question."

"You've been judging me since the minute you got here." He looked angrier than I'd ever seen him.

"Oh, that's the pot calling the kettle black, isn't it?" I countered.

"If that's how you feel, why are you even sitting here?"

"You got me," I said, standing up from the picnic table.

"By the way Gigi, this," he said, holding up the Chipwich, "is absolutely disgusting."

"Then throw it in the rubbish bin," I shouted back at him before walking away.

Fuming, I headed back to my cabin, passing Michelle and Brooke who were still sitting OD. They were making s'mores in the campfire and laughing about something. They stopped when they spied me and shot me dirty looks as I walked past. I was too tired to care. If Michelle hadn't copped such an attitude with me earlier, I would have offered to take their place and give them a reprieve. Now, they could sit there all night. I was going to sleep.

The screen door squeaked as I entered the cabin. I could hear the girls shushing each other and telling Madison to hide something. When I walked in, they were all huddled around a piece of paper that was being passed around along with a flashlight. When the paper got to Madison, she stuffed it down her shirt. "Hi, girls, what's going on?"

"Nothing," they replied in unison.

"Maddy, what's that you stuffed down your shirt?" I questioned.

"Nothing," she answered.

"Nothing? It looked like something."

"I don't know what you're talking about," she said.

I gave her a look that told her I meant business, and she reached down her sweatshirt and handed the crumpled piece of paper over to me. I unfurled it, smoothing it out against the wall as best I could. The minute I could make out what it was, I burst out laughing. How was the Purity Test still floating around Chinooka?

The Purity Test was a self-graded survey that calculated the participant's degree of innocence with regard to sex, drugs, and other sordid activities. It worked on a sliding scale, and each act had an associated point value. For example, a kiss on the cheek with a guy could earn you one point, whereas receiving a hickey would earn you fifteen. When I was a camper, we would take it the first night we got to camp and then see how many points we could rack up throughout the summer. The girl with the highest point value at the end was always idolized by the rest of the girls, most of whom barely cracked the single digits.

I turned the sheet over. On the back were the names of all the girls, with numbers written next to each of them. To my complete astonishment, Emily Zegantz had one of the lowest numbers next to her name and Alana Griffin, the girl I'd pegged as a shy bookworm, had one of the highest. I wondered what kind of points a relationship with my best friend's boyfriend would earn. My guess was that there wasn't even a score that could quantify my past behavior.

The girls looked ready for the lecture they believed was forthcoming. I didn't have one. Part of what made camp so special was getting to live side by side with girls your own age, who were going through the exact same things you were. It was about experimenting, making mistakes, and knowing you had friends to fall back on when you did. I rubbed my hand against my heart and handed the paper back to Madison.

"All right, girls, I've had a long day, so lights out for real this time, including flashlights, okay?"

Madison tiptoed over to me. "You aren't mad about the list, Gigi?"

"No, not mad. I guess if you really want me to comment on it, then all I'll say is this: Once you've done something, be it on that list or in life, you can't undo it, no matter how much you might want to."

The room was quiet for a moment, and then the girls went in separate directions to get ready for bed while I lay restless in my own.

The bunk was stifling hot, and the clip-on fan on my nightstand wasn't doing a thing to help. It was unnervingly quiet in the cabin, and I wished there was a TV I could turn on to distract me from how uncomfortably warm it was. I reached under the bed and pulled my phone out from an empty shoebox. I'd tried not to use it in front of the girls in order to show them it was possible to have fun at camp without any modern conveniences. Tonight, though, I needed a diversion. I scrolled to the new Adele album, closed my eyes and waited for sleep to wash over me, but my mind kept replaying my conversation with Perry. We'd had our fair share of spats, but this one felt different—as if I'd hit a real nerve this time.

Like me, he was obviously using Chinooka as a refuge. But from what?

CHAPTER ELEVEN

The following morning, my phone and fan batteries long dead, I was awakened to Lee Greenwood's 'Proud To Be An American' blasting over the camp's loudspeaker. It was the Fourth of July, and one-hundred degrees, with one-hundred percent humidity. I woke up drenched in sweat.

July Fourth was always a special day at camp. Each year, the different age groups battled it out in a series of events for Gordy points. The competition was followed by a cookout. Then, the whole camp would go down to the lake to watch fireworks before the Rope Burn Battle. The girls were already complaining about the schedule I'd taped to the wall the night before. Now, with the heat wave, they were really moaning. I was less than enthusiastic myself. July Fourth was one of the few days that I enjoyed spending in the Hamptons. Every year, my parents threw an over-the-top party for their friends and the other partners at my father's law firm. The grounds of the house were immaculately decorated, complete with white tents and ice sculptures. At night, the guests would all gather on the shore of Georgica Pond for a bonfire and fireworks.

Every year, Alicia and Joshua came as my parents' guests, but last year, Joshua had come alone, as mine. Certain Alicia was moving to London after all, we'd planned on concealing our relationship just a bit longer, and then coming out to her the next time she was in town. Just being able to sit side by side with him, eating lunch out in the open, had made me feel for the first time that we wouldn't always have to hide. She'd see Joshua and me together—her two oldest friends having fallen for each other—and wonder why she hadn't seen our chemistry all along. It was delusional, but I'd been so in love with Joshua that anything seemed possible.

Still, we weren't ready to go public, so every chance we got, we'd stolen away to dark corners of the house or garden and then returned to the party as if nothing had happened. Under the party tent, he kissed me on the forehead and pulled me in close to his chest. We stood that way for a few seconds before reality, and my mother's voice had pried us apart. We couldn't escape quickly enough, and she cornered us.

"Gigi, I've been looking all over for you," she said, slightly out of breath. "Where have you been?"

"Right here," I answered.

"Thank you so much for inviting me, Mrs. Goldstein," Joshua said from behind me.

"For the millionth time, it's Kathryn. Is Gigi showing you a good time?"

"The best," he answered.

"I'm glad. Gigi, I want to introduce you to someone," she said, pushing a good-looking man in my direction. "This is David Mincher, a new associate at your father's firm. David, this is my daughter, Georgica."

"Nice to meet you," I said, extending my hand.

"David went to Columbia Law School like Daddy. Gigi was accepted to Columbia. She's weighing her options right now."

"Where are you deciding between?" David asked me.

"I'm not really sure law school's for me. I've been designing for Diane von Furstenberg's line."

Joshua chimed in, "Gigi's really talented. You should take a look at this month's issue of *Vogue*. There's a feature on her as an up-and-coming designer."

"Up-and-coming isn't the same as there-and-established, though," I said modestly.

"She's selling herself short," Joshua said. "Her stuff's incredible."

"I'll have to check it out," David said. "This month's *Vogue*?"

"Page seventy-nine," Joshua answered for me.

David took out his phone and typed in the page number. "There. Just sent myself a reminder to check it out."

"Wonderful," my mother replied. "So I'll leave you two to talk. Joshua, why don't you come with me? I know Mitchell wanted to talk to you about a few investments."

My mother pulled Joshua over to talk to my father. Even though she had no idea there was anything going on with us, any woman could see that no other guy could stand a chance in his presence.

"Nice party," David commented after my mother walked away.

"It is," I said, looking around.

"So the invitation asked all the guests to wear white? Sort of like P. Diddy's White Party, right?"

It wasn't *sort of* like P. Diddy's White Party—it was

exactly like P. Diddy's White Party. Every year, P. Diddy, a neighbor of my parents' in East Hampton, threw a huge blowout on July Fourth and required all his guests be decked out in only white clothing. My mother had read about the party and decided to require the same of her guests. Every year, in protest of the sheer absurdity of my mother thinking she could compete with an international superstar, I bucked the dress code and showed up in an obnoxious bold color or print. That year, I'd opted for a tangerine dress.

"Yeah, it's a nice touch," I replied. "I didn't exactly follow the dress code, though."

"I think you look great. Did you design your dress?" he asked.

"No, not this one, it's from a vintage store."

"It looks great on you," David said.

Poor guy. He was trying hard, and there was nothing wrong with him. If the timing had been different, I may have even been interested. But, right then, I was so wrapped up in Joshua that nobody would have been able to get my attention. All I could think about was how I was going to ditch David and get back to the dark corner behind the gardener's shed to pick up where Joshua and I had left off.

I spotted Joshua talking to my father and some of his cronies by an ice sculpture of the American flag. He kept stealing glances at me. I could hardly concentrate on anything David was saying.

"If you'll excuse me, David, I think my mother needs some help," I said.

He looked around at all the servers. "Your mother has an army of help."

"Time for me to report to duty," I said, giving a mock salute. As soon as I was alone again, I caught Joshua's eye, then walked behind the gardener's shed to wait for him. Within minutes, he met me.

"How'd you manage to escape?" I asked him.

"I told your father I had to go meet up with a client who needed my undivided, very close, very personal attention," he said before kissing me. "You're making it tough in that dress, Gigi."

"To what? Restrain yourself?" I teased.

"To be discreet. Bright orange in a sea of white."

"Tangerine," I corrected.

"Tangerine," he conceded. "I got you something." He pulled an unmistakable blue Tiffany box out of his pocket. "I saw it and instantly thought of you. Of us."

I took the box from him and slowly undid the white satin ribbon. Inside was a dainty diamond key pendant on a thin chain. He pulled it out and put it around my neck.

"It looks beautiful on you." He kissed my neck. "Maybe you should go show it to David. See if he likes it."

"Jealous?"

"Who could blame me?" he said, never taking his eyes off of me.

"Well, don't be. I have my sights set on someone else."

Joshua scooped me up in his arms. We went at it like two teenagers behind the bleachers of a high school football game and eventually returned to the party like nothing had happened.

Later that night, my mother stopped me and complimented my necklace.

"Were you wearing that earlier?" she asked.

"Yes." I nodded.

"It's sweet." As far as my mother was concerned, that

was a compliment. "So David's very nice, don't you think?"

"Very," I replied.

"He seemed taken with you."

"I think he's just taken with this party, which, by the way, Mom, is beautiful this year."

"Gigi, you've been at every single one of our Fourth of July parties since you stopped going to summer camp. They're always beautiful."

"This one seems especially nice. Just accept the compliment. I don't have any ulterior motives in giving you one."

She smiled. "Would you mind starting to direct people down to the pond for the fireworks?"

I ushered the crowds away from the bar and down to the grass fields that surrounded our portion of Georgica Pond. As soon as the sun completely set, the first set of fireworks went off. Joshua came up behind me, and I leaned back on him slightly. Not enough for anyone to notice, but enough to feel the steady rhythm of his heart. We stood and watched with everyone else until the last burst fell from the sky. Slowly, the crowd made their way back up to the party tents, but Joshua and I stayed behind. When everyone had gone, he pulled me close and kissed me like we really were the living embodiment of the tragic star-crossed lovers I'd only ever come across in great romantic novels. Deep down, though, I couldn't ignore the small voice in my head telling me my happiness wasn't that different from the magnificent fireworks we'd seen just moments before—a brilliant explosion of passion and color that would eventually fade into nothing.

Now, a full year later, I reached up and touched the dainty diamond key I hadn't once taken off since Joshua had given it to me. In the thick heat on this July Fourth morning, it was like a noose around my neck. I groped for the necklace's clasp and struggled for a few seconds, trying to unhook it. When it was finally off, I opened the tin of Band-Aids on top of my nightstand and slid the necklace inside. It was time to close up whatever Pandora's box that key opened a year ago. All I could do was hope, for Alicia's sake, that Joshua and my secret stayed hidden inside.

After a quick and refreshingly freezing shower, I went to the horseshoe for roll call. The girls eventually emerged from the bunks, dressed in Chinooka T-shirts. It wasn't any cooler outside than it was in the cabin. If anything, the sun made it even hotter. In an effort to rally the girls for the day's events, I did my best version of Mel Gibson's rousing speech from *Braveheart*, which was almost entirely lost on them. The only time I noticed them slightly perk up was when I mentioned the possibility of the day's events being canceled in favor of an all-camp swim.

They got their wish. Halfway through breakfast, Gordy announced that because of the heat, Field Day was canceled. All the campers went back to the bunks to change into their swimsuits and head over to the waterfront or pool. I divided up the counselors between the two areas and decided I'd also split my day. I went down to the lake first and parked myself under a tree, which did little to alleviate the heat. I took off my shorts and T-shirt and found myself in a bikini that was skimpier than I remembered. Suddenly, what seemed appropriate on Georgica Beach was completely obscene on the shores of Lake Chinooka. I noticed some of the waterfront staff looking at me and put my shorts back on.

"I just don't get you, Gigi," Tara said from behind me.

"What's that?" I said, sitting up on my towel.

"You had all those guys' attention and you decide to cover up?" She pointed to the center of my neck. "What's that?"

I reached up and felt around. "What's what?"

She handed me a compact out of her bag.

"That mark on your neck?"

I opened the compact, looked down, and saw the silhouette of the key embossed on my neck. In the year since Joshua had given it to me, the skin around the necklace had darkened, leaving a distinct white outline of the key's shape right in the center of my chest. It was my Scarlet Letter.

"It's from a necklace I always wear," I answered Tara.

"That's why I like to lay out nude, or at least topless. Tan lines are a bitch," she said.

"Not here, okay, Tara? Let's keep it G-rated for the kids," I pleaded. She was already pushing the envelope with a very skimpy string bikini.

"Yeah, fine," she said, obviously disappointed. "You should get out from under this tree, though. Get some sun on that so it disappears."

I reluctantly moved out from under the shade and onto the lawn. I laid out my towel and stretched out under the blazing sun. Within a half hour, I had to go into the lake to cool off. Trying to avoid unwanted stares, I ran into the water as quickly as I could and dove in. I swam up to the dock about a quarter mile from the shore and climbed onto it to dry off and catch my breath. Just my luck, Perry was stretched out on it, watching his group.

"Of course," I muttered. "Look, I just need a minute

to catch my breath and then I'll head back to dry land," I said to him.

"It's a free country, isn't it?" he responded.

"You've spent the last four summers in America. You should know."

He didn't respond and instead continued applying a generous layer of suntan lotion. He lifted his shirt up over his face to wipe away the sweat from his forehead, exposing his washboard stomach. It was like looking at a statue of a Greek god. His tanned body was flawless, and the sun hit the glistening beads of sweat in all the right places. He gestured toward me with the tube of lotion and caught me staring.

"No, thank you, I'm fine," I said, thinking of the mark on my neck I was desperate to erase.

"You sure? Your shoulders are already starting to get red," he said.

"I'm sure. I have dark features. I never burn. I tan."

"The sun's really strong today," he said, stressing the word strong.

"You just think that 'cause you're from London, where it rains like 364 days out of the year."

"Suit yourself," he said, putting the lotion away. "Hey, aren't those yours?" He pointed to a group of girls in the middle of the lake intentionally trying to sink their small sailboat.

It was Candice and her crew. The four of them were standing on the boat, two on each side, rocking it back and forth in an effort to flip it over. I knew this game. I'd played it back when I was a camper. The objective was to capsize the boat so that the very good-looking lakefront lifeguards would come rushing to the rescue. Usually, though, it resulted in someone getting hurt and an expensive piece of boating equipment being damaged.

"Do something!" The dock rocked back and forth as I bounced on the balls of my feet to get a better view of the impending shipwreck.

"No way." Perry jammed his hands into the pockets of his trunks. "I told you I was done rescuing you."

"You aren't rescuing *me,* you're rescuing *them*. Oh, just forget it," I said, diving into the lake to swim toward the girls.

He dove in right behind me. By the time we swam over, it was too late. The small Sunfish sailboat was upside down in the lake, and the four girls were floating next to it, treading water in their life preservers. Since I wasn't wearing one, I grabbed ahold of the underside of the boat to stay afloat. I heard the bullhorn on the shore, but Perry shouted at the lifeguards that we were okay and he could right the boat without them.

Like some sort of superhero, he climbed on top of the dagger board and then asked all of us to grab hold of the sides. Using all of our weight, we managed to right the boat. Then Perry pulled himself into the hull and helped each of us inside. Once we were all safely on board, he dove back into the lake and swam back to shore, leaving us to sail back to the dock.

I turned to look at the girls, who were smiling. Even better than having one of the lifeguards rescue them, they'd gotten Perry to dive in and pull them to safety. Candice turned to one of her friends and asked her if she caught a glimpse of Perry's "hot abs."

"That's enough," I chided her.

"You must be blind or into girls," Candice said, smirking.

"And you must be ready to go home because I can easily call this strike three."

That shut her up for the rest of the time we were on

the boat. Like riding a bicycle, sailing came right back to me, and I remembered everything from when I'd earned my Red Cross sailing certificate well over ten years earlier. I easily navigated the Sunfish back to the dock and tied it up while Candice and her entourage went running off to tell their tale of terror on the high seas.

Before I could thank him for his help, Perry had already jumped onto a Jet Ski and was heading back out onto the lake. After I sent Candice and the other girls off to their bunk, I spent the rest of the day at the pool in the sun, trying to remove my mark of Cain. By the time the afternoon came, not only were my shoulders pretty burnt but so was the rest of me. I'd managed to even out the key mark, but I'd given myself an awful sunburn in the process. Everything hurt, and I had no choice but to go to the infirmary for some aloe and lotion. The camp nurse took one look at me and shook her head.

"I know, I know," I said. "I'm an idiot and didn't wear any sunscreen."

"I'm usually yelling at the kids for this, not the counselors. You should know better," she said.

"If it makes you feel any better, I'm feeling every bit of my stupidity," I said.

"And you will for the next couple of days. Here, take two of these," she said, handing me some aspirin. "They're anti-inflammatories. They'll help with the swelling."

I swallowed the pills along with my dignity and went back to the cabin to change into the lightest sundress I owned. I met the rest of the groups back at the lake for the cookout and fireworks. Jordana spotted me as I stiffly walked down the hill toward the dock.

Her eyes bugged out of her head. "Oh my God, Gigi, you are a lobster."

"Among other things," I replied.

"Can I get you anything?" she asked, pointing to the barbecue that was well under way.

It smelled delicious. I hadn't eaten much all day and my mouth was watering from the tangy sweet aroma of the barbecue sauce mixing with the smoky char of the corn. But then, I looked over at the crackling and burning pieces of chicken on the massive grills and shuddered in my own very burnt skin. Suddenly, it all looked very unappealing.

"I'm going to keep applying this aloe and will probably just grab some watermelon." I said, spying a few large cut-up pieces on a tray.

Jordana ran off to join the line for the barbecue, and I swiped a slice from the picnic table on my way down toward the lake. I sat down under one of the few trees providing shade and bit into the watermelon, letting the sweet juice drip down my chin. I wiped it off with the back of my hand.

"Be careful. If you swallow too many of those seeds, you'll grow a watermelon in your stomach," Gordy said as he approached.

"I'll try to be careful," I replied, smiling.

"While you're at it, you should try to be a little more careful in the sun. You're the same color as the watermelon," he said, sliding down next to me.

"So sunburns aren't covered under workers' comp then, I take it?"

"Unfortunately not, and I had to deduct some Gordy points for the stunt your girls pulled in the lake this afternoon."

"I figured as much. Who ratted them out to you, Perry?"

"One of the lifeguards from the waterfront staff. You know, Perry's not such a bad guy," he said.

"I never said he was."

"You didn't have to say it," Gordy answered.

"Look, I know he's a real hero around here and everyone seems to love him. I'm sure that's why he keeps coming back summer after summer, but I just don't get it," I said.

Gordy's voice turned more solemn. "So nobody's told you the real reason Perry keeps coming back to Chinooka?"

"To keep racking up trophies?" I joked.

"Gigi, are you here because you had a compelling need to suddenly be a camp counselor? These old bunks have proven to be a pretty good refuge for me these last thirty-five years."

I wondered what secret Perry was hiding. It had to be related to the nerve I'd touched the other night by The Canteen. My curiosity was more than piqued.

"Back when I was a camper, I used to wish I had a father who was more like you. You always seem to know the right thing to say to me," I told Gordy.

He turned to face me. "What's wrong with your own father?"

"He knows the right thing to say to everyone else."

He laughed. "Gigi, everyone's father knows the right thing to say to everyone else's children. My own kids can vouch for that."

This was news to me. I never knew that Gordy had a family. "Your kids?"

"Yeah, two sons. Both of them married now with kids of their own," he said.

"I didn't realize you had any children."

"My wife had full custody of them, so I was an every-other-weekend father to them and not even a great one of those. I don't think they've quite forgiven me for that." He pulled himself up from off the ground. "I should go check on the fireworks."

A few hours later, couples of campers huddled together to watch the show off the shores of Lake Chinooka. It was a perfectly clear night and the lake was awash in color and light as the reflections of the firework explosions glimmered off the water.

I rubbed my bare neck and my breath caught in my chest when I realized Joshua and Alicia were probably standing together on the shore of Georgica Pond, giving no thought to me whatsoever.

CHAPTER TWELVE

After the fireworks, the campers gathered by the dock for the Rope Burn Battle. The Rope Burn Battle took place every Fourth of July between Cedar and Birch. The victorious group would be able to add five hundred Gordy points to their ledger. Winning was a complete game changer.

Jordana, the fire leader for Cedar, was selecting five names out of a hat full of volunteers when I walked over to join the team. It was the first time I'd seen so many of the girls eager to participate in anything. Jordana pulled out five slips of paper and read the names out loud.

The girls ran up to the pit, while the rest of Cedar gathered around. The five girls and Jordana huddled together to discuss strategy. Over on the boys' side, I could see Perry and his five campers doing the same. Couldn't he give up even the possibility of glory for one second? Gordy stepped to the center between the two fire pits and laid out the rules for the contest.

"Each team will get one single match to start their fire. The teams may use any natural resources available to them to build up the flames but nothing artificial or man-made. Only one counselor and two members of each team are permitted within the fire circle, and the remaining three must stay outside of it as the designated wood gatherers. The event will start at the dock, where canoes representing each team will race to the shore with the one match. The teams cannot start constructing their fire until they receive the match from their canoe. The first team to burn completely through their rope wins."

Gordy handed Jordana and Perry each a match and then blew the bullhorn. The two of them took off running to the dock on the far side of the lake, where a camper from each team was already seated in the canoe, waiting for them. Perry reached his canoe first and jumped into the back. Jordana was only a few seconds behind him. Birch reached the shore before Cedar, and Perry and the camper jumped out of the canoe to drag it to land. After the nod from a waterfront staff judge, he and the camper sprinted to their fire pit. Jordana had a little bit more difficulty pulling the heavy canoe onto the shore. After the whistle from the judge, she and our camper took off to the Cedar fire pit.

Madison had collected a bundle of tinder and was ripping it into smaller and smaller pieces in the Cedar girls' fire circle. Jordana sprinted over and lit the match. Slowly and carefully, she brought it to the tinder bundle. It immediately started to smoke. Very gently, Madison blew on the bundle, coaxing the smoke into an actual flame. Then, she delicately brought it over to a small pile of twigs in the center of the fire pit.

I looked over to Birch, where the boys were using a completely different strategy. They'd rolled up dried-out tree bark into a torch-like cone. Perry lit the cone with the match, and once they had a significant blaze, they transferred it to the center of a log cabin-like structure in the center of their pit. They placed the torch in the center of it and fed the center small twigs and branches.

The rest of the camp had divided into sides and were cheering for their favorite team. Michelle and Brooke were leading the girls in a chant of, "Burn, Baby, Burn." On the boys' side, the campers were screaming the words to 'The Roof Is On Fire.' The wood gatherers were bringing branches of all sizes to the circle, and Jordana and Perry added them into their respective fires.

I watched as the small flames grew into blazing infernos. It was hard to tell which fire was bigger, although it looked as though Perry's team had a slight advantage. The wood gatherers brought larger and larger pieces to the circles, and both teams built up their rising flames. The Birch fire was first to touch the rope, with the Cedar flames hitting theirs a few seconds later. After another few minutes, the fire on the boys' side completely seared through the rope, and Gordy declared them the winners and the recipients of 500 points. All of Birch rushed over to congratulate them.

Tradition dictated that the losing team had to extinguish their fire while the rest of the camp gathered around the winning fire for s'mores and a sing-along. Jordana glumly carried a heavy bucket of water from the lake up to our team's circle. I ran over to give her a hand. She looked exhausted. It was still at least ninety degrees outside, and being that close to the fire made it feel well over a hundred.

"Why don't you go back to the bunk and change? I got this," I offered.

She gratefully took the cue and left.

I continued walking back and forth between the lake and pit, making sure the last of the fire was completely out. Perry grabbed one of the other buckets and followed suit.

"You don't have to help me. I'm fine," I said.

"Not only you can prevent forest fires," he responded in a deep voice.

I burst out laughing. "Was that your impression of Smokey Bear?"

"Not good?"

"Good. Not great. I think this should do it," I said, pouring the last of the water onto the embers.

Perry filled up his bucket with sand from the lakeshore and dumped it over the pit.

"*This* should do it."

I shook my head. "You just can't let me have the last say where anything is concerned, can you?"

"And you can't accept that not everything I do is a direct challenge to you," he said.

Sweat was running down my neck. I pulled my hair off of it and wrapped it into a loose bun. Perry didn't take his eyes off of me.

"You know, you look really pretty tonight, even if you are the color of a tom-ah-to," he said in his affected British accent.

"Tomato," I corrected in my American one.

"Tomato, To-mah-to, Potato, Po-tah-to—let's call the whole thing off," he mumbled.

"A Gershwin fan?" I recognized the line from one of their classic songs. "Me too. My father plays all the greats, Ravel, Debussy, and Schoenberg."

Perry turned the bucket upside down and took a seat on it next to the fire pit. I did the same and sat down beside him.

"Do you know the story about Gershwin meeting Ravel?"

I shrugged my shoulders.

"The story goes that when Gershwin met Ravel, he asked if he could study with him. Ravel apparently responded 'Why would you want to be a second-rate Ravel when you're already a first-rate Gershwin?'"

"I have heard that story, actually, only in my father's telling, Gershwin asked Schoenberg, not Ravel, if he could study with him. It doesn't matter, though, the takeaway is still the same—nobody is a legend in their own mind or time, I guess? It's funny. There were moments on *Top Designer* I was paralyzed with fear that I'd unknowingly copy someone else's design."

"You were on *Top Designer*?"

"I was the runner-up on the first season."

He raised his eyebrows. "That show's hugely popular in the UK."

"Yeah, it was in the States, too."

"Good experience?"

"It was a crash course in design. Sometimes we were only given a day to complete the challenges. It's actually kind of amazing what you can come up with working in those time constraints. You stop thinking and just feel your way through completely on instinct."

"You know, Gershwin wrote 'Rhapsody in Blue' in less than five weeks and composed most of it in his head on a train going to Boston?"

For the first time since we met, Perry and I were having an actual conversation, free of any quips or jabs. Not wanting to do anything to jeopardize the small amount of progress we were making, I answered, "No, I didn't know that."

"It took him five weeks to write a masterpiece. Five weeks. I've been struggling with my composition for almost three years." Perry pushed his fingers through his hair, which had become a mop of curls from the humidity and his own sweat.

He looked so different from his usual cocky, confident self—like all his bravado had been lifted, leaving him raw and exposed. Yes, he was classically handsome, there was no question about that. But seeing him stripped of all of the coolness, I actually found myself wanting to kiss him. Not in the same way I'd wanted to that night in his cabin—as a means to forget Joshua—but because for the first time ever, I felt a genuine desire to kiss someone other than Joshua. The thought made me shiver.

"You can't be cold?" he said, noticing my tremble.

"Maybe it's the sunburn," I said, taking the tube of aloe out of my pocket and rubbing it into my arms.

"I can get your back for you if you want?"

Since my objective for the day had been to erase the mark on my chest, my back was the only part of my body that wasn't burned. I didn't tell him that and passed him the tube. I moved my bucket in front of him so he'd be able to reach me.

"Bet you're wishing you'd taken my advice, Princess?" he said, rubbing the aloe between his hands.

In that moment, I was happy to have disregarded it so that he had a reason to have his hands on me. My hot skin drank in the cold lotion. He massaged it into my back and shoulders while I leaned into him.

"Tell me if I'm hurting you," he said in an almost-whisper.

"No, not hurting me," I said softly. "You know, three years may seem like a really long time to be working on something, but some artists work for years on their masterpieces. It took Michelangelo more than four years to complete his fresco on the ceiling of the Sistine Chapel."

"Where'd you learn that? On one of those tours that takes American teenagers through the greatest hits of Europe?" he asked.

"No," I replied straightening my back again.

"Did your parents take you as a present when you graduated from high school?"

"For my sweet sixteen," I said.

He started laughing. "See, Princess, you aren't too hard to read."

Eric shouted to him before I could respond. "Yo, Perry, we need you over here with your guitar to play something,"

"I should go."

I nodded. Perry slowly brought his hands up the length of my arms and let them linger on my shoulders for a moment. All the hairs on the back of my neck stood up as I turned to look at him. Our eyes locked for a just a moment before he quickly drew back and away from me. I wrapped my arms around myself, wondering if I was chillier from the sunburn or the sudden cold shoulder from Mr. Gillman as he walked away.

CHAPTER THIRTEEN

True to his word, Jamie came up to see me the following Saturday. I was just finishing breakfast when I heard my name being paged to the office over the camp's loudspeaker. Although I'd only been at camp for a few weeks, it felt more like a few years, and I couldn't wait to see a familiar face. Waiting for me in front of the office, Jaime stood holding a large cardboard box, which I assumed was the sewing machine. He was dressed completely wrong, in white linen pants, a light blue button-down shirt, and aviator sunglasses. Upon seeing me, he put the box down, and I rushed over to throw my arms around him.

"Whoa," he said, putting his foot back to steady himself. "I missed you, too."

I stepped away from him to fully take in his look. "What exactly are you wearing?"

"You don't like? I was channeling Robert Redford in *Out of Africa*. Who are you channeling, Dirty Harry-et?"

I wore ripped jean shorts and a Camp Chinooka tank

top—not at all the perfectly coiffed Manhattanite fashionista he was used to seeing. "I'm just worried your white pants aren't going to make it out of here in the same pristine condition they arrived in. But yes, you nailed it, Robert Redford in *Out of Africa*. I totally see it. You look great."

"Well, you, my dear, look skinny. What have you been eating, or rather not eating?"

"It's not intentional. I've been sustaining myself on s'mores and ice cream. Who knew it would be a better diet than Atkins?"

"S'mores?"

"It's a camp thing. Chocolate and toasted marshmallow squished between graham crackers. So good you always want some more or s'more, get it?"

He pulled out a bag of bagels from H&H, my favorite bagel shop in New York. "Not really, but rest assured, I come bearing carbs."

"And cream cheese?" I asked, my stomach grumbling.

"Two kinds, scallion and vegetable."

"Bless you." I didn't even bother to split a bagel before devouring it, breaking off pieces and dipping them into the scallion cream cheese.

"What's that?" I said, eyeing the familiar green-and-white coffee cup stacked on top of the box.

"A skinny vanilla latte, but it's cold now. I was looking for a place I could dump it."

"No way! What are you crazy?" I said, grabbing the cup and gulping it down. It was cold but delicious. I was convinced I could feel the caffeine hit my bloodstream instantly.

"Addict much?"

"I haven't had a cup of *real* coffee in weeks. I basically had no choice but to do a full detox. It was harder than when I gave up cigarettes."

"You smoked for like a week," he said, laughing. "You know, I think I was wrong to give you a hard time about working here. You've lost weight, given up caffeine, and are clearly putting much less emphasis on your looks. It seems like you should be paying them for these accommodations. In fact, who can I talk to about booking myself a room?"

"This man, actually," I said, pointing to Gordy. I walked Jamie over to introduce him. "Gordy, this is my friend, Jamie Malone. He very kindly drove up my electric sewing machine and some fabric so I can get to work on the costumes for the show."

"Any friend of Gigi's," Gordy said, extending his hand. Then he stood back and stared at Jamie like he was trying to place him. "Do I know you?"

"Jamie was on the first season of *Top Designer* with me," I interjected before Jamie could burst into his usual speech about how he was completely robbed.

"Can't say I watched that. You weren't a camper here?"

"No, sir. My parents sent me to a Bible camp in West Virginia one summer. I got kicked out three days in," Jamie answered.

Gordy shook his head and walked away.

"Nice one, Malone. Now he thinks I hang out with degenerates at home."

"I was eleven. I refused to wear the camp uniform. Brown shorts and a tan T-shirt? Hideous."

"Say no more," I said, putting my hand up. "How was the drive up here?"

"It was great. I was with Joan and Judy."

"Joan and Judy?"

"Joan Jetta and Judy Garmin, the car and the navigation system," he said as if everyone named their modes of transport.

"I have no words," I said through a smirk. "So, you want a tour of the grounds?"

He put his arm around me. "Love one."

I took him to the athletic fields and then showed him all the activity studios. I explained that Saturday was a free day. All the studios were open so that campers could finish projects they may not have had time to finish during the week. Most of my girls were, of course, not taking advantage and were instead tanning down by the lake. Within seconds of seeing Jamie, the girls started firing off questions about *Top Designer*, and he happily embraced his fan base. When they finally backed down, we went to see the Lakeside Amphitheater.

We sat down on one of the wood benches, and I took out my sketchbook. He thoughtfully looked at each of the drawings for a few minutes before turning to the next one. When he was finally done, he said, "These are really great, Gigi, the wedding dress especially. It's magnificent."

For the pinnacle scene in the show—when Tzeitel, the oldest daughter, married Motel the tailor—I'd sketched a lace wedding gown based off of the black-and-white photograph of my great-grandmother on her wedding day that my mother kept on her dresser. It was an ambitious design and the first time I'd ever sketched a wedding gown. I wasn't sure I even had the necessary skills to construct it.

"I may have gotten a little bit carried away for it

being a camp production, but once I put pencil to paper, the ideas just came."

He flipped back and forth between the pages. "There's a lot of work here. More work than one person can possibly complete in five weeks."

"I could maybe see if some of the campers are interested in fashion design and get them to help with some of the garments?"

"That might work for the simpler pieces, but for the wedding gown and the fiddler's suit, you're going to need more experienced hands."

"I'll get it done," I replied.

Deep down, though, I knew he was right. With all my other responsibilities, even if I had another ten weeks, I couldn't possibly get all the costumes finished on my own.

"I'll help you."

"Jamie, when I showed these to you, it wasn't so you'd offer to help me, I swear. But thank you. Seriously." I turned and gave him a hug. We sat in an embrace for a few seconds before I heard the rustle of leaves behind me and someone clearing his throat. I turned around and there was Perry, holding his violin case.

"Sorry to interrupt. We have a rehearsal starting in fifteen minutes. I'm Perry," he said, reaching his hand out toward Jamie.

"Perry?" Jamie repeated as he stood up.

"Have we met?"

"No, I'm Jamie Malone, a friend of Gigi's.

I stood up next to Jamie. "Jamie's a friend from home. He's offered to help me out with the costumes for the show."

"Good for you." He unpacked his violin and walked to the stage, where he began warming up.

"See what I've had to deal with?" I whispered to Jamie.

"I do indeed," he said, staring at Perry.

I nudged his side. "Stop. He isn't *that* good-looking," I said. "Okay, he *is* that good-looking, but he's a piece of work."

Jamie stood up and looked around. "So this is where it all began?"

"Where all what began?"

"A life of pining for Joshua Baume."

"When you say it like that it sounds so pathetic."

He cocked his head to the side. "Well, what would you call it then? Gigi, I supported your ridiculous decision to come here when I believed that some time and distance would give you perspective. What you didn't tell me was that this place is an emotional minefield. Every place you step, you risk getting blown to pieces by a memory that includes Joshua or Alicia or both of them."

"It's not like that."

"It's not? Then why can't you even see what's right in front of you?"

"What's right in front of me?"

He pointed to Perry, who was standing center stage, still playing his violin as if he were giving a concert at the Met and not in the middle of the woods.

"Sweetie, I was with Alicia at Kleinfeld's when she said yes to the dress. I saw her in the big white gown holding the big, beautiful bouquet, rattling on and on to the salesgirl about her incredible fiancé who she's known since she was nine and the best friend who introduced them. This story is only going to have one ending," he said.

"I know that. And I want that ending for her. In my head, I can almost believe there are two Joshuas—the one who has loved Alicia his whole life and the one I loved for all of mine."

"Look, three people in the world know you're here. Me and your parents. You have the freedom to reinvent yourself this summer. Do you know what I'd give to disappear for a few months and reemerge as anybody other than the guy who got kicked off *Top Designer* first because he couldn't construct a couture wedding gown out of toilet paper?" Episode "Code Wed" would haunt Jamie forever.

"Well, it was a pretty ugly dress," I said with a wink.

"Some relationships are all passion and fire, but when the smoke clears, it's just two people looking at each other, realizing it simply can't be."

"Like Rhett and Scarlett?" I said.

"Exactly."

"Although, didn't they eventually get together at the end of *Scarlett*?"

"What have I told you about mentioning that travesty of a novel?"

Scarlett was the widely panned sequel to Jamie's beloved *Gone with the Wind*. The sheer mention of the book usually sent him into a complete tirade. "But those chapters in Ireland are so moving," I said, egging him on.

"Gigi..."

"I hear you. I really do. I'm right there. I'm on the edge of getting over him once and for all. I just need a little more time."

"Darling, take all the time you need." Jamie kissed

my forehead. "Just don't forget to enjoy the incredible scenery while you're doing it," he said, looking over at Perry, who was finishing up his serenade.

I spent the rest of the day showing Jamie around Chinooka and my favorite spots on the property. He especially enjoyed The Canteen and meeting Rita, who instantly recognized him from *Top Designer*. She was completely enamored, offering free ice cream in exchange for any show-related gossip he could remember. I reminded her that I'd been a finalist, but she didn't seem to have any recollection of that.

Jamie was enjoying his D-list celebrity status at Chinooka so much that I practically had to escort him off the grounds at the end of the day. He took my sketch of the wedding gown and offered to send a muslin mockup of the pattern back in a few weeks. Most of the lace detailing would have to be done by hand, as would the construction of the corset top. I was grateful for Jamie's offer to partner with me, especially considering I hadn't even begun work on the fiddler's suit.

During my career, I hadn't worked on much menswear. In order to get the fiddler's suit right, I'd have to devote a large amount of time to it. I asked Davis to have Perry meet me at my makeshift design studio in the back of the arts and crafts cabin, so I could take his measurements and get started. We hadn't spoken much since the bonfire, but time was running out. Perry obliged and came to see me the next night.

I was on the ground hemming a dress from Act One, so Perry didn't immediately see me. I watched as he skimmed through the racks, stopping to look at each costume for a few seconds before moving on to the next one. Finally, I cleared my throat so he'd know I was there.

"You made all of these yourself?" He walked a full circle around the dress I was sitting beneath. "Some of them are really quite good."

"Thank you." I reached out for help getting off the ground, and he politely grasped my hand.

"So what happened?" he asked.

"What do you mean?"

"To the woman *New York Magazine* named their Most Talented Up and Coming Designer?"

"Oh her. She ended up being a big fat failure," I said, pulling a tape measure out of the pocket of my apron. "Arms out. Let's get you measured."

He stretched his arms out and changed his stance, mimicking Da Vinci's *The Vitruvian Man*. I had to laugh. "A little less exaggeration, please. I'm taking your measurements, not giving you a prostate exam."

"Okay, work your magic," he said, adjusting his position.

"You can relax your arms. I'll start with your chest and work my way around." He adjusted his stance as I measured across his broad back.

He tried to turn his head to speak to me. "So who was that guy I saw you with? The one you were showing around camp? Is he your boyfriend?"

"Head straight. Jamie? No, he's not my boyfriend. He's a friend—maybe my best friend now."

He turned around to face me. "Now?"

Nothing got past Perry. He had an uncanny knack for picking up on subtext. "Things are a little complicated with my best friend, Alicia."

"What'd she do to you?"

"You're giving me the benefit of the doubt? That's a first. In this case, though, you'd be wrong. I am entirely at fault. Okay, now arms out."

I came around to his chest and stretched the measuring tape across it.

"I'm listening," he said, taking a hold of both my hands and lowering them. He relaxed his pose and stepped back from me.

I took a deep breath. "I've spent my whole life in love with my best friend's soon-to-be husband. She left for London for work and broke up with him before her trip."

"And the two of you got together?"

I nodded. "When she got home, they reconciled. They're getting married in a few weeks." I looked down at the ground. "She doesn't know anything ever happened between us."

"He didn't want you to tell her?"

"He did. He actually begged me to come clean. I was the one who didn't want to say anything."

"Why? Were you afraid of losing her?"

"Yes, of course. But I was also afraid of losing him," I said with a conviction that took me by surprise.

I'd never uttered that sentence to myself let alone out loud. I'd thought if Alicia found out about my relationship with Joshua she'd pull away from me and, by extension, he would too. I'd naively reasoned that by saying nothing and giving him up, I'd be able to hold onto them both. The truth was, in staying silent, the person I'd really lost was myself. I looked up at Perry, searching his for signs of disdain or contempt. I couldn't find either.

"Thank you," I said.

"For what?"

"Not judging me too harshly, even if I deserve it."

"So is that why you're here? You're trying to get over him?"

"I know. It's stupid to think I could run away from my life."

He lightly touched my arm. "It's not so stupid. So are you?"

"Am I what?"

"Over him?"

All the tears and feelings I'd been holding back for the last year came flooding out like a dam had burst. I tried to wipe them away before Perry could think I was any more foolish than I was sure he already did. I turned away from him, but he pulled me back around so we were face-to-face.

Perry wiped the tears from my cheeks and wrapped his arms around me, drawing me into his chest. He rocked me back and forth while gently running his fingers through my hair. He lifted my chin up and leaned in to kiss me.

He kissed me softly, like he was afraid if he used too much force I might retreat. I moved my body closer to his to let him know I wasn't going anywhere, and he pulled me into him. He reached behind me and untied the apron I was wearing, then pulled it up and over my head and tossed it onto the sewing table.

When things ended with Joshua, I'd tried to lose myself with different men, hoping one would help me forget him. Instead, they made me miss him more as I compared each touch to his and each moment to the ones I'd spent with him.

Now, with Perry—incredibly—it was different. It was like, with one kiss, Joshua faded from my mind. I wasn't thinking about anything other than Perry's perfectly full lips as they brushed over my own. He became more confident, kissing me more forcefully. And I was responsive to all of it. When he lifted up my shirt, I let him. When he pulled off his own, I helped him.

He cleared the top of my sewing table and lay me down on it, then kissed down my collarbone and buried himself in the crook of my neck. Over the last year, I hadn't trusted anyone, including myself. I wasn't sure what had changed or why, but it felt right to let go. Right as we were on the brink of moving one step closer to something we either fervently needed or would ardently regret, I heard a girl's voice calling my name.

"Oh, shit," I said, pushing away from him to snatch my shirt off the floor. "That's Hannah."

"Who?"

"Hannah. Hannah, the girl playing Hodel in the show."

Perry rolled off the table and quickly got dressed. Just as we both finished getting on the last of our clothing, Hannah walked in.

"Hi, Gigi. I thought you could finish measuring me for the second act dress? Oh, hi, Perry." She blushed seeing him standing there.

"Let me just finish taking the last of Perry's measurements," I said, flustered.

He cleared his throat. "That's okay, I'll wait," he said.

I went to pull the tape measure out of my apron, which was now under the sewing table. "Sorry, give me one second." I bent down and picked it up off the floor, then tied it back around my waist and pulled the tape measure out from inside the pocket. As quickly as I could, I took all of Hannah's measurements, spinning her back and forth so forcefully, she told me I was making her dizzy.

"Geez, Gigi, what's the hurry?" she questioned.

Once I finished with Hannah, Perry and I found ourselves alone again. I approached him, anxious to pick up where we'd been interrupted. I started to lift my shirt off when he reached over to pull it back down.

"Don't worry, nobody else is coming by tonight. She was the only other person I asked to come get measured," I said, moving toward him.

"It isn't that. I just don't think this is a good idea," he said.

I was taken aback. "But it was a good idea ten minutes ago?"

"No. It was an impulsive mistake. I can't do this with you. I'm sorry." He reached over to place his hand on my arm.

"Don't touch me," I said, pushing him away.

He'd humiliated me for the last time. I'd revealed parts of myself I hadn't disclosed to anyone. I thought we were two people circling the possibility of there being something real between us, only to find we were still just two strangers staring at each other. "I'm sure you must be very happy. Now you have the confirmation that you were right about me all along. I'm broken and pampered and running away. Is that what you wanted to hear? Guess I don't deserve the *perfect* Perry Gillman, huh?"

"I'm far from perfect, Gigi," he said.

I took out the tape measure. "Let me finish taking these measurements and you'll be free to go."

We stood in silence while I finished. Once I had everything I needed, I moved to the sewing table to write it all down. Perry came put his hands on my shoulders and started massaging them. He leaned in close and whispered in my ear, "You just remind me so much of someone it hurts."

I spun around to face him. "Yeah, well, right back at you," I spat.

Then, before he could see the tears beginning to spring to my eyes, I pushed past him and ran out the door. Perry came running after me, shouting my name, but I never looked back.

CHAPTER FOURTEEN

After the night in the arts and crafts cabin, Perry and I did our best to avoid one another. All my girls picked up on it, and, of course, the rumors about us spread like wildfire from there. The campers assumed we must have had some sort of romantic falling out, and we became the infamous counselor couple that everyone loved to gossip about. Jordana told me we were notorious and they'd even taken to referring to us as "Gerry," a combination of Gigi and Perry. Parents' Weekend was just around the corner, and although it would mean a ton of work for me, I was looking forward to anything that might take the campers' attention off.

The night before Parents' Weekend, there was no planned evening activity so the campers could finish cleaning up the bunks. After dinner, the girls did a sweep of the grounds, and then I went to each of the Cedar cabins for inspections. When I got back to Bunk Fourteen, Jordana was in the center of the room rattling off orders like a drill sergeant, so I went to my area to straighten up my cubbies. I was refolding clothes when

Perry knocked on the open door of the bunk. The girls shrieked at his mere presence.

"Good evening, ladies," he said in his smooth British accent. The girls were completely awestruck. "Might I have a word with Gigi?" he asked, looking around.

"I'm here," I said, standing up from underneath a pile of clothes.

He motioned his head toward the front door. "Outside?"

I followed him to the porch where we stood in uncomfortable silence until he finally spoke. "You have something stuck to your person," he said, pointing to my shorts.

I looked down and saw a pair of my skimpier underwear clinging to me. "Static," I said, balling them up and shoving them into my pocket. "So, what do you want?"

He was fidgeting and pacing like he needed to get something off his chest. It was the first time I'd ever seen him look nervous. He was always so self-assured, so confident. I was determined not to be the one to speak next. As he opened his mouth to say something, I heard my name being called from behind us.

"Who's that?" Perry asked.

I squinted and made out the faint outline of a woman walking toward us. It wasn't until she was closer that I saw the glow of her unmistakable Chanel-red lips in the moonlight.

"*That* is my mother," I said, shaking my head.

"Your mother?" he said, surprised.

"What'd you think, I was raised by wolves?"

He held up his hands. "You said it, not me."

I rushed down the stairs to meet her. Perry followed closely behind. "Mom, what are you doing here?"

"Is that how you greet me? It's Parents' Weekend, isn't it?" She leaned in for a hug.

"For the campers. Even when I actually was a camper, you hated coming up here. Plus, it doesn't start 'til tomorrow morning."

The whole time I was speaking, her eyes were locked on Perry. I could tell she was trying to work out what kind of a conversation she'd just interrupted.

"And you are?" she asked, extending a well-manicured hand toward him.

"I'm Perry Gillman. I work with Georgica."

"What a lovely accent. What part of England are you from?"

She was really laying it on thick. Perry caught me mid-eye roll but continued to be his usual charming self.

"I have a flat in Kensington now, but I grew up in Oxshott. It's a smaller village in Surrey," he said.

My mother looked pleased with his pedigree. "I know it well—some beautiful homes there. And where did you attend University?"

"Mom, what's with the inquisition? I'm sure Perry has things he has to do."

"It's fine. I went to Cambridge and am now working on my DPhil in music composition at Oxford."

"DPhil?"

"A Doctor of Philosophy degree. What you call a PhD."

She was outwardly impressed. "You know, Gigi was accepted to several Ivy League law schools."

I chimed in before she could rattle off the rest of my resume. "Yes, and now Gigi is a summer camp counselor. I'm sure Perry finds this all very fascinating, but it's late, and I have to finish getting the girls ready for tomorrow and then sit OD."

"Yes, excuse me, Mrs. Goldstein, but I need to get back to my post as well," Perry said politely.

"Well, he certainly was charming," my mother said after he was out of earshot.

"I hadn't noticed," I muttered under my breath. "Mom, what are you really doing here? Where's Dad?"

"Your father stayed in the city this weekend, and I felt like getting away for a bit," she answered.

"So you decided to take a three-hour drive to the middle of nowhere?"

"Not to the 'middle of nowhere.' To see you. I thought it might be nice to visit my only child. I don't know why you find this so shocking?"

She looked genuinely hurt by my less-than-warm reception. I softened my approach. "I'm sorry. It's nice to see you, only I'm working tonight. Are you staying in town? Can you come back tomorrow for a few hours?"

"I'm staying at the Stanton Inn. I took a room through the weekend. I have a massage booked for the morning."

"The campers are performing a few scenes from the summer musical at the amphitheater, but I should be finished around two."

She smiled. "Let me guess, *Fiddler on the Roof*?"

"You'd think Gordy would pay for the rights to some other show by now, but I'm doing my best to help raise the bar. I designed and made all the costumes."

"That's nice," she said dismissively. "Walk me out?"

I walked my mother back to her car and told her I'd make some time for us to visit the next afternoon. That seemed to mollify her, and she left to go back to the inn for the night.

I went back to Cedar to sit OD. It was going to be a long, exhausting weekend for the counselors, so I let them have the night off to blow off some steam at The

Canteen. After I lit the fire, I settled down at the picnic table and took out the costumes I was putting last-minute touches on. I pulled the lantern close to me and started attaching the buttons to the fiddler's suit, which had turned out way better than I'd ever expected. It was a fantastic midnight blue I'd chosen so the fiddler would almost blend into the sky—like he was a true fixture of the town and Tevye's life.

The material had some sheen to it that really glistened under the stage lights. Perry'd worn it a few times during rehearsals and it was hard to take your eyes off him. With the exception of the wedding gown, it had taken me almost three times as long to make it as any of the other costumes. When I finished securing the last of the buttons, I slid my arms into the jacket to try it on. I stood up to model it and pulled the collar up to my face and breathed in. It smelled like Perry.

"Looks good on you." A voice said from behind me. I turned around to find Perry standing there. I suddenly felt embarrassed, not knowing how long he'd been watching me.

"It looks better on you," I said, slipping it off and handing it to him. "Sorry about the interruption earlier. I had no idea in a million years my mother would show up here."

"Yeah, that was pretty obvious, Princess."

"So we're back to Princess? You called me Georgica in front of my mother."

"I like your proper name," he said.

"I wouldn't have guessed. You hardly ever use it."

"That's because I like messing with you more."

"Is that what you were doing that night in the arts and crafts cabin? Messing with me?"

He sighed. "No, I wasn't trying to mess with you.

That's why I came by to talk to you earlier. I want to explain."

He motioned for me to take a seat, and I reluctantly did.

"Remember that night when we were eating those ice cream things outside The Canteen and you said nobody my age would come here summer after summer unless they were trying to escape something?" he asked.

I nodded, remembering how he'd reacted after I made that statement.

He rubbed the soft stubble on his face and brushed his fingers across his lips. "You weren't wrong," he said.

"You're admitting I was right about something? Well, that's a first."

"Are you going to let me talk or not?"

"Sorry, Mr. Gillman, you have the floor," I said, motioning for him to take a seat.

He sat down across from me at the picnic table and moved the lantern between us. "My first summer working here, I fell for one of the other counselors. She was American and a real ballbuster. Just so completely different from the girls back home. I swear, I think her parents forced her to work at Chinooka just to get her out of their hair for a few months."

I immediately felt self-conscious, knowing this was the very same impression he'd had of me when we first met.

He continued, "I was attracted to her instantly. Most of the male counselors were. She was beautiful, but it was more than that. Something about being around her made you feel special."

He didn't have to explain. I used to feel that way about Joshua. Being in his presence had made me feel like everyone else in the room must think I was someone exceptional because he'd chosen to be with me.

Perry fidgeted with the buttons closest to his collar and slowly started undoing them. "She dated like three other guys before she gave me the time of day, and I think it was so I'd want her more," he said. "It worked. I was completely smitten. Then, once we started dating, we were inseparable. I slacked on all my duties, and we sneaked away to be together as much as we could."

"So no Gordy Award that summer?" I asked, playfully kicking his leg under the table.

He pursed his lips. "Gigi, please. Let me finish."

I could see his whole demeanor change. He pulled his legs together and clasped his hands in his lap. His lower chin was now trembling and his breathing slowed as the memory washed over him. I promised not to say another word.

"At the end of the summer, I convinced her to travel across the US with me to do one of those big road trips you see all the time in the movies. A drive-your-Chevrolet-across-the-USA type adventure. At first, it was great. We stopped at all these bed and breakfasts up and down the California coast. But then she got restless or bored, with me or with the trip. I don't really know."

He stood up from the picnic table and began pacing. He kept his head down and eyes averted. "A couple weeks into the trip we were in a small town in Arizona. One night we both had way too much to drink with some locals, and she started flirting pretty heavily with the bartender. It wasn't the first time she'd flirted with other men to get a rise out of me. I asked her to go back to the hotel, but she wouldn't. I tossed her the car keys, called a cab for myself, and left.

He sat down next to me and put his head between his

hands. He started talking again, his voice thick like he was holding back tears. He swallowed them down and continued. "In my stupid inebriated judgment, I thought she'd call her own cab or sober up enough to drive herself to the hotel. I'd seen her do it dozens of times after throwing a few back at Rosie's."

Tears streamed down Perry's face. He didn't bother wiping them away. "On her way home, she hit a flatbed truck and the car flipped. She died instantly or so I was told by the emergency room doctor. And it's all my fault. I left her with the keys. I handed her the loaded gun."

He was sobbing now, his shoulders shaking with emotion. I instinctively knew this was the first time he had shared this story with anyone.

I took his hands into my own. "Perry, you couldn't have known that would happen."

He wiped his face with the back of his hand and took a few breaths to calm down. "I waited for her parents to come and collect her body and then flew home to try to return to my life. Only you can't ever really go back after something like that. You just keep reliving the minutes it took for you to do something you wish more than anything you could take back. Her parents didn't want me in New York at the funeral. I never got to say goodbye. I never got a chance to tell them I'm sorry."

It all made sense. His hostility toward me was because I reminded him of her. I'd shown up at Chinooka and stirred up all the emotions he'd been suppressing for so long. I pulled him to my chest, where he continued to let his grief pour out. I stroked his cheek, and he reached up and grabbed my hand, grasping it firmly in his own. We stayed like that until we could hear the far-away voices of the counselors starting to return from The Canteen.

Without saying a word he stood up and led me back to his cabin, where we made love like two people no longer bound by the weight of our offenses. Free from the secrets we'd been trying so desperately to keep buried, we were released from the past. Every one of my encounters since Joshua had been about trying to erase the feeling of his touch and my memories. I'd thrown myself at dozens of men, hoping they'd help me escape my feelings. Finally, I was at ease with a man who made me forget them.

The next morning, I tried to sneak back into the bunk unnoticed, but the girls were up bright and early getting ready for Parents' Weekend. Tara was the first person to confront me as I walked in.

"Where've you been?" she asked.

Jordana shot me a puzzled look.

"I did a final sweep of the grounds, and they look great," I announced as loudly as I could.

Tara looked me up and down. "How come you're wearing the same clothes from last night?"

"I slept in them. I was exhausted when I came in from OD."

Her expression made no secret of the fact she didn't believe me. Madison and some of the other girls were whispering over by their cubbies. I couldn't make out exactly what they were saying, but I heard them say "Gerry" a couple times.

"So I'm going to take a shower before breakfast, and I'll meet you girls over in the dining hall. Jordana, think you can do roll call for me?"

Perry was waiting for me outside the dining hall. He took my hand and held it as we walked inside. Gordy caught my eye and smiled with approval.

As soon as I sat down, the questions started flying

like I was in front of a firing squad. *How long have you been together? When did it start? Is he a good kisser?* I looked over to Perry for some support, but he was holding a mini press junket of his own. I crossed the room to get coffee, and Jordana followed me up to the machine.

"Okay, Gigi, spill," she whispered.

"There isn't much to spill."

"You didn't sleep in the bunk last night. I covered for you the best I could. I even put a pillow under the blanket so it would look like you were there if any of the girls got up to use the bathroom. Now you walk in holding hands with your sworn mortal enemy? *Spill.*"

I took a deep breath. "Can you hand me a sugar packet?"

"Gigi!" she shrieked. Some campers turned to look at us.

"Okay, okay. I spent the night with Perry, and we are certainly not mortal enemies."

"Well, that's obvious," she said, taking her coffee back to the table.

I followed her and looked over at Perry. He glanced up and our eyes met. He winked at me, and I blushed, thinking back to earlier and how I'd woken in his bed to the sounds of him serenading me to Gershwin's 'Rhapsody in Blue.' He'd played in a complete trance, his fingers dancing over the strings of the violin. When he finished, I'd applauded like I'd been watching him perform at one of the greatest concert halls in the world.

"Now, if only I'd written it," he'd said, putting his violin back in its case.

"Who cares who wrote it when you can play it like that?" I responded.

"It's our song, you know," he said, climbing back into bed with me.

"I guess it is now," I agreed, snuggling close to him.

I'd closed my eyes and fallen back asleep in his arms. Several hours later, Perry had woken me to tell me it was going to be light soon. He'd led me through the back path around the lake that my campers had used that first night to try sneaking into his division.

After breakfast, the visitors started to trickle in. I took my post at the camp's entrance gate, greeting the families and directing them to their children's divisions. I watched as bags of bagels and coolers full of sandwiches and sodas went by. At least a dozen pizza pies were being carried in, not to mention trays of designer coffee and boxes of doughnuts. You would've thought these parents were visiting their children at Attica rather than summer camp.

At noon, I went to the amphitheater, where the kids were getting ready to present a few scenes from *Fiddler on the Roof* for their families. Perry was the only character wearing his actual costume, so there wasn't much for me to do. I grabbed a seat on the side of the stage, hidden from view, and watched as he took his place on top of Tevye's house for the beginning of Act One. Jackie and Davis stepped to the front of the stage and explained the cast was going to perform a sampling of songs from the show, and all the parents were invited to come back to Chinooka in a few weeks to see the finished production. Then, Davis cued Perry, who started playing the opening notes. When the rest of the orchestra of campers and local musicians joined him, his superior talent was that much more apparent.

I looked out into the audience, scanning the different

faces, and saw my mother sitting in the last row of the theater, her Burberry coat spread out like a blanket on the log bench. After the final number, she stood up along with the rest of the audience to give the kids their ovation.

When the show was finished, I went into the audience to greet her. She had stains down her cheeks where her mascara had run from crying. I motioned for her to wipe her eyes, and she took out a handkerchief and hand mirror.

"I don't know what came over me," she said, blotting away the dark streaks. "What talented kids. And your friend—the one with the violin—he's remarkable," she said.

"Perry. Yeah, he's very talented," I said.

"That's an understatement. You designed his costume?"

I nodded. "I've finished most of them, but I'm still working on the wedding gown for the end of Act One."

"Oh, I almost forgot," she said, reaching into her tote. She handed me a stack of newspapers and magazines.

When I was a camper, instead of bringing junk food on Parents' Weekend, she would bring the Fashion & Style section from every single edition of the Sunday *New York Times* that had been delivered while I was away. Sometimes she included the newest issues of *Harper's Bazaar* or *Vogue*. When all the families had gone, Alicia and I would lie on my bottom bunk, devouring them along with all the snacks Mrs. Scheinman brought up.

"I can't believe you remembered these, Mom. I can show the costumes to you if you have any interest, or we can find a quiet place to catch up—maybe one of the gazebos?"

Her face softened. "I would love to see the costumes," she said.

The wedding dress was hanging over a form in the back of the arts and crafts cabin. I'd just recently finished draping the bodice with a tea-colored French Chantilly lace. I'd found the bolt of fabric years ago at an outdoor market in Paris and had been holding onto it for just the right project. As soon as I completed the sketch of the dress, I'd known this was it. Three-quarters of the way completed, it was finally starting to resemble the dress from my great-grandmother's picture, with a bit of a modern twist. I pulled off the sheet covering the form, and my mother walked a full circle around the dress, looking at it from every angle.

"It looks like my Grandma Ruby's—"

"Wedding gown," I said, finishing her sentence. "I used the picture on your dresser as inspiration."

"It's absolutely stunning," she said.

I had to admit that it was one of the best pieces I'd ever made.

"The girl who plays Tzeidel will look beautiful in it," I said.

My mother put on her glasses and lifted the lace from the gown, leaning in to examine it more closely. "You'd look beautiful in it."

"Me? No, it's cut too straight. It's not forgiving at all. It's meant for someone with your body type or Alicia's, not mine," I said.

She sat down at my sewing table and flipped through my sketchbooks. The top book had the sketches of the costumes for the show. The rest were filled with sketches of wedding gowns inspired by the one I'd done for the show. As my mother closed the last page, Madison came running into the cabin looking for me.

"Oh, good, Gigi, there you are, I've been looking everywhere," she said breathlessly.

"Mom, this is one of my campers, Madison Gertstein," I said, introducing them.

Madison smiled at my mother, who couldn't take her eyes off of the young girl. From the look on my mother's face, I was certain she was amazed by the likeness between Madison and me at that age. Chubby with unkempt hair she'd tried to tame into a braid, her clothes just a little too tight and not quite on trend.

"Well, you found me. What's going on?" I asked. Madison motioned for me to come closer to her, concerned someone might overhear us. I lowered my voice. "Maddy, I don't think anyone's eavesdropping."

"Alex wants me to meet his parents," she whispered.

"That's great. What's the problem?" I asked.

She chewed on her nails. "What if they don't like me?"

I looked over at my mother, who was pretending not to listen but could no doubt hear us. "Not possible," I said, putting my arm around Madison.

"You're just saying that because you *have* to."

"I have to do a lot of things as head counselor, but trying to convince you that you deserve the attention of some guy isn't one of them," I said.

"It would be so much easier if I looked like Candice or like you."

"It's you he's liked from day one. Not Candice. You."

She still looked unconvinced, but she gave me a hug before running out to go find Alex and his family.

"I had no idea you were so good with kids," my mother said.

I picked up the sheet off the floor and arranged it back over the dress form. "I just told her what I would have wanted to hear at her age," I said, a bit more harshly than I intended.

"She looks a lot like you did at thirteen."

"I know. That poor girl, right?"

"I was just thinking that she was lovely."

I narrowed my eyes. "Mom, what are you really doing here?"

"It's a beautiful day. Why don't we take out one of those rowboats they have at the lake?" she suggested.

It was obvious she didn't want to talk about why she'd come to visit, so I decided not to push her. I followed her down to the lake while she chirped away about the Hamptons' July Fourth party, Joshua and Alicia's wedding, and her most recent trip to Martha's Vineyard. When we reached the dock, we put on life jackets but had to wait a few minutes for a rowboat to be returned. When one was available, a member of the waterfront staff helped us into it and pushed us off. My mother grabbed a set of oars and we rowed out to the middle of the lake.

"I love this. I'm going to ask your father to get us one for the Hamptons," she said.

"A rowboat?"

"Can't you just picture the two of us enjoying lazy afternoons out on Georgica Pond?"

Unfortunately, after that night my father had shown up with his paralegal, the only person I could picture him enjoying Georgica Pond with was Samara. "Dad's staying in the city this weekend?" I asked.

"He had a lot of work to catch up on," she answered. "You know, I had the most wonderful massage at the hotel this morning. I can't remember when I've felt so relaxed."

She was obviously trying to steer away from the

subject of my father. The unspoken tension between us was killing me. We were both dancing around the one topic neither of us wanted to confront. I bit the bullet and spat out, "Is he staying in the city alone?"

My mother dropped the oars out of her hands, and they fell into the lake.

"Damn it," she cried.

"It's okay. I'll flag down one of the lifeguards," I said, turning around to see if any were doing their usual patrol of the lake on Jet Skis. She started laughing hysterically. In my entire life, I'd never seen her come undone like that. "What's so funny?" I asked, turning back around to face her.

"I've been avoiding this conversation for over twenty years, and now there's no getting away from it. Literally."

"We don't have to talk about this," I said.

She took my hands into her own. "Oh, yes, we do."

One of the lake lifeguards came by on a Jet Ski and handed us back the oars, which had already floated pretty far from the boat. My mother thanked him, and then, after he sped off, she put them back in the water. She saw my puzzled look and said, "I might not be brave enough otherwise." She pushed her oversized sunglasses onto her head so we were finally eye to eye. "No, Gigi, I'm sure he isn't spending this weekend on his own. I'd venture to guess that one of his girlfriends will make sure of that."

I tried not to let disappointment register on my face. "One of?"

"Yes, there's more than one."

"How long have you known about his..." I was going to say "cheating," but in that moment, the word seemed too severe.

"Women my age usually say *indiscretions,"* she said, finishing my sentence. "Let's see, I've known for about twenty years."

Just then, the wake from the Jet Ski hit the rowboat. I put my arms to the side to steady it. I wasn't sure if the revelation or wave was making me queasy. I closed my mouth and swallowed hard, hoping to suppress the feeling.

"I'm not sure I understand," I said.

She moistened her lips, the remnants of her Chanel lipstick barely visible. "You know, your grandfather thought your father and I were out of our minds when we decided to name you Georgica, but we didn't care. To us, the name represented a dream, a life we someday hoped to have."

"I know all that," I said.

"Did you know that while your father went to law school at night, I held two different jobs so we could afford having you plus his tuition? He watched you during the day and studied while I worked. There were days we only saw each other long enough for him to tell me what your nap schedule had been or what you'd eaten. We had nothing back then, but I was so in love with him I didn't care," she said.

This was all news to me. I'd always assumed their roles had been neatly defined and carved out from the very beginning. My father, uncompromisingly working toward his career, while my mother happily stayed home, dutifully cheering him on from the sidelines.

She continued, "We were a team back then. He graduated at the top of his class, clerked for a judge, and then became an associate. He climbed up the ladder pretty quickly after that, and we were living our supposed dream."

I picked up on her sarcasm. "Supposed?"

"We had our fancy apartment in the city and our house on Georgica Pond, but funnily enough, I would have given anything to go back to our one-bedroom apartment in Astoria. I hadn't realized how much I gave up in helping him pursue his dreams. The resentment came later. Without even realizing it, I pushed him away. The awful truth is I wasn't all that surprised the first time I saw your father in a dark corner whispering with a young, attractive associate at the firm's Christmas party."

My head was swimming from her confessions. "I don't understand. Then why did you stay with him all these years?"

A smile crept across her face. "Your father can be very persuasive, as you know. It's why they pay him the big bucks."

"Mom..."

She suddenly looked very serious. "I stay because, after thirty-five years of marriage, I don't know how to be anything other than his wife. I *stayed* because I wasn't a noun. And mostly, I stay because, despite all his flaws, or maybe even because of all his flaws, I love him," she said, locking eyes with me.

A warm rush came over my body. It all made sense. Her constant badgering for me to pursue a career she thought would provide me with an independence and fulfillment she hadn't found.

"So then, this is an arrangement the two of you have?" I imagined her and my father negotiating the terms over our kitchen table.

"I've made my life work, Gigi. I'm not unhappy. He fulfilled his end of our agreement and has given me everything I've ever asked for. I can't blame him for the fact that it wasn't quite enough. He doesn't flaunt anything in my face. Our dynamic isn't one I would choose for you, but when you're in love with somebody, you do and accept things you are ashamed to admit to yourself, let alone to anyone else."

My mind drifted back to that day she and I had lunch —when she pleaded with me to demand more from my relationships. Now, having heard her confession, I was ashamed to let her know just how alike she and I were.

I took a deep breath and said, "Mom, I carried on a relationship with Joshua while Alicia was doing that training program in London." The words spilled out in a stream. "They weren't together then, but still. I could never bring myself to tell her. She doesn't know anything about it."

My mother closed her eyes and shook her head, and I prepared myself for the scolding I knew I deserved. "God, you must hate me," she said and I was certain I'd misheard her. "All those times I went on and on about how lucky Alicia was to have found a guy like him," she continued. "So this summer, being here, it's about more than just you being fired from your job then." I noticed for the first time there was no disdain in her voice when she said *job*. Her eyes softened. "Is it over now?"

I stared down into the water. The small waves from the Jet Ski had subsided and the lake was still. "He's not a bad guy. He never meant to hurt me. I don't think he had any idea how long I'd been in love with him."

"They never do," she said, her voice breaking.

I looked up and at my mother's face. Her skin was as luminescent as a teenager's. Her big, dark eyes had only the smallest suggestion of crow's-feet around them. Years of wearing big hats and even bigger sunglasses had preserved her youthful appearance. Her glossy hair, not pulled back into its usual chignon, framed her face in such a way that I could almost imagine that twenty-something girl confidently making her way in the world. I wished I could have known her, although I was grateful to have just discovered she ever existed at all.

I took her hands in mine. "Should we try to get the oars back, or do you want to sit here for a bit longer?"

"Let's float a little bit longer," she answered.

CHAPTER FIFTEEN

Later that day, after my mother left, Perry came to find me at the athletic field, where I was watching a Parents vs. Campers softball game.

"What's the score?" he asked, settling down next to me in the grass.

"Campers four. Parents one."

He pulled a Chipwich out of each of his pockets and handed me one.

"I thought you hated these?"

"It's an acquired taste," he responded with a coy smile. "How did things go with your mum?"

"It was nice to spend some time with her." I noticed his Chipwich melting all over his hands. "You still don't like them, do you?"

He shook his head. I held out my napkin so he could wrap it up. This playful side to his personality was all new to me.

"Are you sitting OD tonight?" he asked.

"No, Jordana's sitting with Brooke."

"Good. I wanted to invite you to my cabin for a proper date."

Just as the sincerity of his invitation was sinking in, one of the parent batters hit a fly ball that landed a few feet from where we were sitting. Perry stood up to retrieve it and threw it back to the pitcher's mound.

"So a proper date, huh? What does that entail, exactly?" I asked.

"Well, I swiped a pizza from Alex Shane's pile and should be able to scrounge up a bottle of wine," he answered.

"Sounds proper to me." I smiled.

He cocked his head to the side and smiled back. "Glad to hear it, Princess. See you later."

The game was a complete bloodbath. The campers beat the parents with a final score of 14-3. When it was over, I went back to the cabin to check in on Jordana and the rest of the campers. Tara was showing her parents and boyfriend around when I walked in.

"Gigi, good. I'm glad you're here," she said, rushing over to me. "These are my parents, and this is my boyfriend, Brian."

Brian was nothing like I'd expected. Based on Tara's outrageousness, I'd pictured an alternative-type guy covered in piercings and tattoos. Brian was the complete opposite. He was wearing khaki shorts, a white polo shirt, and Docksiders. He looked like your average high schooler.

Tara had severely toned down her look for the day. Normally, she liked to tie her CIT T-shirt up in the middle so that her midriff showed and pair it with skimpy jean shorts. Today, she had her shirt untied with khaki shorts similar to Brian's. Her hair, which she'd been highlighting all summer using lemon juice and Sun-In, was neatly slicked back into a ponytail.

"Nice to meet all of you," I said, giving them a small wave.

Tara's mother approached me. She was a petite woman who looked a lot like her daughter.

"So Tara's told us she's been like your right hand all summer?" she said sweetly.

I looked over at Tara, who looked nervous I was going to rat her out for who she really was. "Sure, yeah. She's been a real help."

Jordana walked into the bunk. "Who's been a help to us?"

"I was just telling Tara's parents how great it's been having her as our CIT."

Jordana looked at me like I was crazy.

Tara's mother chimed in, "And she told us she's been helping you make the costumes for the show."

The closest Tara had come to helping me with the costumes for the show was when she begged me to make her a halter top out of some of the leftover lace fabric to wear out to The Canteen.

I nodded and smiled. Jordana made a face. Tara looked thankful I hadn't told them most of her summer had been spent flirting with the male counselors and working on her tan.

"Okay, Gigi, we're going to take a sailboat out before it gets dark. We'll catch you later," Tara said, ushering her family out of the bunk.

A few seconds later, Tara's father came back inside.

"Forget something?" I asked, looking up at him.

"Just wanted to tell the two of you thank you. I know what a handful she can be," he said.

Jordana and I looked at each other before she

responded. "Not at all, Mr. Mann. She's been a pleasure to work with."

He looked relieved. After he left, I turned to Jordana and raised my eyebrows.

"You're right. What's the point? It's camp. Let her be the bad girl here if she has to be the good one at home," Jordana said.

"Well, it doesn't sound like she's exactly a good girl at home."

"Did you catch a glimpse of her boyfriend, Brian? He doesn't scream bad boy to me," she said, changing from her Chinooka staff tank top into the long-sleeved version of it.

"Are you still okay to sit OD tonight?" I asked.

"I'm counting on them crashing hard from the sugar they've been gorging themselves on all day," she said.

After visiting day, the counselors went around to the bunks to seize all the food that could attract animals. It typically ended up at The Canteen, where the counselors happily finished it off.

"I have my eye on some subs I saw in Bunk Eleven. I'll make sure to bring them over to The Canteen for you," Jordana said.

"I actually have a date with Perry tonight," I mumbled.

She whipped around to face me. "You have what?"

"A date. He called it that. We'll probably just hang out in his cabin."

"Call it whatever you want, Gigi, but he asked you for plans alone, in advance. It's a date."

"Okay, *assuming* it's a date, what should I wear?"

"Well, makeup, for a start," she teased.

I appreciated Jordana's not-so-subtle way of telling me my new beauty regime consisting of only tinted moisturizer and ChapStick wasn't cutting it. "I'll wear makeup. What about clothes?"

"I'd probably wear clothes. Although it's Perry Gillman. Maybe not," she said with a wicked smile.

"Very funny. A dress? Shorts? Pants?"

She shrugged her shoulders. "You're the fashion guru."

"What about this?" I said, pulling a white eyelet sundress out from my cubby.

"I love that," Madison said, walking into the cabin holding hands with Alex Shane.

"Maddy, you know boys aren't allowed in the bunk," Jordana chided.

"He just wanted to see what it looked like. Please, Jordana. It's technically still Parents' Weekend, and boys are allowed in the bunk during Parents' Weekend."

Jordana sighed. "You have five minutes."

I was happy to let Jordana be the disciplinarian so I could pull a few more options from my shelves. I held different combinations up to myself in the full-length mirror in the bathroom before firmly deciding on the sundress with flat gold sandals. After Jordana kicked Alex out of our bunk, Madison sat down on my bed to recount the rest of the events from her day. As she prattled on and on, I felt that same rolling fluttering feeling in my stomach I used to feel with Joshua. I guess it really was a date?

Dinner that night was a picnic on the Great Lawn. The dining room staff put out a spread of sandwiches and chips for anyone who wanted it. However, most of the campers and staff were too full from stuffing themselves with junk food all day to eat anything. Instead, everyone hung out on the grass until it was time for them to go to their own divisions for lights out.

While the rest of the camp was busy socializing I quickly showered and let my hair air dry. I applied some light makeup and put on the sundress. When I was ready, I took the secret route behind the lake over to Perry's cabin. I didn't want to unintentionally create any more fodder for the camp gossip mill. When I reached his cabin door, I looked around to make sure nobody was around. Then, I took a deep breath and straightened my dress before I knocked. It seemed like an eternity before Perry answered.

"Wow," I said, peeking in and around at his cabin, which was aglow with lit candles.

"Wow, yourself. You look beautiful, Gigi. Tonight's been a long time in the making, and I wanted it to be perfect."

"I'm not sure I believe in perfect anymore," I said.

"Well, I'll just have to work on changing your mind, then."

He motioned for me to come inside, and I followed him into the main room. It looked completely different. The sheets of music that had been scattered around the floor the night before were piled on the bookshelf in neat stacks, and the records all organized and lined on the shelf. The table was set for two with plates, glasses, and flatware he must have swiped from the dining hall. Perry pulled a chair out and motioned for me to sit. I placed my paper napkin in my lap and watched as he unscrewed the top of the wine bottle before pouring two glasses.

"Screw top. Very classy."

"Only the best for you, Princess," he said, carrying the glasses over to the table.

He handed one to me and then lifted his glass to make a toast. I raised mine to meet it in the air. Perry cleared his throat and said, "Let those now love, who never loved before. Let those who've loved, now love the more."

"Emerson? Keats?" I guessed.

"Abe Gillman. My father. Although I'm sure he stole the line from someone," he said.

I took a sip of the wine and noticed he hadn't touched his own drink. "You know, it's bad luck not to drink to your own toast," I teased.

He looked at me solemnly and said, "I gave up drinking after the accident."

I thought back to the night he'd found me at Rosie's, pounding back tequila shots. I blushed, thinking how immature it must have looked to him. "I don't need to drink either," I said, pushing my glass aside. "So what can I help with?"

"Nothing. Take a seat. I have this under control."

I sat back down at the table and waited for him to bring the food over. He looked relaxed in a loose-fitting pair of jeans, a white T-shirt, and bare feet. He hummed as he skillfully moved around his small kitchen. He announced everything was ready and served us each a slice of the pizza and some salad before sitting down across from me. I picked up my fork and knife and starting cutting bite-size pieces of pizza.

"In the UK, we usually pick our pizza up, like this," he said, folding the slice in half and taking a bite.

"We do that in the US too, just not in the Goldstein house," I said, putting down my cutlery and following suit.

He smiled and leaned toward me. "Tell me more about life in the Goldstein house."

"Not much to tell. You met my mother earlier. That should give you the first clue."

He laughed, exposing his adorable dimples before turning more serious. "Okay then, tell me more about the ex. What's the bloke's name?"

The directness of his question caught me a bit off guard. I put my pizza down and answered, "Joshua." He repeated the name as if saying it out loud might give him some better insight into the man.

"What was her name?" I asked.

"Annie."

I repeated Annie's name for the same reason. Suddenly, it felt as though there were four of us crowded around his very small kitchen table.

"She was a counselor in Cedar?" I asked.

"Yes. She was actually Michelle's counselor back when Michelle was a camper."

That explained his close relationship with Michelle. She was a link to someone he'd loved and lost. Of course, he would cling to her as a way to hold onto his feelings for Annie. An overwhelming sense of relief washed over me. The rumors about him and younger counselors made complete sense now. They'd all been Annie's campers years ago. They knew Annie and could corroborate his memories of her.

Perry stood up to clear the table. I motioned for him to sit back down and he slowly slid back into his chair.

"That night in the arts and crafts cabin when I was fitting you for your costume, you asked me if I was over Joshua," I said.

"I remember."

"I never answered you."

"Your tears did Gigi. I understand."

"No, I don't think you do."

"Then explain it to me," he said, taking my hands into his own.

"I met Joshua at Chinooka. We spent seven summers as campers here—me, him, and Alicia. The three of us were inseparable and at some point along the way, I found myself Joshua's sounding board. He came to me anytime things with Alicia were the least bit rocky and I'd fix whatever was going on. I should've taken myself out of the equation, but I liked that he needed me."

Perry chewed on his bottom lip and waited for my next sentence.

"It was a childhood crush that turned into an adult infatuation. Then Alicia left for London and decided she wanted a break from Joshua."

"That's when the two of you got together?"

I nodded. "We started spending more and more time together. Suddenly, I found myself in a relationship with Joshua and not on the sidelines of his and Alicia's. It was wonderful and fun and exciting, but in the back of my mind I knew I was a placeholder."

Perry reached up and pushed my hair behind my ears. "You could never be a placeholder, Gigi."

"I'm not trying to be self-effacing. I'm not saying he didn't care for me, or even that he doesn't still in some way. But because of the dynamic the three of us had—the one I allowed for so long—I was an easy surrogate for the person he was meant to be with."

"Are you sure that you're not still in love him?"

"I've spent my life chasing a mirage. It almost destroyed me," I said, looking down.

Perry lifted my head up so we were eye to eye. "Gigi," he said softly, "I don't want to win by default."

"I'm not playing a game."

"Good." He kissed me softly. "Neither am I."

After we finished eating, we moved to the couch and continued revealing new things about our pasts, both of us coming clean about our mistakes and culpability. As good as it felt to finally be so honest with someone without self-reproach or shame, I worried maybe we were just two moths being drawn to equally damaged flames. But over the next few hours, the conversation shifted, and we became just two people getting to know one another.

Perry told me about his childhood in Oxshott and more about his father, who'd just retired following an illustrious career as a first violinist with the Vienna Philharmonic. I learned about the years he spent studying at the Royal College of Music and the writer's block that was currently preventing him from completing his doctorate. I told him funny stories from when I was a camper at Chinooka, about being on *Top Designer*, and my dream to one day start my own line.

When we finished clearing the dishes, Perry led me away from the table to the back porch, which overlooked Lake Chinooka. I leaned over the railing and looked out onto the lake. The sun was setting, casting an amazing red-orange hue over everything. "Nice view," I said, admiring the serenity of the scene.

"I agree," he said, gazing at me. He stepped toward me and pulled me in for a deep kiss. Although we'd already spent the night together, in a way, this was the most intimate moment we'd shared so far. I retreated from his grasp.

"What's the matter?" he asked.

I'd convinced myself that the feelings I had for Joshua were incomparable and extraordinary. It was the only justification I could come up with for betraying my friendship with Alicia, and now that Perry had shattered all that reasoning, I had no excuse for what I'd done.

"I don't deserve to be this happy," I said.

"Happiness is a gift. Neither one of us planned for this. If anything, we both fought like hell to stop it from happening. But, here we are, and for the first time in a long time, I want to be happy. So let's be happy, Georgica. Whether it's just for tonight, for a few days, or a few weeks. Let's try to be happy."

I nodded and nuzzled into his chest. There was a cool breeze coming off the lake, and goose bumps formed up and down my arms. Perry went inside and brought me out one of his sweaters. I slipped it over my dress, and, together, we watched the sun set over Chinooka.

"Pretty perfect," I whispered.

"I thought you didn't believe in perfect?"

"I don't know what I believe anymore."

"Let's take it one day at a time while you try to figure it out."

"Deal."

CHAPTER SIXTEEN

As the summer wore on, our relationship eased into a comfortable routine. Perry and I'd been the hot topic around Chinooka for a few weeks, but eventually, the campers grew tired of talking about us and moved on to some of the other couplings. Jordana started officially seeing Jake. Their on-again, off-again romance took some of the spotlight off of us, something Perry and I were grateful for. Although Gordy had given us his blessing, we still tried to stay under the radar. Neither one of us went to Rosie's or The Canteen, preferring to spend our nights off in his cabin—me working on finishing the costumes for the show, and him working on his thesis.

We were just about tied with Birch in points for The Gordy, and the Cedar girls believed I could lead them to victory for the first time in three summers. Color War, a three-day competition where the entire camp was divided into two teams, would be breaking out any day and would determine the final winner. Color War always broke out with a surprise. Gordy spent months planning it. Leading up to the actual breakout were a series of fake-outs meant to psych the kids up even more.

Last year, Gordy had played the sound of a helicopter over the PA system, and when the campers ran out to the tennis courts, they'd found a huge banner that said "Fake Out." This summer, the kitchen staff put blue and yellow food coloring in the milk at breakfast so the kids believed they were being divided into teams based on the color milk they were given. Once everyone got their glass, Gordy went up to the microphone and screamed "fake out" at the top of his lungs.

After all the fake-outs, the campers were completely on edge waiting for the real Color War to begin. For weeks now, "One, Two, Three, Four, we want Color War," had been heard echoing around Chinooka.

Then, it finally happened. The whole camp was seated for dinner when two men dressed in medieval costumes and carrying heralding trumpets walked into the dining hall. They blasted out a tune and announced everyone was to report to the soccer field. The campers took off running, knowing this was finally the real thing.

Gordy had the floodlights on and positioned so they created a spotlight in the middle of the athletics field. It was eerily silent, and then, suddenly, music started playing over the camp's loudspeaker system. Gordy always had a flair for the dramatic. When I was a camper, he and the head of the woodshop had worked all summer, making the façade of a pirate's ship to attach to one of the larger sailboats in the lake. All the campers had stood on the shores of Lake Chinooka as he sailed up in a replica of the *Jolly Roger* from *Peter Pan* to announce the breakout of Color War. The theme that year was Pirates vs. Indians. Alicia and I had both been captains, leading the Indian team to victory.

As the music grew louder and louder, we all looked around, wondering what kind of a surprise Gordy had in store for us this summer. Then, two knights on white horses rode into the soccer field from opposite sides. Both of them carried banners—one blue and one gold. The gold banner had the word "Heroes" written on it, and the blue banner said "Villains." The horses approached the center of the field and stopped so they were facing one another about 50 yards apart. Then, the knights—in full period regalia—charged at one another, screaming out what was on their banners. After a few more passes, Gordy stepped to the center of the field dressed up like a medieval king and asked them to halt their match. The whole camp was on their feet, wondering what would happen next.

The two knights retreated to their respective sides and then came down from their horses. Each one knelt down in front of Gordy and presented their banner to him. Holding one in each hand, Gordy marched forward, and in his best English accent said, "Once more unto the breach, dear friends, once more. In peace there's nothing so becomes a man as modest stillness and humility. But, when the blast of war blows in our ears, then imitate the action of the tiger."

I looked over at Perry and mouthed the words, "Shakespeare?"

He held up his hand so his five fingers showed and mouthed back, "Henry the Fifth."

Gordy screamed into the microphone, "I bid you all welcome to Camp Chinooka's One-Hundredth Color War Games."

The campers went crazy, and it took a full minute before they settled down and Gordy could continue speaking.

"This year's competition will pit Heroes against Villains. The Gold Team, led by General Goldstein, will be the Heroes. Gigi, please come join me."

I ran up to Gordy, and he handed me the gold banner along with a gold T-shirt that said General on the front and Heroes on the back.

"The Blue Team, led by General Gillman, will be the Villains. Perry, can you please come up here as well?"

Perry ran up from the crowd, getting high-fived along the way. He joined me on the other side of Gordy, who handed Perry his blue banner and T-shirt. We both slipped our shirts over our heads and were met with more cheers. Gordy handed me the microphone and a piece of paper that had the names of the counselor sergeants, CIT majors, and the camper captains for my team. I read off my list, and Perry did the same. When we were both finished, the counselors, CITs, and campers from all the different divisions lined up behind each of us.

Gordy announced the first strategy session for the Gold Team would be at the Lakeside Amphitheater in ten minutes. The campers and staff hurried off to their bunks to change into their team colors and go to their respective meetings. Before I left to join them, I congratulated Gordy on another successful breakout.

Perry nodded in agreement. "Where'd you find the knights?"

"Medieval Times. There's one about forty-five minutes away from here. The horses belong to the camp. I hired the actors."

Gordy walked away looking extremely pleased with himself. When he was out of earshot, Perry turned to me and asked, "What's Medieval Times?"

"It's a kind of dinner theater where you watch the

reenactment of a period jousting tournament and eat with your hands," I said, giving him the best description I could come up with.

"Sounds brilliant. Let's go someday," he said.

"It's a date," I said, leaning up to kiss him. "So, General Gillman, is this it for the next four days?"

"Yes, it is," he said, taking hold of my hands. "Fraternizing with the enemy is tantamount to treason."

"Well then, far be it from me to be a traitor." I started to walk away from him, but he pulled me back into his arms for one last kiss. "Think Mussolini and Churchill said goodbye like this?" I teased.

"I hope not. See you in four days," he said.

"Oh, you'll see me before then, General Gillman, and when you do, you and your team should be prepared to retreat."

"Starting with the smack talk already? Bring it," he said.

"Oh, I will."

He raised his eyebrows. "Looking forward to it, Princess."

"That's General Goldstein to you," I said with a playful smile.

He saluted me, and we separated to go to our first team strategy meetings. I walked into the amphitheater and was greeted by a sea of gold. The campers had wasted no time getting into the full spirit of Color War and wore anything they could find in a gold or yellow. Some had even painted their faces, arms, and legs with yellow war paint.

I ran to the front of the stage greeted by massive cheers from the crowd. I reintroduced the sergeants, majors, and captains who were met with more applause. Once the kids settled down, I read through the schedule for the next day, letting each age group know the events they'd be competing in. I asked for volunteers to work on the team's original cheer, song, and plaque. The Creative Trifecta accounted for almost half of the final score and would be presented during the final night of Color War. Knowing their significance to the competition, I asked the volunteers to stay behind a few extra minutes so we could brainstorm some ideas.

As the other campers made their way back to their cabins, most of them still on a high from the breakout, the rest of us sat down on the stage to strategize. Since Davis, one of the drama directors from *Fiddler*, was assigned to our team, I begged him to take the lead on the song. He was hesitant to accept. When I pressed him on the reason, he explained that Perry had single-handedly written the winning song the last three years of Color War.

"Gigi, you don't get it. His songs are incredible," Davis said.

I did get it. Over the last few weeks, I'd been Perry's very willing audience of one. He played different incarnations of his original composition, and I gave him my critiques. Knowing little about classical orchestrations, most of my comments were limited to my gut emotional response to the music. My gut told me he was incredible. So did my heart.

"Just do what you can. You're our best chance," I said, rubbing his shoulders like I was prepping Rocky for his big fight against Apollo Creed.

Davis still looked nervous. I reminded him that Sally, the head arts and crafts counselor, had been assigned to our team too, so we at least had an advantage where the plaque was concerned. That seemed to take a bit of the pressure off, and he finally agreed to help.

All that was left to figure out was the cheer. A few of the girls from my cabin stepped forward with their ideas. I was happy to let them run with it. After admitting she'd been the captain of her high school's cheerleading team, Jordana offered to supervise. I delegated out the rest of the tasks and dismissed everyone back to their bunks.

The next morning, The Beach Boys' song 'Heroes and Villains' played at top volume over the camp PA system to wake the whole camp. The song's lyrics had almost nothing to do with heroes or villains, but I could only imagine how thrilled Gordy had been when he came across the apropos title. For the first time all summer, the girls didn't complain about the early hour or try to burrow back under their blankets. They were ready for battle.

Madison, dressed in tight-fitting yellow shorts and a yellow T-shirt, offered to let me use the gold nail polish she'd brought to camp. It had already become a huge trend with the girls, so the limited supply made it a hot commodity around the bunk. I thanked her and applied some to my own nails. I got dressed in my "General" T-shirt and paired it with cut-off jean shorts. I asked Jordana if she could braid some gold ribbon into my hair and then did the same for her. I walked past the full-length bathroom mirror and stopped right in front of it. I couldn't help but wonder what my very fashionable former colleagues from Diane von Furstenberg would have to say about my look. The truth was, I was having so much fun, I didn't care one bit.

The Cedar girls were competing in water events in the morning and tug-of-war in the afternoon. The water events consisted of swim relays, sailing, and rowing races, and, of course, Ishkabibble.

Ishkabibble was Gordy's favorite Color War event and mine too. All the participating campers stood around the edge of the pool while Gordy read a story over a bullhorn. Every time he said the word "Ishkabibble" the campers had to jump into the pool. To make it harder, the story was always littered with phrases that sounded similar to Ishkabibble, like Ishkasnivel or Ishkadribble. If you jumped in the pool on the wrong word, you were out. The tension was usually pretty unbearable, especially as it got down to the last few campers. From what I'd observed over the years, Ishkabibble was not a game for the faint of heart.

When we arrived at the dining hall for breakfast, I reminded the girls all meals were silent during Color War and points would be deducted from the team caught talking. The dining staff loved to try to get the campers to talk by putting disgusting combinations of food on their plates or heckling them. As a camper, I'd hated the silent meals, but as a counselor, I already loved them. We were only a few hours into Color War, and I was already grateful to have a few minutes to hear myself think between the wall-to-wall cheering.

Most of the team heeded my warnings and ate their meal in complete silence. A girl from Elm cost the Villains some points when she asked one of the kitchen staff to get her a new grilled cheese after a Heroes CIT had covered hers in whipped cream. Madison and Alex Shane lost Heroes a few points when they were caught speaking to each other by the cereal dispensers. Perry caught my glance and stared me up and down. Who would've thought he was capable of saying so much while saying so little? I winked back at him and took my seat. Gordy, the only one exempt from the silent meal rules, made a few announcements and then dismissed us to our first contests.

During the morning, the Villains pretty much slaughtered the Heroes in all events. We did manage to squeak out a win in Ishkabibble. Surprisingly, Candice won the game for the Gold Team. In the final round, it had gotten down to her and a girl from the Villains. The other girl had jumped in the water on Ishkariddle and we were declared the victors. I couldn't believe that the girl who didn't listen to anyone *ever* could actually be the victor in a game designed around paying attention. I was pretty certain Candice just didn't want to get her hair wet.

That small triumph wasn't enough to even the scores. By the afternoon, it was clear we needed to win the tug-of-war to give us a fighting chance going into Day Two.

CHAPTER SEVENTEEN

The next morning, the whole camp came out to watch the tug-of-war, which was set up on the far corner of the athletics field. It started out as a pretty evenly matched game. The Blue Team would gain some yardage, then the Gold. Perry placed their biggest campers at the far end of the rope to anchor it, and the smaller ones closer to the middle and front. From way in the back, he was leading his team in a chant of "One, two, three, heave."

On my side of the moat, I was shouting over the noise to try to get my campers to synchronize, but it wasn't working. The tides turned and we were losing, although putting up a decent fight. For every couple of inches the Blue Team gained, we'd reclaim a few. My hands were being rubbed raw from the rope, and sweat was pouring off of my forehead. I desperately wanted to reach up and put my hair in a ponytail but was too afraid to let go of the rope for even one second. I was so focused, head down, pulling with all my might, I didn't immediately notice Joshua watching me from across the field.

I had no clue how long he'd been standing there. In an instant, everything moved in slow motion. I could barely make out the muffled yelling of my teammates, screaming at me to pick up the rope that I'd dropped. I stumbled over to a nearby tree stump to catch my breath and drink some water. Joshua spotted me and came down the field. My face couldn't hide my confusion. How'd he find me? What did he want?

"You don't seem happy to see me," he said before I could say anything.

"Joshua." Just saying his name again made me feel instantly vulnerable—like I was nine years old on that bus to Chinooka for the first time.

"Your father told me where you were."

I shook my head and sat down on the stump. "My father?"

"I went to his office and pleaded with him to tell me. When he said Chinooka, I didn't believe him at first. It's surreal to be standing here with you. Is Gordy still around? You're head counselor of Cedar?"

"What are you doing here?"

"I'm sorry I just showed up like this, but I didn't think you'd see me otherwise. I had to see you. You look—"

"Like a mess," I interjected, looking down at my sweat-marked T-shirt and mud-stained calves.

"Beautiful," he said, finishing his thought.

I swallowed hard and Perry came up behind me. "Everything okay here, Gigi? He asked, putting his hand on my shoulder.

"I'm fine," I answered.

"If you need me, I'll be right over there," he said, pointing to the tug-of-war match, which—remarkably—was still going on.

"Who's he?" Joshua asked when Perry was out of earshot.

Before I could answer, Gordy shouted that the Heroes had won the tug-of-war. I looked over at Perry. He was panting and pouring water from his canteen over his hands, which were visibly red and raw. He'd conceded the Blue Team's advantage when he left the game to check on me. Over on my side, the Gold Team was high-fiving and celebrating their win. I turned back to face Joshua. "I have to go. My team needs me."

"Gigi, please. I came all the way here to see you."

I crossed my arms and all the muscles in my back and neck tightened. "I said all I needed to say that night on the sidewalk in June."

He lifted his hand up to the side of his face and rubbed it. "Yeah, I know. My cheek's still stinging. Gigi, come on. Five minutes for an old friend."

"I can't."

He stepped closer and stroked the side of my cheek. "Georgica, please."

I softened my stance. "I can't get away now. Maybe later I can, for few minutes."

He raised his eyebrows and flashed a closed-lipped smile. "I'll go walk around and visit some of my favorite haunts. When you're ready, I'll be here."

I left the field to look for Perry and found him at the lakefront giving a motivational speech to his team, trying to psych them up for the competitions that night. When he finished, the campers dispersed to their next activity, and he waited behind to talk to me.

"Was that who I think it was?"

I nodded. "Joshua."

"He's very charming," Perry said while tying a blue bandana around his head.

It didn't surprise me to hear the self-doubt in his voice. Perry was just as handsome and magnetic, but he was rougher around the edges. Joshua was more polished, and he had a swagger and coolness that was noticeable to men and women alike.

"He can be." There was no point in denying what was obvious to anyone who'd met him.

"What'd he come here for?"

"I'm not sure," I said.

Perry nodded and then asked the question I knew he'd wanted to ask from the moment he saw us talking earlier. "Is it really done?"

I leaned in and kissed Perry hard.

"What was that for?" he asked.

"You lost the tug-of-war," I said.

"No. I didn't," he said, touching my cheek.

"No. You didn't."

I spent the rest of the day in a tense daze, wandering among the different Color War matchups and looking around every corner for Joshua. As I was heading back to the Cedar horseshoe, Tara spotted him sitting alone in one of the gazebos on the Great Lawn.

"Gigi, there's your hot friend," she said, pointing to him.

"I should go talk to him," I mumbled.

Jordana gave me a sympathetic smile and ushered Tara and the rest of the girls away so I'd have some privacy. Joshua stood up to greet me as I walked inside the gazebo.

"You sure know how to keep a fella waiting," he said.

"I figured you'd be fine without me," I said and then realized the irony of the statement. I cleared my throat and changed the subject quickly, shaking my head. "I can't believe you didn't go home."

"I've been walking around looking at all our old stomping grounds. It's amazing how much has changed and how little has changed. I ran into Gordy. He at least pretended to remember who I was."

"Oh, I'm sure he remembers you. That man has a memory like a steel trap and you pulled off the most legendary raid of The Canteen in Chinooka history. Campers still talk about it."

He brushed his hand across his lips. "You were the brains of that operation. I was just the muscle."

"Remember how we woke Alicia up afterward and the three of us sat on the dock chowing down on all the snacks we looted?"

Joshua walked to the side of the gazebo and leaned over the railing. "What was it Gordy used to call us? Not the Three Musketeers?"

"The Three Stooges. You were Moe, Alicia was Larry, and I was Curly," I said, holding up a piece of hair. "Funny, he never realized that Curly was actually the bald one."

"The Stooges, that's right," he said, laughing to himself.

I got up and stood beside him. "Do you remember the last time we were here?

He turned from the railing to face me. "In this gazebo? No? Should I?"

"It was our last summer at Chinooka. Alicia was interested in one of the CIT's. I can't remember his name."

"It was Andrew, I think," he said.

I nodded. "You and I'd been spending a lot of time together. Then, out of nowhere, you passed me a note during dinner to meet you here. I read and reread the note trying to decipher what it meant." I finished talking and looked down at the ground.

"What did it say?" he asked.

I rubbed the back of my neck as I paced the gazebo. "I thought you liked me. I thought you wanted to meet here so you could tell me how you felt."

"Right," he said, closing his eyes. "Instead, I asked you to help me get Alicia back." He sat down and rested his back against the railing.

I sat down beside him. "Why are you really here, Joshua?"

He bowed forward and put his head between his hands. "She's having cold feet or second thoughts. I don't know."

"And you came to talk to your old friend, Gigi, about it. You were expecting me to fix it?"

He looked up. "I'm not sure. I didn't think anything. I just wanted to see you. God, being here, I feel like I'm thirteen years old again."

I pointed to Madison and Alex, who were kissing in a dark corner of the field. "Until you realize they're actually thirteen and you're the grown-up."

He took hold of both my hands and said, "So tell me, grown-up, how'd we get to this place?

I pulled my hands back and turned away from him. "All I wanted was to run away from my life and the mistakes that'd been piling up. And where did I run to? Chinooka, where a million memories came flooding back to me every day. You and Alicia. Me and Alicia. You can tell me that you're unsure about this marriage and unsure about Alicia and that you maybe love me too, but I'm the one person you can't lie to. I've been part of your relationship with Alicia for as long as you've had one. I know better than anyone that it's always been, and will always be, her."

He pulled me back around so we were face-to-face. "That night in June outside the restaurant, you asked me if you were just a distraction," he said.

I swallowed hard. "I remember."

"You've been my truest friend, and I put you in an impossible situation. I was selfish. I headed straight for your arms—I knew you'd be there for me the way you've always been there for me. But you weren't a distraction, Gigi, and what I felt for you then was real. I need you to know that."

"I do know that. At least I know it now. It means everything to hear you say it." I took Joshua's hands into my own. "And you didn't put me anywhere. I wanted to be there. It's all I'd ever wanted." I reached into my pocket. "Here," I said, handing him back the key necklace he'd given me last summer. I'd retrieved it from my Band-Aid box earlier in the day.

He closed his fist tightly around it. There was loud cheering off in the distance, and we both turned to see where it was coming from.

"It must be the relay races going on at the athletic field," I said.

Joshua tucked the necklace into his shirt pocket, but when he opened his fist, I could see the key had left a small imprint.

He stood up. "I should let you get back to them," he said, motioning to the field.

I threw my arms around his neck and whispered in

his ear, "She may be having cold feet but be patient, she'll come around. I know it."

"Thank you, Gigi," he whispered back.

"Be good to her, Joshua."

He nodded without saying a word and walked out of the gazebo, heading back to Alicia. Back where he belonged.

CHAPTER EIGHTEEN

Color War raged on for two more days. By the time the final night arrived, the kids were completely battle-worn. I stopped trying to keep track of who was in the lead, instead of putting all of my energy into the Creative Trifecta. The war's final outcome could be completely changed depending on which team won the song, plaque, and cheer. Poor Davis had been up the last two nights, writing and rewriting his song, knowing that Perry had long completed his.

I gathered the team at the lakeside amphitheater so we could rehearse. Davis passed around sheets with the lyrics and then went to the front of the stage. He sat down at his electric keyboard and started playing the intro to 'Holding out for a Hero,' the eighties song by Bonnie Tyler of 'Total Eclipse of the Heart' fame. It was a good song and actually made a great Color War song, but, unfortunately, most of the campers were too young to know it. When we got to the chorus, a few more campers and some of the counselors chimed in, but not many. Not being familiar with the melody, the kids were butchering it. Davis looked horrified. I nudged Madison and asked her if she remembered anything about Perry's winning song from last year.

"It was awesome. The theme was the Future versus the Past, and he wrote a mash-up of all these techno songs with classical music, almost like they were battling each other."

"And if you were to compare it to this song?" I asked.

She shrugged. "No contest."

Davis was doing his best to teach the kids the words. Our eyes met and he gave me a weak smile. Obviously, we weren't winning the song, but we still had a fighting chance with the plaque and cheer, not to mention the final event of the Color War—the trivia contest.

The event pitted the two team generals in a rapid-fire trivia face-off, fielding a series of questions covering a variety of topics, like pop culture, literature, and Chinooka history. As the rounds went on, the questions grew harder and the point values increased. Past generals had become camp legends based on how well they did during the event. Jordana and the rest of Bunk Fourteen had been quizzing me on different subjects over the last few days. Tara took the lead on pop culture, catching me up to speed on reality TV and the latest celebrity gossip, courtesy of the magazines she had her parents send up weekly. The rest of the campers filled in my knowledge gap on some of the more recent changes at Chinooka. I hadn't studied so hard for anything since my LSATs, but by the time the final night came, I felt ready to face General Gillman.

All the evening Color War events took place on the athletic field, except for last night's contests, which were held on the tennis courts. Gordy had hired back the DJ from the dance to help him emcee. When both teams got onto the court, we separated onto our respective sides and waited for Gordy to announce the order of events.

The team cheer was first. Gordy called up the cheer captains and flipped a coin to see which team would go first. He nodded at the Blue Team to take the stage. The cheer captain proceeded to lead the Villains through an inspiring chant. Everyone was on their feet, but there was nothing particularly memorable about it. When they were finished, Gordy nodded to our team, and Jordana stepped forward to lead the Heroes through our cheer.

Jordana had the idea to have the campers leading the cheer dressed up like different movie and storybook heroes. Harry Potter, Robin Hood, and Batman were over on the Villains' side, heckling them, while Ironman, Indiana Jones, and Hercules were rousing the rest of the Heroes and judges. When the Gold Team finished, Gordy's smile told me everything I needed to know. The Heroes had won the cheer round.

Next, each team brought forward their plaques for presentation to the judges. The Blue Team's had different villains from comics, movies, and TV depicted in black-and-white mug shots. Their names and prison identification numbers were printed below each portrait. The word Villains was spray-painted across the plaque in bright blue. I had to admit that it was pretty clever.

Sally and some of the campers who'd helped with our plaque then brought ours to the judges' table. It was well executed, but not nearly as creative as the Blue Team's. It didn't take long for the judges to render their decision, awarding all the plaque points to the Blue Team.

Finally, came the song. We presented ours first. Even after several rehearsals, the kids still didn't know the melody or words. Most of them rushed through the lyrics, getting to the chorus way too fast. I looked over at Perry, who was leaning forward, trying to recognize the underlying tune. Davis stood behind the electronic keyboard trying to conduct. The look of horror on his face was unmistakable. He could not be put out of his misery fast enough. When it was over, Gordy was on his feet clapping, relieved it was finally over.

When it was the Blue Team's turn, Perry led the campers to the center of the tennis court and instructed them to crouch down to the ground. When the lights on the court dimmed and Perry nodded to the DJ to turn on the fog machine, I knew we were in trouble.

Then I heard it. The unmistakable first notes of Michael Jackson's 'Thriller,' blasting over the speaker system. Suddenly, the squatting campers started to rise to the beat of the music. The music alternated back and forth between 'Thriller,' 'Bad,' and then 'Smooth Criminal.' He'd mashed together all three songs perfectly, and his entire team was singing and dancing seamlessly, with Perry leading the way. When it was over, there was no question they hadn't just won—they'd crushed us. I stood up and gave Perry his due. It was an impressive show, and he deserved the win.

When the applause died down, Gordy called Perry and me to the center of the tennis courts for the final showdown. We took our places behind the two podiums set up next to each other. Gordy took his place at a podium facing ours. He took a piece of paper out of his pocket, carefully unfolded it, put on his glasses, and recited the rules.

"Round One will consist of ten questions, each worth ten points. The team generals may confer with any member of their team for the answers. Round Two will consist of three questions, each worth twenty-five points.

Incorrect answers will result in a ten-point deduction. During Round Two, the team generals may only confer with the three designated trivia captains for the answers. Can the captains please take their place behind their team podium?"

Tara, Jordana, and a camper named Hunter from the Pine Group ran up and joined me. Tara was my designated pop culture expert. Jordana had literature, history, and geography. Hunter was my authority for any sports-related questions. On Perry's side, I saw Alex Shane and two campers I didn't know.

Gordy continued, "The final round will consist of just one question worth fifty points. Incorrect answers will result in a twenty-five-point deduction. Team generals will not be allowed to confer with anyone during the final round. Do the team generals have any questions?"

Perry and I both shook our heads no. Gordy nodded to the DJ. The lights dimmed so that there was only a spotlight on the center of the court where we stood, adding to the already tense atmosphere. Once he had absolute silence, Gordy asked the first question. "If all the state capital cities in the US were listed in alphabetical order, what would be the first two?"

The Gold Team was crowded together when I broke into their huddle. The campers were frantically shouting out the names of different state capitals, and I was repeating them back, trying to work out which one came first in the alphabet. "Let's see. There's Boise and Baton Rouge. Baton Rouge comes before Boise. What other capitals besides Albany start with an A?"

Michelle raised her voice above the other campers, who were yelling out names. "There's Atlanta, Augusta, Annapolis, and Austin."

I quickly ran through the letters of the alphabet. "So, the first two would be Albany and Annapolis, right?"

"Right!" she said.

It was the first time all summer that she'd offered me any help, but I was grateful for it. I ran back to the podium, hit my buzzer, and shouted out, "Albany and Annapolis."

"Correct, ten points awarded to the Heroes," Gordy yelled into his microphone. The Gold Team erupted in cheers. I mouthed "thank you" to Michelle, who smiled back.

Gordy rattled off a few more questions and then announced we were moving on to Round Two. He switched out his index cards for a new set and read off the first question.

"What American playwright wrote screenplays for the films *Ronin, Wag the Dog, The Spanish Prisoner*, and *Glengarry Glenn Ross*?"

I turned around to my trivia captains, expecting Jordana to give me the answer, but instead, Tara jumped in and said, "David Mamet."

"Are you sure?" Jordana asked.

Tara put her hands on her hips. "Positive."

I hit the buzzer. "David Mamet."

"Correct!" Gordy said, jumping up and down.

I turned around to Jordana, who looked completely mystified by Tara's aptitude. Tara whispered that *Glenngary Glenn Ross* was her boyfriend, Brian's, favorite movie.

"Final question. Which two teams were involved in the thrown 1919 World Series?"

I turned around to my experts, and Hunter quickly said, "The Chicago White Sox and the Pittsburgh Pirates."

I hit the buzzer and repeated his answer.

"I'm sorry, but that's incorrect. Ten points deducted from the Heroes. Do the Villains have an answer?" Gordy asked.

Perry conferred with his captains and then answered, "The Chicago White Sox and the Cincinnati Reds."

"That's correct. Twenty-five points are awarded to the Villains. Now on to the final round. Remember, the generals will have to answer this one on their own without help from their teams or the trivia captains. Captains, please return to your seats."

While Tara, Jordana, and Hunter sat down, Gordy took a sealed envelope out of his pocket. He opened it and unfolded the paper inside, laying it flat on the podium. Reading carefully, he said, "This sewing machine has been a fixture in the arts and crafts cabin ever since I took over as director. What is the nickname of this sewing machine?"

I looked over at Perry and hit the buzzer with lightning speed. "Big Bertha?"

"Correct," Gordy cried.

The Gold Team came rushing up to the podium as Perry tipped his imaginary hat to me. When the excitement died down, Gordy sent everyone back to their seats so he could announce the final scores and the winner of Chinooka's one-hundredth Color War games and the coveted Gordy.

The tennis court was dead silent as Gordy conferred with the other judges on the scores. They stood in a semicircle, comparing notes from their clipboards. After what seemed like an eternity, Gordy walked over the podium. He tapped the microphone a few times to make sure it was on, and then said, "I've been the director of Camp Chinooka for thirty-five years and head judge of thirty-five Color Wars. Never before have I seen such a close matchup between teams. However, it is with great pleasure that I announce that the winner of the Camp Chinooka Centennial Color War—the Heroes!"

The Gold Team went absolutely crazy at the news, cheering, hugging, and high-fiving each other. A few of the younger campers were even crying, simply overwhelmed with excitement. Over on the Villains' side, one of the camper captains was leading their team in a cheer to boost their spirits. When they finished, Gordy gave them the nod that it was okay to go join the Gold Team. The formally divided Chinooka was once again a united camp. Out of the crowd of campers, I spotted Perry walking toward me, waving a small white flag.

"General Goldstein, I applaud your victory," he said, clapping as he approached.

"Thank you, General Gillman. Does this white flag mean you're surrendering?"

"Completely," he said, taking me in his arms for a long and passionate kiss.

"I missed you, too," I whispered back to him when we finally broke apart.

Gordy returned to the microphone and asked everyone to take their seats again. It took a few more minutes for the noise to die down. At last, Gordy spoke. "As many of you know, tradition dictates that, on the final night of Color War, I also announce the winner of The Gordy. This year was especially close, with two groups taking the lead early in the summer. I've carefully reviewed the point totals, including the bonus points awarded from the Rope Burn Battle and the winning Color War team general."

I looked around the tennis courts and saw pockets of

Cedar girls with their eyes closed, holding hands, anxiously waiting for the winner to be announced. I closed my eyes and grasped Perry's arm.

Gordy continued, "The winners of this summer's Gordy Award are the Cedar girls *and* the Birch boys. For the first time ever in Chinooka's history, it's a tie."

Both groups jumped to their feet. Perry pulled me in for a quick kiss before running off to celebrate with his staff. The Cedar counselors hurried over to congratulate me. Not only had I survived the whole summer as head counselor for the Cedar girls, a feat accomplished by only a small handful of my predecessors, but I'd led them to a Gordy win.

CHAPTER NINETEEN

Color War was always followed by Lazy Day. After a week of wall-to-wall events and activities, on Lazy Day, the campers were able to sleep in, hang by the pool or lake, and just relax. With the winner of The Gordy already announced, there were no points or titles at stake. The kids could do as much or as little as they wanted with no consequences.

Gordy left three different itineraries in my mailbox: one for Washington DC, one for Boston, and one for New York City. Perry and I were going to present each one to the campers and let them vote on the trip they wanted. When we gathered everyone later that day, some of the CITs were already making pitches for the city they wanted to visit. I could hear Tara trying to talk some of the girls in Bunk Fourteen into voting for New York.

Perry took the stage and congratulated the campers on their win while the trip itineraries were passed around. As he started to read the New York itinerary, I noticed the dates printed on the top of the page. The trip fell smack over Alicia and Joshua's wedding weekend. If the campers voted for New York, we would be staying just blocks from their reception at The St. Regis Hotel. Jordana noticed me clutching the piece of paper in my hand to the point of white knuckles and asked me if I was all right. I motioned for Tara to come sit next to me on one of the benches.

"What'd I do?" she asked as she sat down.

"I'm just curious why you're pushing so hard to go to New York City?"

"New York's awesome," she said.

"It's definitely awesome, but DC and Boston are pretty great, too."

"They're okay," Tara said, shrugging her shoulders.

She wasn't going to be any help in trying to convince the other campers to choose one of the other cities, so I took matters into my own hands and joined Perry on the stage. When he finished the New York spiel, I grabbed the other two papers from his hand and made the very best cases I could for DC and Boston. Perry looked at me like I'd lost my mind.

"What's with the hard sell? You getting kickbacks from the DC and Boston Chambers of Commerce I don't know about?" he whispered when I took my seat.

"I can't go to New York."

He instructed the counselors to pass out the ballots and pulled me to the side of the stage. "What's going on, Gigi?"

"Joshua and Alicia are getting married that weekend."

His eyes opened wide with surprise. "I thought she was having cold feet. Isn't that what he came here to tell you?"

"When I spoke to Jamie last night, he said as far as he's heard, the wedding's still on," I said.

Perry's big brown eyes softened. "Are you okay?"

"I just can't imagine being so close and not actually being there to see Alicia walk down the aisle."

"Maybe you should go see her and explain yourself. She still doesn't know the real reason her best friend isn't going to be there to see her get married. You owe her that, don't you think? Doesn't she deserve some sort of closure on your friendship?"

I stood up to face him. "Our friendship isn't over. I needed a break from it. From them."

"It *is* over, Gigi. It was over the minute you didn't tell her about you and Joshua. To pretend otherwise is just selfish."

His detachment was so hypocritical. His half-completed symphony spoke volumes about the fact that he'd never found closure after Annie died. Anyone he let close to him could see his guilt had morphed into an insurmountable writer's block. "You told me Annie's parents want nothing to do with you, right? That you've never explained to them what happened that night? How come?"

He stood up and placed his pointer finger lightly over my mouth. "Gigi, don't do this."

I pushed his finger away more forcefully than intended. "No, really. Tell me, Perry. Where's your closure?"

Before he could answer, Tara came hurrying over to us. Almost breathless, she told us that the votes had been tallied and that Cedar and Birch were going to New York City.

"Looks like we're going to your hometown, Princess," Perry said, trying to break the tension between us.

I raised my eyebrows. "And Annie's."

Perry interlaced his fingers with mine. He pulled me toward him so that we were eye to eye. I could feel his breath on my neck as he leaned in and whispered in my ear. "I'm ready for closure. Are you?"

I nodded, and he kissed me on the forehead, as if to seal the deal we'd just made—to go to New York and confront our pasts.

Only a week later, Perry and I stood with the Cedar and Birch campers and counselors in the lobby of the Times Square Marriott Marquee. We'd taken them to see the Broadway musical *Wicked* and decided to split up for dinner. I took half the campers down to Chinatown, and Perry took the rest to a restaurant in Little Italy. Jamie was planning on meeting me at one of my favorite Chinese restaurants, Wo Hop, so we could catch up a bit before I went back to his apartment to pick up the rest of the finished costumes for the show.

Getting thirty kids safely through Times Square and down to Mott Street was no easy feat. The air was thick and steamy. I'd forgotten how muggy New York City could be in the summertime compared to the Poconos. We squeezed onto the N train and were met by a wall of heat. The air-conditioning wasn't working in our car, but there were too many of us to switch to a different one. Finally, we got to Canal Street, and I led the way out of the subway station toward the restaurant.

When we finally arrived, Jamie was standing outside waiting for us. He looked impossibly cool in his jeans, T-shirt, and blazer. I ran and threw my arms around his neck. My hair and clothes were noticeably damp from the humidity. He was bone dry. "How are you not even a little bit sweaty?" I asked in amazement.

"Botox."

"Seriously?"

"Just a little in each arm pit. Shall we?" he said, holding the door open and ushering us in.

Wo Hop was one of my favorite Chinatown spots. Open all night, they had two dining rooms, one downstairs and one upstairs. The roomy upstairs restaurant had tablecloths and laminated menus. The tiny basement restaurant held only a handful of booths covered with paper tablecloths and paper menus. I was of the opinion it had better food than its upstairs counterpart, but you couldn't make a reservation there. It was cramped and no frills but also one of the few places I remembered going to with my father as a little girl. On nights my mother had a charity event or committee meeting, we'd take the subway from our uptown apartment down to Mott Street. I'd hold his hand as we walked down the dark and hidden staircase to the restaurant. When a table finally opened up, he'd order us each a Hot and Sour soup and two dishes to share as he pointed out the famous signed headshots that made up the wallpaper of the room. Having dinner there felt special—like we'd wandered off the beaten path to our own exclusive eatery. He loved how removed it was, and I loved how undivided his attention was in a place where we never ran into anyone he knew.

The hostess greeted Jamie and me at the entrance and asked if we wanted a table upstairs or downstairs. Jamie looked to me for instruction.

"I have a reservation for upstairs," I said, ushering the kids to the top of the staircase.

Jamie and I followed the hostess to three large, round

tables. After making sure I'd distributed enough counselor chaperones, I took a seat next to Jamie at the largest table.

"So what's good here?" he said, perusing the menu.

"Everything, although just about anything would taste good to me after eating camp food all summer. Want to share the hot and spicy shrimp?"

"Speaking of hot and spicy, how's Mr. Gillman?" Jamie teased.

I blushed all over. "He's good—great, actually."

"So then, where is Mr. Wonderful tonight? Didn't you say he's in New York with you?"

"He's taking the rest of the campers to a restaurant in Little Italy," I said.

"Should we all meet up after dinner?"

"He has something he wants to take care of tonight."

Jamie nodded. "What about you? Are you planning to see Alicia?"

"All those months ago, I told you I was running away to Chinooka to protect Alicia. It was a lie. I was protecting myself. It was wrong of me to disappear then, but it would be even more selfish to suddenly reappear now."

Jamie raised his eyebrows and offered a questioning gaze. "You told me she's having cold feet, right? There's a very big piece of this puzzle she's still missing. You still don't think she deserves to know the truth?"

"I should've told her about me and Joshua. I know that, but it's too late now."

"It's never too late for honesty," he said, sipping his tea.

Jamie put his arm around me and turned the conversation to Chinooka. As delicious heaping plates of Moo Shu Chicken, Lo Mein, and Beef and Broccoli were ushered out on platters, I told him about everything from Color War to the final rehearsals of *Fiddler*. When the waitress set down orange slices and fortune cookies for dessert, Jamie reached over to the center of the table and took two of each. He set them down in front of us. As was our tradition, we counted to three and then opened the fortune cookies at the exact same time. I motioned for him to read his aloud.

He cleared his throat and read off the small paper. "You have the skills and experiences that will equip you for a whole new adventure."

I raised my eyebrows. "That sounds promising. Now mine," I said, breaking the cookie in half. "The heart of a true friend is a deep abyss, at the bottom of which you will always find forgiveness."

We both were silent. Jamie raised his teacup in the air for a toast. I lifted mine to meet it.

I paid the check and sent the campers back to the hotel with the other counselors so I could go to Jamie's apartment. Jamie pointed me to the bedroom where the costumes were hanging on a foldable clothing rack. I unzipped the garment bags to examine each one.

"I'm gonna open a bottle of red, want some?" Jamie shouted from the kitchen.

"Just a small glass. We have an early day tomorrow," I yelled back.

The downstairs buzzer rang and Jamie called out to me to ask me to grab the door.

I walked over to answer it. "Expecting company?"

"It's probably Thom," he said. "Want some cheese with the wine? That thing about being hungry an hour after you eat Chinese food is totally true. I'm starving."

"How have you not given him a key yet? You guys have been dating for what, four years?"

"Three and a half," he said.

I poked my head into his galley kitchen as I passed. "You're unbelievable. He's a good guy. Commit to him. Be happy."

Jamie reached up to a high shelf to pull down two wine glasses. "You're giving me love advice? That's rich."

I stuck out my tongue and went to answer the door.

I opened it and Alicia looked absolutely shocked to see me standing there. Before I could react, she threw her arms around me and pulled me into a tight embrace.

"I knew you'd show up," she said excitedly. "I knew you wouldn't miss the wedding."

I looked into her eyes, which were warm and welcoming. I hugged her again, my own eyes welling up with tears. It was the complete opposite of the reaction I'd expected, and the full realization of just how much I'd missed my best friend bubbled to surface like a teakettle that'd been left on the stove too long.

"Gigi, what's wrong?" Alicia asked, stepping back and away from me.

"I'm just so happy to see you," I managed to choke out. "What are you doing here?"

She walked past me and into the living room, holding a large garment bag over her head. She laid it down across the couch and sank down into Jamie's big armchair. I sat across from her.

"I don't know what came over me, but I decided to try on my wedding dress. It fit like a glove when I bought it. I literally didn't need one thing altered, but I slipped it on tonight and it's...it's just all wrong. Jamie was the first person I thought of who could help. Well, actually you were, but I didn't know you were in New York."

"Alicia…"

"It's okay. Joshua told me he tracked you down at Chinooka."

I shook my head in disbelief. "Joshua told you he came to see me?"

"I'm sure he told you we hit a bit of a rough patch. He knew how much it would mean to me to have you at the wedding. I can only guess you showing up is my wedding gift from him?"

My head was swimming with questions. "You think I'm his gift to you?"

"Gigi, I know why you had to disappear this summer. Your parents put all that pressure on you to go to law school, and then you got fired from your job. I'm sorry I wasn't there for you more when you needed me. Maybe if I was, you wouldn't have felt like you had to run away."

Jamie stepped into the living room holding two glasses of wine and a small cheese plate. His mouth dropped open when he saw Alicia sitting in his favorite chair.

Alicia stood up, gave Jamie a kiss on each cheek, and continued talking. "You don't have to be embarrassed. Ever since Joshua told me you were at Chinooka, do you know how many afternoons I've sat at my desk wishing I could quit my job and go back to camp with you?"

My eyes pricked with tears. I blinked them back. "Do you know how many afternoons I've wished that too?"

She smiled warmly, stood up, and started unzipping the gown from its the bag. "I don't know—things have just felt so different with you away, but I can't put my finger on it. I wanted to have the wedding before my promotion started, but then it all started to feel too rushed and I told Joshua I wanted to postpone. I think that's when he went to find you at camp."

"He told me you were having cold feet."

"He came home and I came to my senses. I realized I was acting crazy. How can an eighteen-year relationship feel rushed? Who wouldn't want what we have?"

Alicia looked over at me for some unique insight, the kind I used to ungrudgingly provide, but I remained silent. She walked into Jamie's kitchen to pour herself a glass of wine and kept talking. "It's funny, I'd always suspected he was seeing someone when I was in London, but he was never honest about it, so a few weeks ago I called him out. He finally came clean about the fact that he'd dated someone. I can't be mad, though, right? I mean, *I* ended things with *him*. I was seeing someone else too. But still, he should have told me. The truth is I'm actually glad it happened. We've been together so long it was good for us both to have that time to explore other people, have other experiences."

She walked out of the kitchen, put the wine glass down on a coaster on the coffee table, and looked over at Jamie. "Should I try the dress on in your room? I don't know what it is but something's just not right with it. I need your expert hands, Jamie. Actually, since I have both of you here, even better."

"Did he tell you anything about who she was?" Jamie asked.

"No, not much. Some girl he met out at a bar or something. I think he was looking for something meaningless to help get over me."

Jamie looked over in my direction, his eyes wide with insistence. Maybe he was right? What if her cold feet weren't actually nerves, but doubt? I was the reason for it, only she had no idea. I squeezed my eyes shut and blurted out, "It was me."

"What was you?"

I swallowed hard. "I was the girl."

Alicia narrowed her eyes. I could tell she was trying to convince herself that what I'd said had a different meaning than the obvious. She stepped away from the dress and stood in front of me. "What are you saying, Gigi?"

"I was the girl Joshua was with while you were in London." I stepped back and braced myself for whatever was going to happen next. Nothing came but stunned silence. It was worse than any impact would have been. "Please, Ali, say something," I begged.

"That doesn't make any sense. You would never do that to me."

I reached for her. "I didn't mean to. No, that's not true. I did want it to happen—I just never expected it to. You told him you were moving on, that you might even be moving to London. I actually convinced myself you'd even be happy for us. It sounds insane to me now. God, how can I explain this to you in a way that you could ever understand?"

"I'm not an idiot, Gigi. I know you've always had a crush on him, I just never in a million years thought you would act on it," she said, her jaw clenched so tightly she looked distorted. "How long did you wait before you made a play for him?"

Alicia's face was ashen. My always-composed best friend was shaking with anger, trying to grasp how the two people she loved most in the world had hurt her in the worst way possible. I looked over at Jamie and knew what I had to do for her, the person who had always been there for me so unconditionally, supporting me through every moment of my life. Before I could think twice, I fell on my sword.

"Not long. A few days after you ended it, he came over to the apartment to pick up some of his stuff. Things just spiraled from there."

"And what happened? As soon as he got there, you just threw yourself at him?" she asked.

"Yes, I threw myself at him," I said resolutely.

"Did you even think about me?" she asked, the tears rolling down her cheeks. "How it would hurt me?"

I wanted to tell her that I'd thought about her a million times. That guilt and regret had enveloped my life and I'd only recently begun to dig myself out of that darkness. I wanted to explain how sorry I was, and how deeply I missed her. Instead, I said nothing and let her keep on believing that I was the instigator, the predator, the one who'd pursued Joshua, and not that our wrongdoings had been mutual.

"You're disgusting. I can't even look at you. I have to go. Jamie, I'll come back for the dress tomorrow," she said, fighting her way to the door.

"Ali, please." I grabbed her shoulder.

"Get off me!" she screamed like a wounded animal.

I peeled my fingers away and she raced to the front door. Her hand was on the knob when she suddenly turned on her heels to face me.

"Why'd he go see you at Chinooka?"

"Ali…"

"Is it over Gigi?"

"It is. It has been for months. Ever since you got back from London. He chose you."

She let out a long low sigh. "Did he?"

She opened the door and slammed it hard behind her. After I heard the elevator door close, I stepped out into the hallway. I made it a few feet before I slid to the floor, my body shaking with sobs. Jamie came out and sat with me until I'd calmed down enough to be able to leave. He offered to help me get a cab, but I told him I wanted to walk. I set off uptown and somehow, after wandering for what felt like hours, found myself in front of my parents' apartment building. I went inside and took the elevator to their floor. I got to their door and knocked softly. A few seconds later, my father called out, "Who's there?"

He'd always been a much lighter sleeper than my mother.

"It's Georgie," I answered as he unlocked the deadbolt. He was the only person who ever called me that. It used to make me feel as though he hardly knew me, but now I wondered if it wasn't something special, something only he and I shared.

"Georgie, what are you doing here? What's the matter?" he asked, wrapping his robe tightly around himself.

"Hi, Daddy, can we maybe go somewhere to talk?"

"Just give me a second to throw something on," he answered.

I appreciated his calm nature. Other parents might panic at their child showing up at their door so late at night, especially when they were supposed to be in Pennsylvania. Not my father. With him, nothing was a problem until it was a problem. I used to interpret his composure as disinterest, but now I knew it was just his way. I nodded and waited in the hallway for him. A few minutes later he came out in jeans and a Columbia University sweatshirt.

"Where to?" he asked.

"Anywhere. I don't care where we go."

"Have you eaten today?"

"I had dinner at Wo Hop."

"Upstairs or downstairs?" he asked.

"Upstairs."

"Then you didn't really eat. Let's grab a cab."

We jumped in a taxi and headed back down to Mott Street and Wo Hop. This time, when the hostess asked where we wanted to sit, I took his hand, and we descended down the long, dark, narrow stairway to the basement restaurant. It was a little after midnight, but every table was full. When two off-duty police officers finally finished, we slid into their booth.

My father handed me the paper menu, but I put it down and asked him to order for us. When the waitress came over, he ordered two Hot and Sour soups and a Moo Goo Gai Pan. He poured some tea and sat back in his seat as if to tell me I had the floor to speak. I blew on the hot tea but put it down without taking a sip. I looked up at my father and realized that, for the first time in a long time, I had his full and undivided attention.

"I'm not sure where to begin," I said.

"I usually tell my clients to just start at the beginning."

I inhaled deeply. "Joshua came to see me at Chinooka."

"I know. He came to my office and pleaded with me to tell him where you were. I hesitated at first, but then I remembered that night in the Hamptons."

"Dad, we don't have to rehash that night," I said, thinking of the conversation with my mother on the rowboat.

The Hot and Sour soup came. My father passed me the plate of crispy noodles, and we both crunched them up and let the pieces fall into our bowls. I took a few spoonfuls of the soup and then let the whole story of

Joshua's visit to Chinooka pour out. When I was finished, he simply said, "So their wedding's on?"

"I hope so," I said, as tears started rolling down my face. My father picked the napkin off his lap and wiped them away. "I saw Alicia tonight. She had no idea about Joshua and me. I told her I instigated the whole thing."

He leaned into the table. "You gave Joshua a pass?"

"No, no, I finally told the truth. I did instigate it. I may not have invited him over that first night, but I'd been ready to act on those feelings for years, long before the thought ever crossed his mind. I'm so sorry, Dad."

"For what?" he asked.

"For thinking I knew everything I needed to know when I saw you with that girl in the Hamptons. I know now it's not that black and white."

"Things with me and your mother are incredibly complicated, but that doesn't excuse all of my behavior and many of my decisions."

I nodded. Even though my mother's visit had revealed things about my parents' relationship that I was just beginning to wrap my head around, one thing was clear—they'd both played a part in its breakdown. His acknowledgment of his role in it all was more than I expected, but just what I needed to hear to put us back on an even plane.

The Moo Goo Gai Pan arrived, but I was too full to eat any. My father took two large helpings and covered them in duck sauce. Between forkfuls, he asked me about the rest of my summer at Chinooka. I gave him the highlights and then told him about Perry.

"Are you happy with him, Georgie?" he asked.

"I am," I answered.

"And he's a good guy?"

"He's a Gershwin fan," I said.

"So he's a very good guy," he said, winking at me.

"Dad, do you think Alicia will ever forgive me?"

He took hold of my hands from across the table. "You'd be surprised at some people's capacity to forgive, Georgie."

"You really believe that?"

He laughed, and I asked him what could possibly be so funny.

"You know, when you were a little girl you'd ask me a question, and that question would lead to another question, which would lead to ten more questions. You were convinced I had the answers to all of them," he said.

"Didn't you?"

"Not even close, but I never wanted to disappoint you," he said in a tone softer than I'd ever heard him use with me. He picked the check up off the table. "Shall we?" he said, leading the way out of the restaurant.

The sidewalk was wet and I could see we'd missed a summer storm. The rain had broken the humidity, and the air was much cooler and more forgiving. We took a taxi back uptown, and he dropped me back off at the hotel. As I climbed out of the car, he pulled me in for a hug. It felt good to have his big arms around me like I was a little girl again. When he finally let go, I got out of the cab and watched it drive away.

Perry was sitting in the lobby when I walked in. As soon as he saw me, he put his arms out. I gratefully let him pull me close to his chest. His shirt smelled like the cheap detergent they used at camp. I breathed it in and missed Chinooka.

"Let's take a walk somewhere. The kids are all in their rooms, and I have counselors stationed on all the floors to make sure they stay there," he said.

He took my hand, and I let him guide me through the double doors, out to the noisy street. It was well after midnight, and Times Square was as lively as if it were mid-day.

"This is your city. Lead the way, Princess," he said, trying to make me smile.

We turned onto Seventh Avenue, and I let the whole story pour out. Perry listened to every word, starting with what happened with Alicia and through the conversation with my father. When I was done, he told me he was proud of how honest I'd been with them both.

Then, he took over, telling me everything about his meeting with Annie's parents. He'd told them all about his relationship with Annie and how much he'd loved her. He'd gone into detail about that fateful night in the desert, when he left her at the bar. He answered every question about those last few hours and the role he'd played in them. When he finished, they'd thanked him for his honesty and candor. Most importantly, they forgave him, admitting that they'd known their daughter liked to push boundaries and live on the edge.

Perry looked like a different man. His eyes were brighter. His stance more assured. The shame he'd been carrying around since that night might never totally be gone, but it had, for the moment, been eased. Time would do the rest.

We continued walking until we reached the fountain at Lincoln Center. We sat down on the edge of the pool and people-watched.

"Is it always like this?" Perry asked.

"All the people, you mean? Yeah, on a beautiful summer night like this one, you can count on it," I said. "Remember one of the first nights of camp, when we played the Dating Game?"

"Of course, I remember. You couldn't stand me then," he teased.

"Remember that question about your perfect date and your answer about Little Venice and The Whispering Gallery?"

He nodded.

"Well, this is mine," I said.

"What is?"

"Sitting here like this. Both of us, just like this."

He put his arm around me and pulled me close to his chest. "Even with the taxis honking and the sirens screaming?"

"Just close your eyes and listen." I looked up and saw his eyes were tightly closed. A smile crept across his face "It's the symphony of the city," I said.

"It sure is," he replied.

He kissed me, and we walked back to the hotel. The next few days in New York were hectic, but we accomplished everything we'd set out to. And when it was time to get on the bus to go back to camp, I was ready to go home.

CHAPTER TWENTY

When we got back from New York, there was only one full week left at camp. The kids would perform *Fiddler on the Roof* on the last night, leaving only a few more rehearsals and just days for me to finish the rest of the costumes. All around Chinooka, things were winding down. At the lake, the lifeguards were administering Red Cross certification tests. At the different activity cabins, campers were finishing up their projects. At night, in the gazebos, the Birch boys and Cedar girls were trying to make up for lost time, becoming bolder and more strategic in their tactics toward the opposite sex. Everyone wanted a good story to take home with them.

Gordy agreed to let Jamie spend the last week of camp in one of the empty off-season cabins so he could help me with the final preparations for the show. Although he'd been an absolute lifesaver, I couldn't help but wonder why Jamie was giving so much of his time and energy to this project. When I finally got him alone the night before the show, I confronted him. He was working on Big Bertha, finishing Motel the tailor's suit for the wedding scene while I was hand sewing the lace trim on Tzeidel's wedding veil. When he took out his earphones, I seized the opportunity and brought the finished veil over to him so he could inspect my work.

"This is gorgeous, Gigi," he said, studying every inch of it.

"How's the rest of the suit coming along?" I asked.

"Almost finished," he said, holding up a pant leg to show me. "I see why you asked me to bring up your sewing machine. Big Bertha's kind of a bitch."

"Wow, it's incredible," I said, admiring all the details he'd added. His abilities still astounded me. "Jamie, can I ask you a question?"

"Sure," he replied.

"Why are you here?

He folded the jacket and laid it on top of the sewing machine. "You needed my help," he answered.

"I know, and I can't thank you enough for all you've done, but really, Jamie, is there another reason?"

He sat back down. I could see his eyes searching for the right answer. "I guess for the same reason you're here."

I nodded in understanding. He'd been unhappy with the direction of his career for a long time. He'd confided in me more than once that he felt stuck and stalled, doing mediocre work that he didn't believe in. He'd been looking for an escape for a while, and, like me, he'd found it at Chinooka. I sat down beside him and took his hand in mine. "The show's over tomorrow night. Camp's over on Sunday. In forty-eight hours, we both turn back into pumpkins," I said.

An electrified smile crept across his face. "We don't have to."

"I don't know about you, but I don't think I have the stamina to be a professional counselor. These girls have worn me out."

"That's not what I mean. Gigi, look around at what we created together," he said, motioning to the racks and racks of costumes.

I stood up and took a turn around the room. He was right. In a little less than eight weeks, we'd produced some pretty extraordinary pieces. The wedding gown was our crowning achievement. It could easily be on a mannequin at any high-end bridal boutique. "You're right. We did good, partner."

"Exactly my point. What if we really tried it?"

"Tried what?"

"To be partners. Designing partners."

"Are you crazy? We can't be partners! What are you talking about? Starting our own label?"

"Badgley Mischka did it. And Georgina Chapman and Keren Craig started Marchesa together, didn't they?"

I hadn't seen him looking so excited since the day we met for our first challenge on *Top Designer*. I felt bad bursting his bubble, but I had to acknowledge the truth. "I'm currently a fashion pariah, and you're the guy who got kicked off first."

"Frankly, my dear, I don't give a damn," he said, quoting the famous line from *Gone with the Wind*.

"Jamie, we could lose everything," I said.

"You just said it yourself, you're a pariah, and I'm the guy who got kicked off first. What do we have to lose? Do this with me, Gigi. Take a chance on us."

He was right. What did either of us really have to lose? In a few days, I'd be back to being an unemployed designer, and he'd be returning to a job he hated. We'd both poured more heart and effort into these costumes than we'd given to anything else in memory. The end result spoke for itself. "Okay, let's do it."

Jamie pulled me in for a hug. "Can you break the news to Big Bertha that she isn't joining our new company?"

"I think she knows that her place is here."

We worked straight through the night to finish the costumes. As the sun came up over Lake Chinooka, the last of the buttons were tightened, threads snipped, and the final skirts hemmed. Exhausted, we congratulated ourselves on a job well done and what we hoped would be the first of many completed collections.

Later, I went back to the cabin to catch a few minutes of shut-eye. I'd only been asleep about forty-five minutes when Hannah woke me, chirping away about how nervous she was for the show later that night. I reassured her she'd be great and promised to meet her at the amphitheater early to run some lines. I climbed out of bed and looked around the room. Trunks and duffle bags were strewn all over the floor. Most of the girls were busy packing and cleaning before breakfast. I tiptoed around the mess to grab my bathrobe and shower caddy. Then, for the last time, I sprinted across the field to the shower house, the one place at Chinooka I was definitely *not* going to miss.

When I was dressed, I met up with the rest of the camp in the dining hall. Breakfast was well underway, and Gordy was at the microphone about to make some morning announcements. Perry saw me walk in and motioned for me to come sit next to him as Gordy whistled to get the room's attention.

"I'm sad to say this is our last full day together," Gordy said. "The activity cabins will be open all day, so make sure to go pick up your projects. Counselors, please ensure that your groups have their packed trunks and duffle bags on their bunk porches no later than 3:00. Maintenance will be around to pick them up. Tonight, *Fiddler on the Roof* will be performed at the Lakeside Amphitheater, starting at 6:00. The performance will be followed by the final banquet and slide show. Have a great last day at Chinooka."

The campers went back to eating and talking. Perry passed me over a cup of coffee.

"Bless you," I said, stirring in some milk and sugar.

"I saw Jamie coming back to his cabin around 5:00 this morning. The two of you were really burning the midnight oil."

"We finished everything." I yawned. "The costumes are done. What were you doing up at that hour?"

"Composing. I think I finally broke through my writer's block. About eight weeks too late, but better late than never. At least I'm going back to London with a direction to take my composition in."

"London," I repeated. We'd both been actively avoiding that topic for the last few weeks.

He kissed me on my forehead and stroked my hair. I was snuggling into him when Hannah ran over, interrupting us.

"Gigi, can we run lines now?" she pleaded.

"Sure, just give me a second," I said. She backed a few feet away but had her eyes firmly on us. Perry let go of my hand.

"Go. I'll see you at the amphitheater later," Perry said.

"You don't want to get in a last-minute rehearsal?"

He picked up his violin case from the ground. "Did you forget I'm a ringer?"

"What I forgot was just how modest you are," I said.

When Hannah and I arrived at the amphitheater, the backstage crew was putting the finishing touches on the sets while Davis and Jackie directed them where to place the props and pieces of scenery. When they were done, the space was completely transformed. Davis and Jackie were not only using the center stage but also the surrounding areas to turn the whole amphitheater into the fictional town of Anatevka. Davis had told me the design was intended so that everyone in the audience would feel like they were living in that small Russian village along with the characters in the play. I'd never seen the show performed like that and knew it would be something special.

When I got back to the cabin, Jordana was helping Madison get a summer's worth of stuff into her trunk and two duffle bags while the rest of the girls were helping each other carry their bags out to the porch for pickup. I walked to each of the Cedar cabins and made sure the girls were on schedule for the luggage pickup. Most of the girls had long finished and were sitting on the beds, writing out their goodbye messages in each other's autograph books. When I got to Michelle and Brooke's cabin, Candice ran over to me and asked me to write something in hers. I thought carefully, and then scribbled out, "To my favorite troublemaker, thanks for keeping me on my toes." I handed the book back to her and saw a big smile creep across her face. I made the rest of my rounds and headed back to the amphitheater to help get the kids ready for the performance.

As I was doing one last inspection, Perry walked in. His dark wavy hair was tied back in a neat ponytail, and the stubble he'd been letting grow out for the show was now a neat beard. He led me behind one of the racks and leaned in to kiss me.

"Is the beard scratching you?" he asked.

I rubbed my hand across his chin. "No, I like it. You look very dignified."

He smiled. "Maybe I won't shave it off tomorrow, then. I'll go back to London a bearded wonder," he said, leaning into me for another kiss.

I turned away from him. "Maybe."

He pulled me in close, and I nuzzled into the lapels of his jacket. We stood together, locked in an embrace, as the cast started trickling in. When Hannah called my name, I pulled away to help her.

"See you at curtain time?" Perry called to me as he walked toward the boys' side.

"I'll be the one cheering your name from stage left," I answered.

He flashed a smile and ducked under the dividing curtain.

Around six, the entire camp filed into the amphitheater. Gordy took his usual place in the center of the front row, and the rest of the senior staff sat down on both sides of him. I peeked out from behind the stage curtain and saw the Cedar girls and Birch boys strategically picking their seats for the two-and-a-half hour performance. When the campers and counselors were finally seated, Jackie and Davis stepped to the center of the stage and welcomed all of Camp Chinooka to the opening—and closing—night of *Fiddler on the Roof.*

Then, they cued the camper operating the spotlight to the back of the amphitheater, where Perry stood, waiting to begin his cadenza.

When the spotlight hit the iridescent material of his fiddler's suit, reflecting the blue-gold hue into the audience, I heard actual gasps. He looked amazing—like a star that had just fallen out of the sky. Without a moment's hesitation, Perry picked up the bow of his violin and played the familiar and haunting opening of the show. Every eye in the audience followed him as he danced and played up and down the aisles, inviting all the onlookers to be transported to Anatevka with him. When he finally got to the stage and took his perch atop Tevye's house, the rest of the orchestra joined him, playing the show's overture while the cast took their places for the opening number. Perry hit the final note, and the entire audience was on their feet cheering. I tipped my imaginary hat to his brilliance and blew him a kiss. He pretended to catch the kiss in the palm of his hand and put it in the pocket of his suit. Then, he turned his attention back to the show, which was now fully underway. I gave him a small wave and retreated to the hidden backstage area to help Jamie prep the costume changes for the wedding scene at the end of Act One.

Like two old theater pros, Jamie and I worked as a perfectly synchronized team, helping the cast into the costumes. I'd only seen the cast rehearse during the day. From what Jackie had told me, seeing this particular scene at night was going to be a totally different experience.

Davis had staged it so the wedding processional would come down the two main aisles of the amphitheater, the men on one aisle, and the women on the other. The entire arena would be lit up with candles as they sang the famous song 'Sunrise, Sunset' and walked toward the large wedding canopy in the center of the stage.

I closed my eyes to listen to the powerful lyrics of 'Sunrise, Sunset' and immediately thought of Alicia on her own wedding day. How nervous and excited she must have felt as her parents escorted her to her own wedding canopy. How beautiful she must have looked in her dress, surrounded by votive candles and white flowers. I opened my eyes and looked out into the audience and saw many of the girls, and even some of the boys dabbing the corners of their eyes. Then, I spotted her.

Alicia was sitting in the last row of the theater, staring right back at me.

All the blood rushed to my feet. I grabbed hold of the curtain to steady myself. I took a deep breath and glanced back out into the audience. Our gazes met again and then drifted over to the center of the theater. Together, we watched as the bride and groom walked underneath the chuppah—a symbol of the home the new couple would build.

Together, Alicia and I witnessed them exchange rings and drink from the same kiddush cup. We listened to the show's choir sing the beautiful and poignant lyrics. Tears streamed down both of our faces as the groom lifted the bride's veil to kiss her before stepping on the glass, signifying the end of the ceremony. In my heart, I knew this would be the one and only wedding Alicia and I would ever attend together. The look on her face told me she knew it too.

I watched the rest of the show in a fog, fixated on Alicia in the audience, and terrified that if I lost sight of her for even one second she'd be gone forever. Then, in the second act, Hannah stepped forward to sing her character's big number, 'Far From The Home I Love,' the same song Alicia had belted out when she was thirteen years old. The second the spotlight hit her, Hannah looked like she was going to be sick. The orchestra played the opening notes, and it was obvious she'd forgotten the words. Ashen, she looked over to me, and I mouthed the first few to her. The orchestra restarted the song and the color returned to her face. This time, she started exactly on cue. When I looked back out into the audience, Alicia was gone.

The rest of the show flew by, and suddenly, it was time for the curtain call. Hannah looked genuinely shocked and thrilled when the audience stood up and gave her a standing ovation. Perry, the final member of the cast to come out for a bow, got the longest and loudest applause. Jackie and Davis took the stage and thanked Sally from arts and crafts for her help with the sets and the members of the Milbank Orchestral Society, who'd generously given up their time to perform the score. Then they invited Jamie and me to step forward. Jackie gushed about the costumes and all of the hours of work we'd put into the show. Perry stepped forward and presented me with a bouquet of flowers tied together with a measuring tape.

Gordy leaped onto the stage to give his standard congratulatory speech, and I ducked away to find Alicia. Perry saw me sneaking off and cornered me backstage.

"Where are you tiptoeing off to?" he asked.

"Go to the banquet with everyone. I'll meet you there," I said.

"Don't you want to go together? I mean, after tonight, I'm pretty much a bona fide celebrity around here," he teased.

"I'll meet you there, Mr. Celebrity. I have to take care of something," I said, turning from him.

He grabbed ahold of my arm. "Gigi, what's the matter?"

"I saw Alicia," I said.

"Where?"

"She was in the audience during the show. I turned away for a second and she was gone. I don't know if she's even still on the grounds. I have to try to find her."

He nodded and let go of my arm. "I'll be in the dining hall waiting for you."

I didn't have to look far. Alicia was sitting in the large gazebo on the Great Lawn, staring off toward Lake Chinooka. She didn't even turn her head when I sat down beside her, her gaze fixed on the distance. There were a million things I wanted to say, but I remained silent. We watched as the entire camp came up from the amphitheater and crossed the Great Lawn into the dining hall. When the last camper was inside, she finally spoke.

"When I got into my car tonight, I never expected to end up here. I just started driving. Then, all of a sudden, I found myself on the road to Chinooka," Alicia said. "I should've turned around right then and gone home. But, that night at Jamie's keeps playing over and over in my head. I have dreams where I ask you a million questions about how this happened. Then I have these other dreams where I scream and scream at you, and say all the things I couldn't say to you that night."

"So scream at me. Whatever it is, just say it now. Tell me I'm a terrible friend. Tell me I betrayed you and you hate me," I said, pleading with her.

She drew in a slow and steady breath. "I'm not going to ease your guilty conscience for you."

She was right. Hearing her say those words—that I

was a terrible friend who'd betrayed her—would be far easier than it'd been to admit them to myself. So, I offered her the only thing I could. "Ask me all your questions. Ask me anything."

Alicia looked surprised by my voluntary candor. She pushed her hair behind her ears. "Tell me the truth. You didn't really throw yourself at him, did you?"

"After you left for London and ended things with him, Joshua came over to the apartment to grab some of his stuff and get some advice. We had dinner and things progressed from there. I went to see him a few nights later, and we agreed it had been a mistake and would never happen again."

"But it did happen again?"

"Yes."

"And continued the whole time I was away?"

"Yes."

"I see," she said softly. "So that's the whole of it?"

I inhaled deeply. "Ali, I spent my whole life in love with him. My whole life watching from a distance. Then, suddenly he looked at me. He wanted me. It's not an excuse—it's the truth."

"Did you come here to get away from him and the wedding? Are you still in love with him?"

"When I came here, I fooled myself into thinking I was running away from Joshua and the mistakes we'd made. But this place is full of ghosts. You were everywhere I turned. What I did was inexcusable, but I swear, losing you, not him, has been the worst heartbreak of my life."

She broke down and swung her arms around herself like a hug, her shoulders shaking with sobs. I slid closer to her, and she buried her head in my chest. I wrapped my arms around her, and we stayed like that, not moving or saying a word until she finally lifted her head and took a few deep breaths to compose herself.

"I postponed the wedding. I told Joshua I need some time to figure this all out." She took a tissue out of her bag and wiped her eyes.

"I'm so sorry. That's the last thing I wanted."

She stood up, crossed the gazebo, and looked up at the sky. It was a full moon and a clear night. The light coming down illuminated the whole lawn so the old worn gazebos looked freshly painted.

"When I accused you of being jealous of me and my relationship with Joshua, I didn't mean it—at least not the way it came out. I've always known your feelings for him, right from that very first day of camp when he sat with you on the bus. I just never thought about how hard it must have been all these years, and I'm sorry for that. What I've come to realize is that we—me and Joshua—don't work without you."

I crossed over to where she stood looking out over the lawn. "Of course you do."

"No. We don't. It was never clearer to me than when you were gone. A good relationship shouldn't require an interpreter." She turned to me. "The costumes and the show were beautiful, Gigi. The wedding and wedding dress, especially. It was exactly what a wedding should be."

I hadn't told her I had anything to do with making the costumes, but because she was Alicia, she knew.

"You know, it's funny," Alicia said. "This place looks just the same as it did when we were campers, but it feels different to be standing here now."

"I know exactly what you mean."

"I'm jealous you were able to squeeze out one more summer here."

"You feel that chill in the air?" I said, wrapping my arms around my body. "Summer's practically over."

She slipped her arms into a light coat. "Practically, but I think we have a few good days left ahead of us."

"I hope so," I said.

"Me too."

CHAPTER TWENTY-ONE

I collected myself and went into the dining hall, where the banquet was well underway. I searched the room and saw Jordana sitting with most of the girls from Bunk Fourteen. She'd saved me a place next to her, and when I slid onto the bench, she pushed a plate of food toward me.

"I figured you'd want to get in your last bites of camp food," she said, rolling her eyes.

I pushed the food around my plate until Gordy went up to the microphone and asked one of the kitchen staff to turn off the lights in the dining hall. Perry walked to the front of the room, where the large white viewing screen was set up. As the first picture flashed onto the screen, he brought his violin up to his chin and played the opening notes of 'Rhapsody in Blue.' He looked out into the audience, caught my eye, and winked right at me. It would always be our song. Then, he seamlessly transitioned over to his guitar and more current tunes, while dozens of photos appeared behind him.

The photography counselor had done a great job

capturing so many moments from the summer. From Parent's Weekend to Color War, rehearsals for *Fiddler on the Roof,* and the Rope Burn Battle, everything was there. Then, to my horror, Perry started playing Gershwin's 'Let's Call the Whole Thing Off' as a photo montage depicting our summer-long rivalry popped onto the screen. Finally, Perry played a slowed-down version of 'Summer Nights' as photos of Chinooka couples appeared on the screen. First up were Madison and Alex Shane, who had defied all the skeptics—me included—by staying together throughout the summer. I looked over at them. Madison was leaning back and into Alex Shane's chest, watching the show. She'd never looked happier or more at ease with him. She finally believed what Alex Shane had known all along—she was special.

When the slide show was over, Gordy thanked Perry and invited him to join him at the microphone. Perry looked confused as he made his way to the center of the dining hall. Gordy put his arm around him and spoke. "For one-hundred summers, we've welcomed campers and staff through the gates of Camp Chinooka who've made it their home away from home. I'm sad to say this is the last summer one of our most beloved counselors will be making Chinooka his home. For four summers, Perry Gillman has been head counselor for Birch. He's led his group to four Gordy Award wins and been our resident musician. Last week, Perry informed me he won't be returning next summer so that he can really focus on his music career. I wanted to take the opportunity to personally thank him for always going the extra mile and being the living embodiment of what Chinooka spirit is all about."

Perry was beet red. He thanked Gordy for his words, shook his hand, and tried to sit down.

"Not just yet, young man, we're not through with you," Gordy said, pulling Perry back up to the microphone stand. "We created this special trophy, the first actual Gordy Award, for you to take back to jolly old England and place on your mantle."

Gordy presented Perry with a large cup, similar to the one awarded to the winner of the Kentucky Derby. It was large, flashy, and a bit pretentious. It was Gordy. Perry looked mortified but thanked him graciously.

Gordy turned more serious and continued, "Some of you here may not remember, but several years ago, we lost a member of the Chinooka family and someone close to Perry, Annie Brandeis. In honor of Perry's years of service, and to honor the life of one of our former staff members, along with Annie's parents, I've set up the Annie Brandeis scholarship. Each summer, one deserving child will be chosen by Annie's parents to spend the summer at Chinooka free of charge."

Perry looked genuinely touched. He pulled Gordy in for a hug, and they spent a few seconds in a tight embrace. Annie would live on at Chinooka. Perry wouldn't have to keep coming back to make sure of that. Gordy had just given him the best gift of all—closure.

Perry hugged him one last time and took a seat next to me. He grabbed my hand under the table, and we joined Gordy and the rest of the camp in singing the Chinooka alma mater at the very top of our lungs.

After my final check that all the Cedar campers and counselors were in their cabins for the night, I made my way to Birch for the very last time. Perry was sitting alone on the rotted-out bench, throwing sticks into the fire just like he'd been doing on the first night when I showed up looking for the missing campers from Bunk Fourteen. I stepped on some dried leaves, and he turned to look at me.

"Announce yourself," he said, squinting into the fire.

"It's Georgica Goldstein, head counselor of Cedar, winning general of Color War, your one-time nemesis, and now, I hope, your always friend," I said, approaching.

"You may enter Birch," he said, standing up from the bench. "You just had to get in that last dig about winning Color War, didn't you?" He pulled me into his arms.

"You're the one who asked for my credentials," I teased.

We sat down, and he added more wood to the dying fire. There was a definite chill in the air and he wrapped a blanket around me.

"Did you find her?" he asked, referring to Alicia.

"She was sitting in the large gazebo on the Great Lawn, waiting for me. It was a hard conversation, but all the skeletons are out of the closet."

"Is the wedding on?"

I shook my head. "I think she needs some time to figure it all out."

"And the two of you?"

"She needs some time to figure it all out, but I have a feeling we'll find our way back."

Perry wiped my teary eyes and held me in his arms. I used the back of my hand to wipe my face. Perry handed me a Kleenex from his pocket and I sat up.

"What is all this?" I asked, looking over at the big shopping bag by the fire.

"Before summer is officially over, I need your help with something," he said, smiling.

"Anything," I replied.

"I've never had a s'more."

"You've spent four summers at Chinooka and never had a s'more? How is that even possible?" I asked.

He shrugged his shoulders. "Are you going to help me or not?"

"Pass over the bag. Let me make sure you've got everything we need."

I pulled out the marshmallows, a chocolate bar, and graham crackers. "Okay, we have all the necessary ingredients. Now we each need a stick."

"I can do you one better," he said, pulling two metal skewers with thick wooden handles from behind him. "I swiped them from the kitchen this afternoon."

"Just follow my lead." I loaded two marshmallows onto my skewer and placed it into the campfire. When the marshmallows turned from white to golden brown, we pulled them off the skewers and smashed them between the chocolate and two pieces of graham cracker, making a sweet, gooey sandwich.

"Ready for one of the best first bites you'll ever have?" I asked.

"You may not want to hype it up too much. I've tried one of your Chipwich things," Perry said with a wide grin.

"This is totally different," I said. "Ready? One... Two... Three."

We both took a bite at the same time, the marshmallow squeezing out the sides of the graham crackers. "So? What do you think?"

He wiped some marshmallow from the corner of his mouth. "I think it's better than I could have ever possibly imagined." He finished off his last bite.

"Yeah?"

"Way better. In fact, I think I need another taste," he said, going in for a kiss.

We polished off the bag of marshmallows and talked until the campfire went out. When the first streaks of morning light broke through, Perry walked me back to Cedar along the hidden path we'd made use of so many times before. He put his arm around me, and we stood together to watch the sun come over Lake Chinooka one last time.

CHAPTER TWENTY-TWO

For the first morning all summer, not a single girl complained when the alarm went off. All of them wanted to squeeze out every last possible second of camp. Some were even out of bed already, folding up the last of their things. The buses would start arriving in a few hours to take everyone home.

I only had a few things of my own left to pack. I wrapped up the alarm clock and placed it in my trunk. Then, I took one last look at the picture of Alicia and me that had been sitting on my nightstand all summer and carefully packed it away. When I was finished, Jordana sat down on the bed next to me.

"You okay?" she said, putting her arm around me.

"I will be. If I haven't said it before, thank you for everything this summer."

"Don't mention it," she said.

"No, really. You've been a great help, and more than that, a great friend."

A smile crept across her face. "Yeah, I think we did

good. Especially once they stopped short-sheeting our beds."

"I almost forgot about that," I said, thinking back to the torturous first few weeks when we'd been the repeat victims of Bunk Fourteen's unrelenting assaults.

"I didn't. In fact, I am taking that nugget with me to Brown, just in case I end up hating my roommate," she said, laughing. "If that doesn't work, I'll just have to find a boyfriend who has his own apartment."

"So things are over between you and Jake?"

"Our story ends here. He's heading back Down Under, and I'm heading off to Rhode Island. We'll always have Chinooka, though."

Jordana and I exchanged information and e-mail addresses. I made her promise to update me regularly, and in exchange, she made me promise to design her a dress for her first sorority formal.

"You're that confident you'll get through all the sorority hazing?" I teased.

"After this summer, piece of cake," she said, walking out of the bunk.

I locked up the last of my things in my trunk and went outside for the final Cedar roll call. After all the campers were lined up, I took a minute to thank the counselors and CITs for their hard work. Then, I addressed the almost fifty campers who had been in my care these last eight weeks.

"I don't know about all of you, but for me, these have been the longest and shortest eight weeks of my entire life. So much happened this summer. We won The Gordy and Color War. Our trip to New York. But, what I want you to remember most of all are the lifelong friendships you made. Some of the best people you'll ever know, you met right here at Camp Chinooka. Respect those friendships. Treasure them, value them, and appreciate them. Don't for one second take them for granted. Be good to yourselves, but more importantly, be good to each other. Nothing else matters."

I glanced around and saw a bunch of the girls nodding in agreement. A few of them were hugging each other, while the rest looked teary at the thought of saying goodbye. "I watched you walk into Chinooka as girls, but today, you are leaving as Cedar women. So, in honor of that transformation, let's hear it one more time. 'We are Cedar, we couldn't be prouder, and if you can't hear us, we'll shout a little louder.'"

By the third verse, all of Cedar had joined in. I led the cheer a few more times until I saw Perry and Jamie walking toward us with their bags in hand. "Okay, as loud as you can. 'We are Cedar, we couldn't be prouder, and if you can't hear us, we'll shout a little louder!'" I screamed.

"You won Color War and the Gordy. Give it a rest, Gigi!" Perry yelled from behind the girls.

"Not a chance," I yelled back before leading them through the chant one last time. When we finished, I motioned for the girls to quiet down and then dismissed them to the Great Lawn to wait for their buses home.

"What time do you want to head out?" Jamie asked, walking toward me.

"I have to stay until the last bus leaves. Probably around noon," I replied.

"What about you?" Jamie said, turning to Perry. "Can we drop you at the airport on our way back to the city?"

"Thanks, but Gordy ordered me a cab. It should be here soon," Perry said.

"Ducking out of your final responsibilities, Head Counselor Gillman?" I teased.

"Believe me, I wish I could stay here forever," he said.

"Me too," I said

Jaime interjected. "Well, I don't, partner. We have a lot of work to get to, and I haven't had a decent cup of coffee in days." Clearly, this was his best effort to pull me out of a difficult moment.

"Well, why don't you get started by loading your stuff in the car? I'll meet you up there in a little bit," I said.

Jamie shook Perry's hand, wished him luck, and then left us alone to say our goodbyes. I looked down at all of Perry's bags. "So you were able to pack the Gordy Award after all? I was worried you wouldn't have room and might have to leave it here."

"I almost had to sacrifice the violin for it, but there was no way that golden treasure wasn't coming home with me. Luckily, I managed to fit it in," he said.

"That word again, *home*."

"Chinooka's home. London's just the place where I live for now," he said softly. "Walk me to my car?"

I walked him all the way to the front entrance of Chinooka. When we got there, his taxi was already waiting. He pulled me in for a kiss and then whispered in my ear. "The way you changed my life, no, no, they can't take that away from me."

"Irving Berlin?" I whispered back.

"Gershwin, Gigi, always Gershwin."

I smiled and pulled away. "Call me when you get to London? Let me know you got there okay?"

"I'll call you from the airport." The taxi driver honked, and Perry swung his backpack over his shoulder. "I don't know how I'm supposed to say goodbye to you," he said, pulling me back in for one more kiss goodbye.

"Me neither."

"N*ei*ther," he said, correcting me with his posh accent.

"Neither, N*ei*ther, Either, *Ei*ther, let's call the whole thing off," I said lightheartedly.

"Not a chance, Princess. Not a chance. I love you, Georgica."

"I love you, too."

When I got back to the Great Lawn, most of the buses had already been called, and just a handful of campers were still waiting around. I noticed Madison sitting by herself in the gazebo, her face red and tear-stained. She had her knees pulled tightly against her chest and looked like she was having trouble catching her breath. I sat down and slid close to her. She immediately buried her head in my neck, and I wrapped my arms around her.

"Did you say goodbye to Alex?" I asked, already knowing the answer.

"He just got on his bus," she said through choking sobs.

"That must have been really hard," I said, smoothing her hair.

She sat up and took a few deep breaths to calm herself down. "What do you think will happen with us?"

"That's hard to say. Some summer romances are like the summer itself, too short, too perfect, and exactly what we need to be able to go back and face the rest of the year."

"What about the other kind?"

"You didn't let me finish. Then there are the *other* summer romances. The ones that are so special, so extraordinary, they outlast the summer and go on maybe even for forever."

"What kind do you think you and Perry have?" she asked.

"Only time will tell."

"And me and Alex?"

"Only time will tell."

Madison dried her eyes, and Gordy called her bus number. She stood up to leave but then ran back to give me a last hug goodbye.

After the final bus pulled away, I was alone on the Great Lawn. I closed my eyes and breathed in the last few minutes of camp.

"Open your eyes. I need you to help me spot a Starbucks off the highway," Jamie yelled out the window as he pulled up to me. After we loaded the last of my things into the car he handed me a pair of aviators out of the glove compartment. "Ready to go home, partner?"

"Not home, New York City," I said, correcting him.

He smiled and pulled out onto the dirt road. As we drove out the camp gates, I looked in the rearview mirror one last time, silently thanking Camp Chinooka for giving me a second chance, a new romance, and just one more summer.

THE SERIES CONTINUES WITH S'MORE TO LOSE, BOOK TWO IN THE CAMPFIRE SERIES!

Four years after her life-changing summer, Gigi Goldstein thinks saying goodbye to Camp Chinooka means saying hello to a brand new life. Now faced with a second chance at her career, she is filled with more hope than she's felt in a long time. Her design house is taking the fashion world by storm, even attracting notice of Victoria Ellicott, the fashionable British socialite who just happens to be engaged to the future king of England. When Gigi is chosen to design the royal wedding dress in London, she is forced to confront her ex-fiancé, Perry Gillman, now a successful composer with a hit show on the West End.

But when Gigi learns Perry's been dating Victoria's sister, who rivals her in looks, style and sophistication,

Gigi can't help but feel inadequate in *everything*. Her world begins to crumble as she develops a creative block so debilitating, she fears that a wedding dress of royal proportions is *never* going to happen. Even a budding relationship with the handsome, wealthy, and rich Viscount of Satterley can't make her forget about Perry and her inability to get over him. As the world gears up for the wedding of the century, Gigi is on the brink of buckling under the immense pressure of the uncertainties of her future and failures of her past.

Will she be able overcome her creative paralysis to design the dress of Victoria's dreams, or will she break down now that she has even s'more to lose?

AND BE SURE TO GRAB THE THIRD INSTALLMENT OF THE CAMPFIRE SERIES, LOVE YOU S'MORE!

Having successfully designed the wedding gown of the century, Gigi Goldstein is on top of the world – that is until it all suddenly comes crashing down around her. When the paparazzi captures her and Perry Gillman in a compromising moment the night of the royal wedding, she finds herself entangled in a scandal of global proportion. Convinced her carelessness has ruined every relationship in her life, she's surprised and moved by her boyfriend, Gideon's, sudden proposal of marriage and accepts it without a second thought.

Four months later, Gigi's living at Badgley Hall contemplating an entirely new kind of life, while guilt, regret, and obligation keep calling her back to her old one. Will Gigi stay in South Gloucestershire, marry Gideon, and become the Countess of Harronsby?

Or, will unfinished opportunities and an old flame bring her back across the pond to confront her past and reclaim her future?

WAIT, ANOTHER CAMPFIRE BOOK!?!

GRAB TELL ME S'MORE, BOOK 4 OF THE CAMPFIRE SERIES - THE "OTHER SIDE" OF THE STORY.

Camp Chinooka was supposed to be a place of inspiration, the place where Perry Gilman would finally compose his symphonic masterpiece. But four years later, Perry Gillman isn't any closer to his dream of becoming a world renown musician.

Instead, he fell love in with Gigi Goldstein and he thought that love would be enough. Now, struggling to find the right subject for a new musical while hustling as a piano player at a local jazz bar, he can't help but measure his own shortcomings to his famous father's monstrous success. So, when he stumbles onto the idea to write a musical about the life and times of Elizabeth I, everything finally changes. The musical is an international sensation and suddenly, Perry is on the fast track to super stardom.

However, fame and success come at a price. When his relationship with Gigi is thrown into a tailspin, he must decide whether to follow his dream for which he fought for so long or sacrifice it all for true love.

Told from Perry's perspective, Tell Me S'more shows that there are two sides to every story and a cost to every choice.

WHAT'S NEXT FOR BETH MERLIN?

BETH MERLIN'S FIRST NOVEL AFTER HER HIT CAMPFIRE SERIES - YOU WON'T WANT TO MISS IT!

Break Up Boot Camp

After weeks of training to whip Joanna Kitt into shape for her big day, her picture-perfect relationship is torn in two and Joanna is left out on her perfectly toned rear end. In an effort to put the past and her heartache behind her, she gears up for a whole different kind of boot camp – but will 12 steps be enough to get her life back on track?

Or will her getaway to get over him prove healing the heart takes a whole lot more?

THE KEY WEST ESCAPE SERIES

LOOKING FOR A NEW SERIES WITH A HEAVY DOSE OF ADVENTURE AND A BIT MORE STEAM? CHECK OUT THE KEY WEST ESCAPE SERIES BY TRICIA LEEDOM STARTING WITH RUM RUNNER.

English socialite Sophie Davies-Stone has been longing to meet her father since she was a little girl. When he sends her a mysterious medallion and asks her to forward it to him in Miami, she can't help herself from doing something totally un-Sophie-like. Rather than mailing it as instructed, Sophie hops on a flight to Florida.

But the family reunion never happens. Instead, Sophie is attacked and almost kidnapped by her father's enemies. Her savior is Jimmy Panama, a cocky and annoyingly handsome former Navy SEAL. Sophie isn't the only one who's annoyed. After years of trying to find a way to pay back his CO, Jimmy never thought his debt would get him mixed up with his commander's uptight, British daughter. He just wants to put her on the next flight home and get back to his low-stress life in Key West, but fate has other plans.

As Sophie and Jimmy embark on a heart-pounding adventure through Key West and the Caribbean, Sophie finds herself falling for the snarky American. Still, her head says Jimmy is all wrong for her, and the more she finds out about him – and her father – the more uncertain she is about who she can trust.

One thing is clear. Sophie is in way over her head, and her greatest adventure might be her last.

REVIEW REQUEST

Dear Reader,

Reviews are like currency to any author – actually, even better! As they help to get our books noticed by even more readers, we would be so grateful if you would take a moment to review this book on Amazon, Goodreads, iBooks - wherever - and feel free to share it on social media!

We're not asking for any special favors – honest reviews would be perfect. They also don't need to be long or in-depth, just a few of your thoughts would be so helpful.

Thank you greatly from the bottom of our hearts. For your time, for your support, and for being a part of our reading community. We couldn't do it without you – nor would we want to!

~ Our Firefly Hill Press Family

ACKNOWLEDGMENTS

I wrote the first chapter of *One S'more Summer* sitting on the NYC subway. Over the next ten years, I wrote the rest during stolen moments and any extra bits of time I could find between building a career and starting a family. In all those years, I experienced more than a few setbacks, but I never gave up because of my husband, Mashaal. Thank you for never wavering in your belief I would accomplish my dream. You've been my loudest and proudest cheerleader, my willing audience, my most honest critic, my voice of reason, my champion, my rock, and very best friend. Your love and support keeps my half empty glass not only full, but overflowing.

Thank you to my incredible editor Danielle Modafferi. You believed in this story from the flawed first (second and even third) draft and have helped me push myself in ways I didn't know were possible. Your support, advice, and guidance has been invaluable to this book and my writing. I am so grateful for our friendship and collaboration.

I am so appreciative to the friends and family who have encouraged me every step of the way. My brother, Robert, and sister, Leslie, who have shown me through their choices and successes what it is to follow your dreams and live out your passions. My best friend, Alyson Weinick Schwartz, my life touchstone. I will forever be grateful to you for letting me tag along with you to sleepaway camp and about a million other places these last thirty years. My grandparents, Ruth and Bernard Hollander, who unselfishly provided me with so many life experiences. Alice, my mother-in-law and friend.

I would not be who I am without my mother, Diane Zamansky, my very first editor who would routinely return my camp letters with corrections and revisions, red-marked for spelling and grammar mistakes. You taught me how to write and the value of the written word. Some of my earliest memories are of hearing you typing away articles and press releases on our Panasonic Word Processor at 5am. You inspired me in more ways than you realize.

A special thank you to my camp friends (special shout out to Rebekah Flig)-- for being nice to me when I had frizzy hair and wore tie-dye from head to toe. Thank you for sticking by my side when we got in trouble. Thank you for keeping my secrets and staying up late at night even when the counselors told us to go to sleep. Thank you for sharing your canteen snacks with me. Thank you for listening to me cry about ridiculous things like the boys I liked or losing out on the lead in the camp play. Most of all thank you for teaching me to embrace my true self and loving me all the more.

Thank you to my beautiful Hadley Alexandra, the light of my life and the bright spot of every single day.

And finally, thank you to my father, Arthur Zamansky, who changed everything for the better.

ABOUT THE AUTHOR

Beth Merlin, a native New Yorker, loves anything Broadway, romantic comedies, and a good maxi dress. After earning her JD from New York Law School, she heard a voice calling her back to fiction writing, like it had during her undergrad study. Amidst her days in The George Washington University's School of Media and Public Affairs, where Beth majored in Political Communications, she found herself wandering into Creative Writing classes, and ended up earning a minor in the field. After 10 long years laboring over her first manuscript, her debut novel, *One S'more Summer*, released May 2017. International bestselling author Kristin Harmel called it "a fast paced, enjoyable read."

Find Beth on Twitter @bethmerlin80, Instagram @bethfmerlin, and at www.fireflyhillpress.com

And keep up to date on all of Beth's future releases, book bargains, sneak peeks, giveaways, special offers, & so much more by subscribing to our newsletter!

Printed in the United States of America

Firefly Hill Press, LLC
4387 W. Swamp Rd #565
Doylestown, PA 18902
www.fireflyhillpress.com
info@fireflyhillpress.com

Print ISBN: 9781945495045
E-Book ISBN: 9781943858200